Virgil's Aeneid: A Retelling in Prose

David Bruce

Published by David Bruce, 2022.

VIRGIL'S AENEID: A RETELLING IN PROSE

First edition. July 6, 2022.

Copyright © 2022 David Bruce.

ISBN: 979-8201867942

Written by David Bruce.

Table of Contents

Virgil's Aeneid: A Retelling in Prose

***

Educate Yourself
Read Like A Wolf Eats
Be Excellent to Each Other
Books Then, Books Now, Books Forever

***

Do you know a language other than English? If you do, I give you permission to translate this book, copyright your translation, publish or self-publish it, and keep all the royalties for yourself. (Do give me credit, of course, for the original retelling.)

I would like to see my retellings of classic literature used in schools, so I give permission to the country of Finland (and all other countries) to buy one copy of this eBook and give copies to all students forever. I also give permission to the state of Texas (and all other states) to buy one copy of this eBook and give copies to all students forever. I also give permission to all teachers to buy one copy of this eBook and give copies to all students forever.

Teachers need not actually teach my retellings. Teachers are welcome to give students copies of my eBooks as background material. For example, if they are teaching Homer's *Iliad* and *Odyssey*, teachers are welcome to give students copies of my *Virgil's* Aeneid: *A Retelling in Prose* and tell students, "Here's another ancient epic you may want to read in your spare time."

A Note

When Virgil died in 19 B.C.E., he had not quite completed his *Aeneid*; therefore, some minor inconsistencies remain. For example, one particular prophecy is made by the Harpy Celaeno in one section, and by Aeneas' father in another section. However, the *Aeneid* is well worth reading. In addition to being *the* epic of ancient Rome, the *Aeneid* contains the fullest surviving ancient account of the fall of Troy. It also contains the story of the tragic love affair between Aeneas and Dido, the Queen of Carthage — a story that Virgil apparently invented. On his deathbed, Virgil requested that the manuscript of the *Aeneid* be burned. I am grateful that Caesar Augustus did not honor that request.

Chapter 1: Arrival at Carthage

My theme is war and a particular man — a man driven by destiny to abandon Troy and sail to western Italy to fulfill his fate of founding the people who would build Rome. Fulfilling his destiny was not easy. Juno, the wife of Jupiter, the king of gods and men, opposed him, as did many warriors. They did not want him to bring his household gods — the Penates — to Latium on the western coast of Italy, to marry Lavinia, to found the city of Lavinium, and to become the ancestor of the Romans.

Muse, remind me of the reasons why Juno hated Aeneas, a man renowned for his *pietas*, for his devotion to duty, whether to the gods, to his family, or to his destiny. Aeneas had respect for those things to which respect is due. Why did Juno make his fulfilling his destiny so difficult? Are the immortals capable of such anger?

Phoenicians from the city of Tyre founded a city named Carthage on the coast of north Africa. Carthage and Rome were the two competitors for worldwide empire, and Juno loved Carthage even more than her beloved island of Samos. In Carthage, Juno kept her armor and her chariot. Juno was willing for Carthage to have a worldwide empire, but the Fates were not. Juno did all she could to make Carthage strong, but gods and goddesses know fate, and Juno knew that a city founded by the descendants of men from Troy would conquer Carthage. Rome, not Carthage, would have a worldwide empire. For that reason, Juno hated Aeneas.

Juno also hated Aeneas because she hated all Trojans. A jealous wife, Juno hated the many affairs that her husband, Jupiter, had had over the centuries. She especially hated the children who resulted from these affairs. One of these illegitimate children, Dardanus, became an early king of the city of Troy.

Also, Paris, prince of Troy, had insulted Juno. Asked to judge a beauty contest of the goddesses Juno, Minerva, and Venus, Paris had accepted a bribe from Venus, the goddess of sexual passion, who offered him the most beautiful woman in the world. Paris went to Sparta and ran away with the most beautiful woman in the world: Helen, the lawfully wedded wife of Menelaus, King of Sparta. Helen became Helen of Troy, and the Trojan War was fought so that Menelaus could get Helen back. Because Juno's beauty had been insulted, Juno hated the Trojans.

Juno also hated the Trojans because of Ganymede. A jealous wife, Juno hated the many affairs of her husband Jupiter, who chased more than just skirts. Ganymede was a beautiful young son of Tros, a king of Troy, and Jupiter kidnapped Ganymede to be his cupbearer and his paramour.

For these reasons, Juno hated Aeneas and the other Trojans, and she did her best to keep them away from western Italy, forcing them to wander the seas and strange lands despite their destiny. Founding the Roman people was a huge burden borne by many people.

Aeneas and his Trojans had set sail from Sicily in twenty ships. Their mood was good; Juno's mood was not. Juno said to herself as she watched Aeneas' ships, "Am I powerless to cause trouble for Aeneas and keep him away from western Italy? True, he has a destiny, and fate decrees that he will fulfill that destiny, but at least I can make that difficult to do. Why should it be easy for Aeneas to reach western Italy?

"I have power, as does another goddess: Minerva. Minerva was angry at Little Ajax, the Greek who during the fall of Troy raped Cassandra in a temple dedicated to Minerva. Anyone in a temple is under the protection of the god or goddess whose temple it is — the mortal has sanctuary. By raping Cassandra in Minerva's temple, Little Ajax disrespected Minerva. Minerva got revenge when Little Ajax attempted to sail home to Greece after the fall of Troy. Minerva hurled one of Jupiter's thunderbolts at Little Ajax' fleet, and she caused a storm with high waves. Little Ajax' ship burned and a cyclone swept him up into the air and then impaled him on a rock.

"Minerva got her well-deserved revenge — quickly! But I am the queen of gods and men, and I have to battle Aeneas and his Trojans continually — for years! Don't I have more power than that? Who among men will worship me unless I show that I can triumph over Aeneas and his Trojans?"

Juno flew to Aeolia, the island ruled by Aeolus, king of the winds. In a cave, Aeolus keeps the winds. They howl and want to break out and cause storms, but Aeolus calms them enough to keep them from breaking out of the cave and destroying the world. Jupiter had been afraid that the winds would cause massive destruction, so he shut them up in a cave, put a mountain over the cave, and gave the winds a king to rule them. Aeolus decides when to keep the winds shut up in the cave and when to allow them to blow freely.

Juno said, "Aeolus, Jupiter gave you great power over the winds. You can either calm them or rouse them. Right now, Aeneas and the Trojans — all of whom I hate — are on the sea carrying their household gods from Troy to Italy. I want you to release the winds and allow them to attack the Trojans' ships and sink them.

"I will reward you if you do what I say. I will give in marriage to you the most beautiful of fourteen sea-nymphs I have much influence over: Deiopea. She will live with you as your wife and bear your children. I reward well those who serve me."

Aeolus replied, "You, Juno, should have everything you want. I, Aeolus, should do everything you tell me to do. You have always been good to me. You are responsible for making me the god of the winds. You have made sure that Jupiter treats me well, and you have made sure that I am invited to the feasts of the Olympian gods. Because of you, I am the lord of the storm winds."

Aeolus struck the mountain over the cave holding the winds with his spear and created a hole through which the winds rushed to the sea. They made huge waves, and they made clouds that blotted out the sun. The sailors shouted, and the ships rose and fell on the huge waves. Thunder roared and lightning bolts crashed, and sailors saw death everywhere.

Aeneas, in private, groaned and said, "So many Trojan warriors died on the plain before Troy as they defended wives, children, parents, and city. They were the lucky ones. They died an honorable death in battle, not an ignoble death by drowning. I would have been better off if the Greek Diomedes had killed me on the battlefield. I would have been better off if I had been buried at Troy with Hector, the greatest Trojan warrior, and Sarpedon, a Trojan ally from Lydia, and other heroes!"

The winds and waves battered Aeneas' ship, breaking oars, and the waves poured over the decks. Waves rose and fell, sometimes rising above the ship and sometimes exposing the sand at the bottom of the sea.

The South wind stranded three of Aeneas' ships on the mid-ocean rocks the Italians called the Altars. The East wind stranded three more of Aeneas' ships on the dangerous coastal reefs called the Syrtes.

Aeneas saw another ship — captained by Orontes — wreck after a huge wave crashed on it. Orontes fell headfirst into the sea, and his ship circled three times in a whirlpool before sinking. In the water, sailors and cargo floated.

The winds and waves battered and damaged four more ships — those captained by Ilioneus, Achates, Abas, and Aletes. Their joints split open and the waters rushed in.

Neptune, the god of the sea, sensed the storm above him. He realized the violence of the winds and the waves — violence not approved by him. Neptune raised his head above the water and saw the scattered ships of Aeneas — the Trojans had been attacked by the violent winds and the violent waves.

Immediately, Neptune realized that this was the work of Juno. He ordered the East wind and West wind to come to him, and he said to them, "You seem awfully sure of yourselves to trespass so on my domain. You have caused destruction in my area of influence. If you ever cause a storm on the sea, you must do so only with my permission. This time I will let you off with a warning, but the next time this happens you will pay. Go back to your cave and tell Aeolus that I — not he — am the god of the sea. Jupiter, Pluto, and I shook lots to see who would rule what. Jupiter became the god of the sky, Pluto became the god of the Land of the Dead, and I became the god of the sea. Aeolus is the god of the island on which he usually keeps you winds imprisoned in a cave. Let him stay in his own area of influence and stay out of mine unless he has my permission."

Neptune then calmed the sea and sent away the clouds so that the sun would shine. Triton, who was one of Neptune's sons, and the sea nymph Cymothoë lifted Aeneas' ships from the rocks while Neptune himself used his trident to raise the ships. Neptune also cleared a passage for the ships that had been grounded on the reefs, and he drove his chariot over the waves to calm them.

Neptune calming the waves was like a statesman calming an unruly crowd. The crowd is full of passion and rage — of *furor* — and it throws rocks and burning torches. But a statesman worthy of respect comes to the crowd of people and talks to them, and they listen to him and become calm and law-abiding. Just like that statesman, Neptune calmed the unruly waves.

Aeneas' men, weary from battling the storm, headed for the nearest land. Driven off their course, they headed for the north African country of Libya. An island there provides a shield for the mouth of a bay, creating a safe haven for ships. The island shields the haven from high waves, and twin towers of rock protect the sides of the harbor.

On the mainland is a forest and cut in a cliff is a cave that is the home of sea nymphs. The harbor here is so safe that ships need not use anchors.

In this harbor arrived Aeneas and seven of his ships — perhaps the only ships left to him out of his entire fleet. Happy to be on land again, the Trojans lay on the sandy beach. Achates used flint to make a fire, and the Trojans began to grind grain to make a meal.

Aeneas climbed a hill and searched the sea, hoping to see the ship of Antheus or of Capys or of Caicus. No ships were in sight. But Aeneas did see three stags and a herd of deer. Using the bow and arrows that his aide Achates kept for him, Aeneas shot the three stags and then began shooting does. He did not stop shooting until he had killed seven deer — one for each of his ships. A good leader provides food for his men.

Aeneas gave the deer to his men and set out wine that Acestes, the king of Sicily, had stocked in the ships.

Before he and his men ate, Aeneas spoke to his men to raise their spirits: "Friends, we have endured much worse than what we are enduring now. This, too, shall come to an end — a god will help us. We have survived the man-eating monster Scylla, and we have survived the boulders thrown by the Cyclops. Once again, we need to be courageous and to resist grief and fear. Someday, we shall look back on this and be proud that we have survived. We still have a destiny: We shall reach Latium in western Italy. Fate has promised us a homeland there, and there the city of Troy shall rise again. Be courageous."

The public Aeneas put on an act of confidence for his men, but the private Aeneas worried.

The men skinned the deer and cut off strips of meat. They cooked the venison, and then they ate and drank. No longer hungry, they talked, wondering about the other ships. Were their shipmates still alive? Aeneas privately mourned for Orontes, Amycus, Lycus, Gyas, and Cloanthus.

Jupiter gazed down on Libya, looking at Aeneas and his Trojans, and witnessed their troubles. Venus, the goddess of sexual passion and of laughter, approached him. Usually a happy goddess, Venus, the mother of Aeneas, was sad. One way for her to help her son was to intercede in his behalf with Jupiter, the king of gods and men.

Venus said to her father, Jupiter, "You rule the lives of gods and of men. Has my Aeneas committed a crime against you? Have the Trojans done any harm to you? Why are Aeneas and the Trojans barred from Italy? Haven't you promised that in Italy the Romans will arise, a people descended from the Trojans? Haven't you promised that the Romans will be a powerful people — the most powerful people? Have you decided not to keep your promise? I was saddened by the fall of Troy, but I consoled myself with the thought that their descendants would be the Romans. So why are the Trojans still enduring so many hardships? Will you set an end to their hardships?

"Antenor, one of the old men of Troy, managed to escape from the city with some other Trojans. They made their way to Italy, and they founded the city of Padua. Now they live in peace.

"But what of Aeneas and the Trojans he leads? How many ships are lost? Because of one enemy — Juno — Aeneas and his Trojans are kept away from Italy. Is this the way you reward the Trojans who worship you? Is this the way you give them power?"

Jupiter kissed his daughter gently and said, "You need not worry, Venus. Aeneas' fate has not changed; he and his Trojans still have the same destiny. They will found the city of Lavinium, and Aeneas' fame will reach the stars.

"To ease your mind, let me tell you more of what fate holds for your son and his Trojans. Aeneas will land on Italy, and he will fight a war there and win. He will build the city of Lavinium in the territory of Latium, and he will govern for three years. Ascanius, his son, who also holds the name of Ilus for Ilium or Troy and who in Italy will also be called Iulus, a name that will later become Julius, will rule Latium for thirty years. Ascanius will build the city of Alba Longa and rule from there. For three hundred years, the Trojans will continue to rule in Latium, and then the priestess Ilia will sleep with Mars, the god of war, and give birth to twin boys: Romulus and Remus. They will be raised by a she-wolf, and they will found Rome. Romulus will name the city, and its citizens will be called Romans.

"On the Romans I set no limits on their power, either in space or in time. Their empire will have no end.

"Juno now hates the Trojans, but eventually she will reform and not resist the toga-wearing Romans. All of this, I decree. Eventually, the Romans will even conquer Greece, land of Achilles, the greatest warrior of the Trojan War, and land of the city of Mycenae, once ruled by Agamemnon, leader of the Greek forces against Troy.

"A Trojan Caesar will arise from the House of Julius, a name that will come from Iulus. This Caesar — the Emperor Caesar Augustus, nephew and adopted son of Julius Caesar — will have an empire that is bounded only by the Ocean. He will receive treasure from the Orient. His fame will also reach the stars. He and Aeneas will be worshiped, and in the reign of Caesar Augustus, Rome will be known for the rule of law and will find peace after centuries of warfare. The gates of the temple of Janus, which are kept open during times of war, will finally be closed as the civil wars come to an end."

Jupiter then sent Mercury, the messenger of the gods, down to Carthage in Libya. Mercury's job was to make sure that the Trojans would find welcome there. Jupiter did not want Dido, the Queen of Carthage, who did not know her fate, to be an enemy to Aeneas and his Trojans. Mercury quickly accomplished his goal: He filled the Carthaginians and Dido with peace and good will.

That night, Aeneas wrestled with worry. When the morning came, he ordered his ships moved to a narrow place where rocks and trees hid them, and then he explored the countryside with his aide Achates by his side. For protection, Aeneas carried two javelins.

Another way for Venus to help her son was by meeting with him, even when she was disguised as a mortal. That way, she could give him information and advice.

Having assumed the form of a young woman, a huntress who could be from Sparta or from Thrace, Venus met Aeneas and Achates in the woods the two men were exploring. She carried a bow and a quiver of arrows. Her hair was not tied up, and her knees were bare — she had tied her skirt so it would not catch on bushes.

The disguised Venus said to Aeneas and Achates, "Have you seen my sister? If you have, where did she go? She is wearing the skin of a spotted lynx and carrying a bow and a quiver of arrows. You may have seen or heard her hunting a boar."

Aeneas replied, "I have not seen any of your sisters. How should I refer to you? You can't be a mortal, not with your physical features and the quality of your voice. You must be a goddess. Are you Diana, Apollo's sister? Are you a nymph? Be kind to us, and help us, please. Where are we? A storm at sea drove us here, and we don't know where we are or who lives here. If you help us, we will sacrifice many animals to you."

Venus lied and said, "I am not a goddess, so I don't deserve sacrifices. We young women from the city of Tyre carry bows and arrows and wear red hunting boots. This land is a kingdom ruled by Phoenicians. The city here is Carthage, and Dido is its queen. She sailed here with her people from Tyre, fleeing from a crime. I will tell you the story.

"Dido's husband was the richest man in Tyre: Sychaeus. He was her first and only husband. Dido's brother is Pygmalion, the ruler of Tyre. He is evil, and he hated Sychaeus and wanted his gold. Pygmalion killed Sychaeus with a sword at an altar, spilling his blood in a holy place. Pygmalion hid his guilt; he did not care about his sister's grief. He lied to her.

"One night Dido dreamed: The ghost of her husband — who was still not buried — told her about his death and ordered her, 'Flee from the city of Tyre!' He also revealed the hidden location of treasure — silver and gold — to help her be able to flee.

"Dido planned her flight and gathered followers. They were easy to find because they hated the tyrant Pygmalion. They gathered ships and loaded them with what Pygmalion desired most: gold. They then set sail with Dido as their commander. They reached this land, and they have started to build a new city: Carthage. To get land to build on, they bought as much land as a bull's-hide would enclose. A tricky people, they cut the bull's-hide into very thin strips so that it would encircle a large hill.

"But who are you? Where did you come from, and where are you headed?"

Aeneas replied, "Goddess, to tell my entire story would take until nightfall. Briefly, we come from Troy. You may have heard of it. We sailed over the sea until a storm drove us here. I am Aeneas, and I seek to fulfill my destiny. On board our ships, we carry our household gods that we took from

Troy when the city fell to the Greeks. My name is famous, and I seek Italy. We set out with twenty ships, but after the storm I have only seven left. Here in Libya, I am a stranger, an exile."

Venus, still disguised as a mortal, said, "Whoever you are, not all the immortals hate you. You are still alive, and you are near Carthage. Walk on this path: You will arrive at the city, and you can see the queen.

"Also, I have good news. I can read bird-signs, and the signs tell me that most of your ships and friends are safe. The winds drove them into a safe port. Look up, and you will see a dozen swans flying together. An eagle had attacked them and sent them in all directions, but now these dozen swans have regrouped and are flying together and are looking for the other swans. Twelve more of your ships are safe. You have seven ships, so in the storm you lost only one ship.

"Now follow the path and go to Carthage."

Venus moved away from Aeneas and revealed herself as a goddess. Her skirt was long and reached the ground, and her appearance and movements revealed that she was a goddess.

Aeneas recognized that she was his mother, and he — all too often isolated — called after her, "Why must you disguise yourself when we meet? Why can't we know each other and hug each other and talk together as mother and son?"

Aeneas and Achates took the path to Carthage. Venus created a fog to hide them. No one could see them, and so no one hindered them. She then flew to the city of Paphos on the island of Cyprus. There her worshippers burned Arabian incense to her on a hundred altars. Paphos was one of her favorite cities.

Aeneas and Achates followed the path, which took them to the top of a hill on which they could look down and see Carthage. Once nothing had been there but a few huts, but now the Phoenicians were building gates and cobbled streets. They were building walls, raising a citadel, and setting boundaries for buildings. They were building a civilization with laws and judges and a senate. They were dredging a harbor and building a theater and quarrying rock to make columns. They were working as hard as bees work in early summer, raising a new generation and harvesting honey and making a living hive.

Aeneas was impressed. He said, "The walls are rising, and this will be a great city."

Aeneas and Achates continued walking. Wrapped in fog, they passed unseen among people. They came to a famous grove. There the Phoenicians had dug after landing on the shore and had unearthed a sign put there by Juno: the head of a fiery stallion. Afterward, the stallion's head appeared on Carthaginian coins. The sign meant that for ages the Carthaginians would have power in war and ease in life. In this sacred grove, Dido was building a temple for Juno, lavishing on it bronze doors, a bronze threshold, and bronze doorposts.

In this grove, Aeneas saw something that gave him hope — hope that he had found a haven. Juno's temple was a place for works of art. The city's artists had created depictions of the Trojan War — a war that was known throughout the world. Depicted in these works of art, Aeneas saw Agamemnon and Menelaus, Priam the king of Troy, and Achilles.

Aeneas said, "Achates, the entire world knows of the hardships of Troy. I see a depiction of Priam here. Here in this city, people's hearts are touched by Trojan troubles. The fame of the Trojan War will offer us respite here."

Aeneas looked at the depictions of the Trojan War on the walls of the temple of Juno. He had known the living, breathing people, and their depictions were empty and lifeless, but they still had the power to arouse memories and grief. He groaned as he looked at the Greeks attacking Troy. In one work of art, the Trojans routed the Greeks. In another work of art, Achilles routed the Trojans. In yet another work of art, Aeneas saw the white tents of Rhesus, a king allied with the Trojans. Diomedes had slaughtered Rhesus and many of his warriors the night they had arrived at Troy. Splattered with the warriors' blood, Diomedes had driven Rhesus' horses back to the Greek camps.

Aeneas also saw Troilus, a young son of Priam. Achilles had ambushed Troilus, who fell out of his chariot but who still held onto the reins and his javelin, which drew a jagged line in the dust.

Aeneas also saw a depiction of the Trojan women praying to the goddess Minerva for her help. The Trojan women were suppliants who beat their breasts in the ancient way of showing grief and who offered Minerva a robe, but the goddess turned away and would not listen to their prayer.

Aeneas also saw the body of Priam's son Hector, the greatest Trojan warrior. Achilles had killed Hector, had dragged his corpse three times around the walls of the city of Troy, and now was selling his corpse. Aeneas groaned as he saw the lifeless body of his friend and as he saw Priam, Hector's father, grieving.

Aeneas also saw a depiction of himself fighting in battle. And he saw the Ethiopian Memnon who had fought for the Trojans and been killed by Achilles. And he saw Queen Penthesilea leading her Amazons into battle; Achilles had also killed her. In the work of art, she cinched a breastband under her bare breast. She and the other Amazons were women who fought like men.

As Aeneas looked at the works of art, Queen Dido came to Juno's temple with several escorts. She was like the goddess Diana walking with a thousand mountain nymphs. Dido sat on her throne with an honor guard by her side. Here she ruled. She made laws and decrees, and she assigned the work that needed to be done. Sometimes she used lots, and sometimes she used her sense of what was right.

Aeneas saw some of his lost Trojans approaching her: Ilioneus, Antheus, Sergestus, Cloanthus, and other Trojans who had been separated from Aeneas and the seven ships that had stayed with him.

Aeneas and Achates wanted to greet the lost Trojans, but they restrained themselves and stayed silent and hidden in fog. They wanted to learn whatever they could learn. Where are these Trojans' ships? Why have these Trojans come to Dido?

The lost Trojans approached Dido, and Ilioneus said to her, "Your majesty, Jupiter has blessed you by allowing you to build a new city here. We are Trojans, and we ask you to welcome us and not set fire to our ships. We worship the same gods that you worship. We have not come to attack your people and to loot your city. We are not in a position to do that; we have suffered many troubles.

"We are in search of a land to settle in. The Greeks know of a land they call Hesperia, but it has another name: Italy. We had set sail for Italy when a storm arose and scattered our ships. We had twenty ships, but now we have only twelve ships left — twelve ships that landed on your coast after the storm.

"Here we have not been welcomed. We have not been treated as guests. Sailors have a right to shore, but your people have forbidden us a footing on the beach. This is not the way to treat sailors. Remember the gods. Remember what the gods say about how to treat other people. Remember the duty that gods have given to mortals.

"Our king was Aeneas. He was devoted to duty. He understood *pietas*, and he did his duty to the gods, to his family, to his city, and to his city's survivors. He was also a formidable warrior. We do not know whether he still lives, but if he does live, you will not regret helping us.

"We have places in the world where we are welcome. In Sicily is a king named Acestes who was born to Trojan parents. Allow us to pull our storm-damaged ships onto shore so that we can repair them and make new oars, and then we shall set sail for Italy, where — fate permitting — we shall land at Latium.

"But if fate does not permit us to sail to Latium, if Aeneas has drowned in the waters off Libya, then we shall sail back to Sicily and we shall have Acestes as our king."

Dido welcomed the Trojans: "Have no fear, Trojans. We have a new kingdom, and we are cautious. That is why you were not allowed — at first — to pull your ships onto the shore and repair them.

"But we, like all people, have heard of Troy and know its story and its fame. We know the fame of Aeneas.

"Wherever you choose to sail to — Italy or Sicily — I will provide safe escorts for you. Or, if you prefer, you can settle here at Carthage. I now allow you to pull your ships onto shore. The Trojans will be equals with the Carthaginians if you choose to settle here.

"I will also send out men to search the coast to try to find Aeneas. He may have been shipwrecked and then reached the shore."

Aeneas and Achates were ready to reveal themselves. Achates said to Aeneas, "This is good news. Dido and the Carthaginians are welcoming us, and we have lost only one ship instead of the thirteen ships we feared we had lost. Your mother, Venus, told us the truth."

Venus melted the fog around Aeneas and Achates, and the two Trojans stood visible in the presence of Dido and the others. Venus made her son handsome and strong; he was like a god. His beauty was of the kind that an artist can add to ivory, or of the kind that an artist can create by working with silver and marble and gold.

Aeneas said to Dido, "I am Aeneas, and my followers and I survived the fall of Troy. You have pitied the fate of Troy and the Trojans, and you have welcomed us to Carthage. We have suffered much, and we cannot adequately reward you for your kindness. But we can ask the gods, who understand right and wrong, to reward you. You are a good person, and your parents have been blessed by giving birth to such a daughter as you. Your name and your goodness will be remembered as rivers flow to the sea, shadows move across mountains as the sun moves, and stars shine in the night sky."

Aeneas then greeted his fellow Trojans whom he had thought were lost: Serestus, Gyas, Cloanthus, Ilioneus, and others.

Aeneas' appearance and his words impressed Dido. She said to him, "Why does your destiny include such troubles as those you have suffered? How is it that you have landed on our coast? Are you really Aeneas, the son of the goddess Venus and the mortal Anchises? Were you really born at Troy?

"I remember the Greek archer named Teucer. He suffered banishment from his native land, and he visited Sidon, the major city of the Phoenicians. Belus, my father, who had sacked Cyprus, was able to help him. Because of this, I have long known of Troy and the Trojans. The Greek Teucer traced his ancestors back to the first king — who was also named Teucer — of the Trojans.

"Trojans, you are welcome here. I have had hard times in my past, and they led me here. Because of the hard times that I have experienced, I have learned to help other people who need help."

Dido led Aeneas into the halls of her palace, and she arranged for sacrifices to the gods. She sent to the Trojans on the shore twenty bulls and one hundred boars and one hundred lambs. This would be a day of feasting, a day of joy.

Dido's palace was regal and splendid. Servants set out a feast in the central hall. Gold and silver and the color purple abounded. Works of art memorialized the deeds of her father and other heroes of Phoenicia.

Aeneas, a loving father, wanted his son, Ascanius, to be with him, so he sent Achates to the ships to get him and bring him to Carthage. Aeneas also ordered Achates to bring gifts from the ships for Dido — gifts taken from the ruins of Troy. The gifts included a gown with gold embroidery and an embroidered veil. These had belonged to Helen, who took them with her when she left her lawfully wedded husband and Sparta and went with Paris to Troy. Helen's mother, Leda, had embroidered these articles of clothing. Aeneas also ordered Achates to bring a scepter that the oldest daughter of Priam, Ilione, used to bear, and he ordered him to bring a necklace of pearls and a two-banded crown — one band was decorated with gems and the other was made of gold. Achates went to the ships to carry out his orders.

Another way for Venus to help her son was to use divine supernatural powers — the powers of the gods and goddesses. She decided to have Cupid, her immortal son, take the place of Ascanius. Cupid, the god of love, could make Dido fall in love with Aeneas, thus ensuring his continued welcome at Carthage. Cupid could make Dido burn with love for Aeneas. Venus feared that the Phoenicians could be untrustworthy, and she feared that the hatred of Juno could cause trouble for her son Aeneas.

Venus said to her son, Cupid, "You, son, are powerful. Jupiter once killed Typhoeus, the hundred-headed, fire-breathing monster, with a thunderbolt, but you laugh at Jupiter' thunderbolts. Help me, please. I need you, and Aeneas, your half-brother, needs you. Aeneas has been traveling the Mediterranean and has suffered many troubles thanks to the hatred and anger of Juno. Now he is in Carthage, where Dido rules, and Dido has him at her mercy. I am worried that Dido will keep him at Carthage, away from Italy and his destiny. I am also worried that Juno will take action to hurt Aeneas — she does not want him to fulfill his destiny. My plan is for Dido to fall in love with Aeneas. That way, she will not hurt him.

"Listen to my plan and how you can help. Aeneas has sent for his son, Ascanius, to be brought to Carthage, along with presents for Dido. I will cause Ascanius to go to sleep, and I will take him somewhere safe — to the island of Cythera or the town of Idalium on Cyprus. Both places are devoted to me.

"I want you to assume the form of Ascanius — gods and goddesses have that power. Take on his form for only one night. That way, when Dido sets you on her lap and kisses you, you can make her fall passionately in love with Aeneas. She will never know that a god caused her to fall in love."

Cupid was willing to do as his mother asked. He shed his wings and assumed the form of Ascanius. Venus put the real Ascanius into a soothing sleep and carried him off to the town of Idalium on Cyprus and placed him on a bed of aromatic marjoram.

Achates led "Ascanius," carrying gifts, to Carthage. Dido sat on her throne, and Aeneas and the Trojans entered her throne room. Servants brought water so that everyone could wash their hands, and they set out a meal. As all ate, they admired the gifts that Aeneas gave Dido and they admired the boy whom they thought to be Ascanius.

Dido especially was enthralled with the gifts and with the boy. Cupid hugged Aeneas and then he went to Dido. She held him in her lap, and the god slowly dissipated her memory of Sychaeus, her late husband. Her heart had long been closed to love and passion, but Cupid began to open it.

Servants cleared the tables of food, and they brought out more wine for all to enjoy. Conversation abounded, and servants lit lamps and torches.

Dido ordered that a golden, bejeweled bowl filled with wine unmixed with water be brought to her, and she prayed aloud to the king of gods and men, "Jupiter, you are the god of hospitality. You are the god of hosts and of guests. Please allow this day to always be a day of joy for Carthaginians and for Trojan exiles. Please allow this day to be remembered with happiness by our children. May Bacchus, god of wine and giver of bliss, and Juno give us their blessings. And now let us celebrate with happiness."

Dido poured out wine for the gods, and then she sipped the wine and passed the bowl to the nobleman Bitias, who drank with pleasure. Then the other nobles drank from the bowl.

The bard Iopas played his lyre and sang songs of epic glory. His teacher had been Atlas, a Titan. Iopas sang about the phases of the moon and the eclipses of the sun, the origins of humans and beasts, the sources of storms and lightning bolts and the constellations, and why winter days are so short and winter nights are so long. The Carthaginians and the Trojans applauded his genius.

As Venus had planned, Dido fell in love with Aeneas, and she asked him many questions about Priam, about Hector, about the Ethiopian king Memnon who had fought for the Trojans, and about the Greek warriors Diomedes and Achilles.

Dido then said to Aeneas, "Please tell us your story from beginning to end. Start with how Troy fell and then tell us your wanderings for the seven years from the fall of Troy to your coming to Carthage."

Chapter 2: The Fall of Troy

Everyone fell silent and stared at Aeneas, who sat in a seat of honor. Aeneas said, "Queen, you ask me to renew a terrible sorrow. You ask me to tell how the Greeks conquered Troy, once a great city but now destroyed. I was there, and I saw horrors. No one who was a witness can refrain from crying at the memory of the fall of the city — not even a Greek, not even Ulysses, the Greek with the hardest heart.

"Now night is falling, but if you want to hear my story and the story of the fall of Troy, I will tell it.

"In the tenth year of the Trojan War, the Greeks were exhausted. So many years had passed. But Minerva gave them the skill to build the Trojan Horse. It was huge, hollow, and wooden. The Greeks pretended that it was an offering for a safe voyage back to Greece, but that was a lie. The Greeks picked their best and bravest warriors, and they hid them and their weapons in the hollow Trojan Horse.

"Within sight of Troy is the island of Tenedos. The Greeks sailed away from Troy and hid behind the island. We Trojans thought that the Greeks had gone back to Greece and that we had won the war. We were wrong. It was all a trick.

"But we opened the gates and walked onto the plain before Troy. We wandered the abandoned camps of the Greeks. We stood on the shore. We stood where Achilles had pitched his tents. We looked over the place where the Greeks had drawn their ships out of the sea. We looked at the battlefield, the place of killing.

"Some Trojans looked at the Trojan Horse, a gift for Minerva, the unwed virgin goddess. Thymoetes urged the Trojans, 'Drag the Horse inside the walls of Troy!' The fate of Troy and the end of Troy were coming closer.

"But some Trojans resisted moving the Horse inside the city walls. Capys and other Trojans, saner than Thymoetes, advised, 'Either throw the Horse into the sea or set it on fire! Or else break open the Horse and see whether warriors are inside!'

"Some Trojans sided with Thymoetes; some Trojans sided with Capys.

"Laocoön, a priest of Neptune, arrived from Troy. He said to the Trojans, 'Are you insane? Do you really believe that the treacherous Greeks have sailed back to Greece? Do you trust any Greek gift? You know the reputation of Ulysses. Do you trust that he has left Troy? This Horse either hides Greek warriors inside, or it will be used to batter our walls, or it has some other treacherous purpose. Do not trust that the Trojan Horse is harmless. I do not trust the Greeks, especially when they are giving gifts.'

"Laocoön hurled his spear at the Trojan Horse. It struck the Horse's side, which echoed, showing that the Horse was hollow. Fate opposed us Trojans, and our own wits also opposed us. If not, we would have listened to Laocoön and broke open the Horse, and Troy would still be a rich center of civilization today.

"Suddenly, in the midst of the arguments the Trojans made, both pro and con, for destroying the Horse or taking it inside the walls of Troy, some Trojan shepherds brought a Greek man to Priam, our king. They had come across him by what they thought was accident, and they had captured him.

"It was a trick. The Greek had made sure that he would be captured. He had a purpose that demanded that he be captured. He wanted to lie to us Trojans and ensure our destruction and the destruction of our city.

"He was a liar, but he was a courageous liar. If his lies had not been believed, he would have died.

"Young Trojan males came up to him and mocked him, and he stood there, helpless, and groaned. Looking at the Trojans who surrounded him, he said, 'What will happen to me now? There is no safe place anywhere for me. Not on land. Not on sea. The Greeks want me dead. So do the Trojans.'

"We Trojans are a merciful people. Instead of killing him, we asked him for his story: 'Who are you? What is your birth? Who is your family? What is your story?'

"He replied, lying, 'I will tell you all, and all of it is truth. Fortune may be against me, but I won't allow Fortune to make me — Sinon — a liar. You may have heard of the Greek named Palamedes, whom the other Greeks charged with treason — falsely. He was innocent of treason, but he opposed the Trojan War. Because of that, the Greeks put him to death, an action they regretted later. I am related by blood to Palamedes, and I opposed the charge of treason. A young man, I had come to Troy as the companion of Palamedes.

As long as he had the respect of the Greeks, they gave me some respect as well. Once they had killed Palamedes, I was no longer treated with respect.

"'Ulysses, whose treachery you well know, hated me. I had opposed the charge of treason made against Palamedes, and now, grieving his death, I swore aloud that if I ever returned to Greece I would get revenge for his death. I swore an oath that I would do this.

"'From that moment, Ulysses tormented me by making charge after charge against me and by starting rumor after rumor about me. He was mainly guilty of the death of Palamedes, and he wanted to ensure that I would not get the revenge that I had sworn to get. Ulysses was determined that I would die at Troy, and so he formed a plan with the prophet Calchas.

"'But do I need to tell you what happened next? If you think that all Greeks are guilty and deserve to die, then kill me now. That would make Ulysses happy. Agamemnon and Menelaus would even pay you to kill me.'"

Ulysses had hated Palamedes because Palamedes was responsible for making Ulysses go to the Trojan War. Ulysses had not wanted to leave his home island of Ithaca, and so when the Greeks came to recruit him for the war, he pretended to be insane and plowed his land with salt. Palamedes guessed that he was faking insanity, and he put Ulysses' infant son, Telemachus, in front of the plow. Rather than kill his son, Ulysses turned aside the plow, proving that he was sane.

Aeneas continued, "We Trojans wanted to hear the rest of his story. We did not know exactly how treacherous a Greek could be.

"Trembling, he continued to tell his lying story: 'After ten long years of fighting, the Greeks grew tired of the war. They wanted it to be over. They wanted a respite from war. How I wish that they had immediately returned home to Greece! But when they wanted to set sail, the waves and the winds were against them. Even after we built this Horse you see before you, the waves and winds were unfavorable for sailing back home to Greece.

"'Therefore, we sent Eurypalus to consult the oracle of Apollo. Oracles can foretell the future and can tell how to gain the favor of the gods. We sought the knowledge of what we should do to ensure favorable waves and winds. Eurypalus brought back the words of the oracle: "When you sailed to Troy, you sacrificed a human being to ensure favorable waves and winds.

Now that you want to sail back home to Greece, you must sacrifice a human to ensure favorable waves and winds."

"'News of the oracle's words spread among all the Greeks. Someone must be sacrificed. Whose life did the gods demand? Who would be the human sacrifice?

"'Ulysses brought the prophet Calchas before the Greeks and demanded that he tell whom the gods wanted to be the sacrifice. The Greek warriors also wanted to know. Even then, the Greek warriors thought that I would be the sacrificial victim because of Ulysses' hatred of me.

"'For ten days, the prophet Calchas refused to name the sacrificial victim. Finally, he seemed to give in to the demands of Ulysses, but actually it was a part of their plan. He named me as the sacrificial victim. The Greek warriors were happy — none of them would be the one to die. They were happy to live, and they were happy that I was the one who was supposed to die.

"'The day set for the human sacrifice soon arrived. The Greeks prepared to sacrifice me. They performed the religious rites, they got ready the salted meal, and they tied the sacred bands around my head. But I escaped. I broke the bonds holding me and ran away and hid all night in a marsh until they set sail.

"'I have no hope now of ever returning to Greece and seeing my children and my father. Maybe the Greeks will punish them because the Greeks failed to sacrifice me.

"'Pity me, king. I have suffered what no man deserved to suffer.'

"Sinon cried, and we Trojans pitied him. We Trojans are merciful. We Trojans have the quality of *clementia*: mercy. Priam ordered that the bonds that the shepherds had put on Sinon be removed. Priam then said to the lying Greek, 'From now on, you are a Trojan. Please, answer my questions. Why did the Greeks build this huge Horse? What is the Horse's purpose? Is it a gift to the gods, or is it a weapon of war?'

"Sinon's hands were now free from his bonds. He raised his arms and prayed, 'Bear witness, stars and sun and gods. Bear witness, altar and knives and the other implements of human sacrifice. Bear witness that I am right to break my oath to the Greeks to fight against Troy. Bear witness that I am right to detest the Greeks. Bear witness that I am right to reveal the purpose of the Trojan Horse. Trojans, keep your promise to me that I will be one of you — a Greek no longer — and I will tell you the truth about the Horse.

"'The Greeks' hopes of conquering Troy have always rested on the good will and the help of Minerva. But her good will toward the Greeks came to an end when Ulysses and Diomedes snuck into Troy and stole the Palladium, the sacred statue of Minerva belonging to you Trojans. Ulysses and Diomedes killed several guards in Troy, and when they reached the Palladium, they touched it with bloody hands — a sacrilege and affront to Minerva. From that moment, Minerva no longer helped the Greeks.

"'Minerva sent omens to show the Greeks that they had offended her. When Ulysses and Diomedes brought the sacred statue into the Greeks' camp, fire shot forth from the statue's eyes. Sweat ran down the statue. Minerva herself, bearing her shield and spear, appeared to the Greeks three times.

"'The prophet Calchas knew that Minerva was offended. He knew that she no longer had good will toward the Greeks. He knew that she had withdrawn her help from the Greeks.

"'He advised the Greeks, "You cannot conquer Troy unless you first return to Greece and make amends to the goddess. Take the Palladium to Greece, propitiate the goddess, and then bring the Palladium back to the plain before Troy."

"'The Greeks obeyed him. They set sail for Greece. They have left Troy — temporarily. They plan to acquire new weapons, persuade the gods to be on the Greeks' side, and then return to Troy and defeat you.

"'Calchas also ordered the Greeks to build this Horse. It is an offering to Minerva. The Greeks hope that she will forgive them for the theft of the Palladium.

"'Calchas ordered that the Horse be built on a massive scale so that you Trojans could not take the Horse inside the city's walls. Calchas knew that you Trojans would either desecrate the Horse or respect it. If you should desecrate the Horse — this offering to the goddess — disaster will come to you and your city and your futures. But if you should respect the Horse — this offering to the goddess — and bring it inside your walls, then you will take the war to Greece. Instead of Greece attacking Troy, Troy and the rest of Asia will attack Greece. So says the prophet Calchas.'

"We believed Sinon, the lying Greek. Achilles could not defeat the Trojans, ten years of war could not defeat the Trojans, the thousand ships that the Greeks had brought to Troy could not defeat the Trojans, but our good nature and our pity for the tears of Sinon ended up defeating us. Our *clementia* ended up defeating us.

"An omen from the gods also defeated us. Laocoön was sacrificing a bull at the altar of Neptune when out of the sea came two huge sea-snakes. Their crests were the color of blood, and the Trojans ran away from them. Each sea-snake coiled itself around one of Laocoön's young sons. Each sea-snake bit the young boy it was killing. Laocoön tried to save his sons. He ran to the sea-snakes and slashed at them with his sword. The sea-snakes trapped him in their coils, wrapping themselves around his waist and his throat. Laocoön tried to push them away. He could not. He screamed, but his screams did not sound human. He sounded like a bull that had been wounded at the sacrificial altar. The bull had not been quickly killed. The ax did not hit a mortal spot. A wounded bull will fight to escape from the altar.

"Having killed Laocoön and his two sons, the sea-snakes went to the shrine of Minerva at Troy and vanished under her shield.

"We Trojans were afraid. We believed that Laocoön had offended the gods. We believed that he deserved the punishment that the gods had given him. Laocoön had thrown his spear at the Trojan Horse, desecrating it.

"We did not know that the gods were determined that Troy should fall.

"We Trojans shouted, 'Haul the Trojan Horse to the temple of Minerva inside the city of Troy. Let us honor the goddess.'

"We Trojans worked to make that happen. The Trojan Horse was too big to fit through the gates, so we tore down part of our own walls to enlarge the opening so that the Horse could come inside the city. We put rollers under the Horse and we tied ropes around its neck so that we could drag the Horse inside Troy.

"Trojan boys and girls were happy. They sang and danced as the Horse rolled toward the city gates.

"Four times the Horse came to a halt, and four times the armor of the Greek warriors hidden inside clanged, but we Trojans were deaf, blind, insane, ill-fated. We kept working until we had the Horse inside Troy.

"Cassandra, the daughter of Priam, prophesized the fall of Troy, and she prophesized correctly, but no one believed her. Later I learned that she had promised the god Apollo that she would sleep with him if he gave her the power of prophecy. He swore an inviolable oath that he would give her that gift, but she reneged on her promise and would not sleep with him. Because Apollo had sworn an inviolable oath, he was forced to give her the gift of prophecy, but he gave her an additional 'gift': She would prophesize correctly, but no one would ever believe her prophecies until after the events she had foretold had actually occurred.

"We Trojans foolishly believed that this was a day of joy, a day to be celebrated. We decorated the city with festive garlands.

"Night came. We Trojans, wearied by our celebrations, slept. The Greeks sailed back to Troy from the island of Tenedos. They arrived at their campsites that they knew very well. The Greeks sent up a flare that signaled Sinon to go to the Trojan Horse and let out the Greek warriors, who slid down a rope to the ground. The warriors inside the Horse were Thessandrus, Sthenelus, Ulysses, Acamas, Thoas, Pyrrhus (Achilles' son, who is also known as Neoptolemus), Machaon, Menelaus, and Epeus, who had built the Horse. The city was quiet, it had few guards, and the Greek warriors killed those guards and opened the gates to let the waiting Agamemnon and his Greek warriors inside the city.

"I was asleep, and I dreamed that Hector, the greatest warrior of the Trojans and one of the warriors whom Achilles had killed, came to me. Tears streamed down his face, and he looked the way that he had looked when Achilles had dragged his corpse behind the chariot. I saw the holes that Achilles had pierced in Hector's ankles so that he could tie his corpse to the chariot and then drag the corpse on the ground. Hector did not look the way he had looked when he proudly wore Achilles' armor that he had stripped from the corpse of Patroclus, Achilles' best friend. He did not look the way that he had looked when the Trojans had set fire to one of the Greeks' ships. He looked the way he had looked when he had been defeated and killed. His beard was matted, his hair was bloody, and his body displayed many wounds.

"I dreamed that I talked to Hector, saying, 'We Trojans are happy that you have returned to us. We have missed you. You were always our best hope for defeating the Greeks. But what is wrong? Your face and body are bloody and wounded.'

"Hector groaned and said to me, 'Now is the time for you to escape from the fires of the city. Troy has fallen. The Greeks have conquered our city. You have served your king and your city valiantly, but it was not enough. If anyone could have saved Troy, it would have been me. Now, you must preserve the city's household gods. Take them with you as you escape from the Greeks and leave Troy. Sail the sea and found a new city where the household gods can reside.'

"In my dream, I saw Hector carry the image of Vesta, the goddess of the hearth, away.

"Noise came from the city. Cries of pain filled the air. I was asleep in my father's palace, which was located in a place with trees, away from the main city, but the noise woke me up. I climbed up on the roof and listened. I heard a roar. It sounded like fire burning a field of wheat or like a flooding and rapidly flowing river dragging full-grown trees into its waters. A shepherd can hear such a roar and be amazed. I understood immediately the treachery of the Greeks.

"I saw the house of Deiphobus. It was on fire, and it crashed to the ground. The house next to his — the house of Ucalegon — had also caught on fire. I saw the fires reflected in the water of the sea. I heard the sound of fighting warriors and of trumpets.

"I seized my armor and weapons. The city had fallen, but I wanted to kill Greeks. If I had to die that night, I wanted to go down fighting. To die defending your city is a noble death.

"I saw Panthus, a priest of Apollo. He was carrying the holy items used in the worship of Apollo. He held the hand of his little grandson as they tried to escape.

"I asked, 'Panthus, where are the Trojan warriors? Where are they making their last stand?'

"Panthus groaned and said, 'It's all over. Troy has fallen. Troy no longer exists. The glory of Troy has vanished. Jupiter now gives glory to the Greeks, who are burning our homes. The Trojan Horse was filled with Greek warriors. Sinon exults as our city burns. Our gates are open wide so that the

Greeks can easily enter. Greeks fill our streets and use their weapons. A few Trojans — only a few — are fighting back. They cannot last long.'

"I headed toward the fighting, toward the cries of war. I met other Trojans: Rhipeus, Epytus, Hypanis, Dymas, and Coroebus, who had come to Troy to marry Cassandra. Not even he understood her prophecies.

"We were ready to do battle and kill Greeks. I told them, 'This is a battle we cannot win. Look around, and you will see that the gods have deserted us and gone over to the side of the Greeks. But let us send some Greeks to the Land of the Dead. We know that we are defeated and we cannot live. Let us not fear the arrival of death because death has already arrived for us.'

"We moved on. We were like a pack of wolves whose hunger drives them to kill so that they can feed their young. Shielded by darkness, we went into the center of the city.

"We saw so much slaughter. We saw so many dead bodies — not just in homes and on the streets but on the altars of the gods as well. The Greeks should have respected the gods at whose altars the Trojans had taken refuge — the Greeks did not.

"Not only Trojans died. Many Trojans sent Greeks to the Land of the Dead.

"The first Greek we saw was Androgeos, who was with his warriors. He was happy and celebrating, and he mistook us for Greeks. He called to us, 'Hurry up. Kill some Trojans. Do some looting. You're late. You must have just come from the ships.'

"Suddenly, Androgeos realized that we were not Greeks. We had given him no friendly words. He was like a man who walks in the woods and steps on a snake that gets into biting position. Androgeos cringed away from us and tried to flee.

"We attacked. The Greeks panicked, and we killed them. In this first encounter with Greeks, we were completely triumphant.

"Coroebus said, 'Trojans, let us trick the Greeks. Let's use these dead Greeks' distinctive shields and their weapons. That way, the Greeks will think that we are Greeks, and we can surprise them with death. Why shouldn't the Greeks supply Trojans with shields and weapons that they can use to kill Greeks?'

"Coroebus put on the armor of Androgeos: his helmet and shield. He also strapped a Greek sword on his hip. We other Trojans also commandeered Greek armor and weapons. Rhipeus and Dymas armed themselves with the possessions of the warriors they had just killed.

"We kept encountering Greeks and killing them. Some Greeks turned coward and fled back to their ships. Other Greeks climbed the rope dangling from the Trojan Horse so that they could hide themselves in its womb.

"But the gods were against us. We saw Cassandra — she was a prisoner, and her hands were tied. Greeks were dragging her by her hair from the temple of Minerva. Later I learned that Little Ajax had raped the virgin Cassandra in the temple — an outrage to Minerva, a virgin goddess. Because Cassandra was in the temple of Minerva, she was under the protection of the goddess. Little Ajax did not respect Minerva.

"Because Cassandra could not raise her hands to the heavens, she raised her eyes. Her fiancé, Coroebus, was infuriated by the sight of the Greeks leading her away as a slave, and he hurled himself at them, knowing that he would die.

"We followed Coroebus, and now we suffered disaster. Our fellow Trojans saw our Greek helmets and shields, and they attacked us. From the roof of the temple, Trojans threw spears at us, thinking that we were enemy soldiers. Our ruse tricked both the Greeks and our fellow Trojans.

"Not only did the Trojans attack us, but so did the Greeks. Briefly, we freed Cassandra, but Little Ajax, Agamemnon, Menelaus, and other Greek soldiers attacked us. We were attacked from above and from all sides.

"The Greeks were as fierce as a whirlwind that howls in the forests. The Greeks were as dangerous as the high waves created by Nereus, the father of Achilles' mother, Thetis, and the other sea-nymphs.

"We had routed many Greeks, but now they regrouped and fought against us, aware that the Greek helmets and Greek shields we wore were lies, aware that the common language we shared with them had a different sound when spoken by Trojans.

"We were outnumbered, and Coroebus was the first Trojan whom the Greeks killed. Peneleus killed him, and Coroebus fell onto the altar of Minerva. Next to die was Rhipeus, the most righteous man in Troy, the Trojan most devoted to justice. Even so, the gods allowed him to die.

"Hypanis and Dymas also died at the end of weapons, but the weapons were in the hands of Trojans. In the chaos of a falling city, the weapons of friendly warriors can be as dangerous as the weapons of enemy warriors.

"Even Panthus, the priest of Apollo, whom I had seen trying to flee the city, fell. Apollo did not save him.

"I survived, but I swear that I did not stay away from the fighting. I sought the enemy, and I killed the enemy. If I had been fated to die that night, fate would have easily found a way for me to die.

"Two other Trojans were still alive with me. Iphitus was an old man, and his old age slowed him down. Pelias was also slow because Ulysses had wounded him. We made our way to the palace of Priam.

"At the palace, a battle roared! Here was death, frequent and in many violent forms. Mars, the god of war, enjoyed the blood and the battle.

"The Trojans were on the roof, being assaulted by the Greeks. On the ground, the Greeks made a tortoise shell of their shields for protection. They also climbed ladders, trying to reach the roof, each carrying a shield on his left arm for protection and climbing higher with his right arm.

"The Trojans ripped off pieces of the roof — tiles and wooden beams — to hurl down on the Greeks climbing the ladders. The Trojans knew that they wouldn't last much longer. Other Trojans defended the doors below. These Trojans also had little time left to live.

"I ran to the palace, eager to defend it.

"In the palace of Priam is a secret passageway that Andromache, the wife of Hector, used to take their son, Astyanax, to visit his grandparents Priam and Hecuba. I used the passageway to climb up to the roof, where Trojans were throwing their spears.

"On the roof was a tower. We used tools to detach it from the roof, and then we tipped it over to crash it onto the Greeks. But more Greeks came to replace those we had killed. The battle continued; we had no respite.

"I saw Pyrrhus, the son of Achilles. Pyrrhus was like a snake that had hibernated and now had come forth to be a danger to men. He had been absent for most of the Trojan War but came to Troy after his father had died. Pyrrhus stood at the front gates with Periphas and Automedon, who had been Achilles' charioteer.

"The Greeks hurled fire onto the roofs. Pyrrhus grabbed an ax and started attacking the doors that led inside the palace. He attacked the doorposts and the doors, and he opened a breach that led inside the palace. Pyrrhus and other Greek warriors saw the Trojan guards who were defending our king.

"Inside the palace was despair. The women, afraid, were crying. Mothers did not know where to go to find safety.

"Pyrrhus and other Greeks kept battering the doors. The doors split and caved in. They fell. The palace was open to the enemy.

"The Greeks rushed in and killed the Trojan guards. The Greeks were everywhere. From a hole we had made in the roof when we were tearing it apart to find things to throw on the enemy, I was able to see everything.

"No flooding river bursting its dikes and overflowing its banks and sweeping away animals and barns could match the flood that was the Greeks sweeping away the Trojan resistance.

"In the palace, I saw Pyrrhus, and I saw Agamemnon and Menelaus. I saw Hecuba, the wife of Priam, with her hundred daughters and daughters-in-law. And I saw Priam.

"Fire was destroying much of the palace. The fifty bridal-bedchambers in the palace fell to fire. Whatever parts of the palace that did not fall to fire fell to the Greeks.

"Do you want to know how Priam died? I can tell you. I saw him die. I wish I had not.

"When Priam realized that the Greeks were inside Troy and were conquering the city, he put on his armor, which he had not worn for decades. As he put it on, his hands shook with old age. He strapped his sword to his hip, and then he went to meet the enemy.

"Inside the palace was an altar, a shrine to the household gods. Hecuba and her daughters had fled there in hopes to find refuge. They were like doves that a storm has thrown to the ground. Hecuba saw her aged husband wearing armor and carrying a spear and said to him, 'Armor and weapons are useless now. Not even our son Hector, if he were alive, could save us. Come to the altar. It is our last and our best hope. Either we will live under the protection of our household gods, or if the Greeks disrespect the gods, we will die here, together.'

"Hecuba took her husband's hands and led him to the altar.

"But Polites, one of their young sons, ran into the room, pursued by Pyrrhus, the son of Achilles. He was already badly wounded by Pyrrhus, who wanted to finish killing him. Polites reached his parents and the altar, Pyrrhus speared him, and then Polites vomited blood and died.

"Angered by the death of yet another of his sons, Priam said to Pyrrhus, 'You are vicious! I hope that the gods repay you for your outrage! You have forced me to witness the death of my son at the altar! You say that you are the son of Achilles? You lie! Achilles was capable of goodness. He honored me when I was a suppliant, and he allowed me to ransom the corpse of my son Hector so I could give him a proper funeral. He allowed me to return safely home to Troy with the body of my son.'

"Priam then threw his spear with all the strength he had at Pyrrhus. It feebly struck his shield and did no damage.

"Pyrrhus told Priam, 'I want you to take news to Achilles, my father, down in the Land of the Dead. Tell him about my outrages and my bad character. Now it is time for you to die!'

"Pyrrhus dragged Priam to the altar. Priam's feet slipped on the blood of his son. Pyrrhus grabbed Priam's hair with one hand, and with the other hand he plunged his sword all the way to the hilt in Priam's side. Hecuba witnessed the death of her husband. So did their daughters.

"So died Priam, King of Troy. So died Troy itself. Priam had ruled Asia, but now it was as if he were a headless corpse lying without a name on a shore.

"Seeing the death of Priam reminded me of my own father — the two men were the same age. I also thought of my wife, Creusa, and my son, Ascanius. They were alone in our house without a warrior to defend them. I looked around. I was alone. The other Trojans had died. They had fallen in battle or had been overcome by the fires.

"I was the only Trojan warrior left there, and suddenly I saw Helen of Troy in the light of the fires destroying Troy. She was clinging to the image of Vesta, hoping for protection from the goddess. She was silent, hoping that no one would notice her. She was terrified of the Trojans, whose city had fallen because of her, and she was terrified of her husband, whom she had deserted.

"Helen had good reason to be terrified. I wanted to kill her.

"Why should Helen live when Troy, its king, and its warriors had fallen? Why should Helen live when Troy's women and children were going to become slaves?

"Should Helen be allowed to go back to Sparta and live an easy life, served by Trojan slaves? No.

"Killing a woman is not honorable. Warriors receive no fame for killing a woman. But Helen being Helen, she should die. Her death would bring comfort to conquered Trojans.

"*Furor* — the passion of rage — conquered me, and I moved with my sword toward Helen, but my mother, Venus, stood before me. I saw her clearly. She wore no disguise. She is a goddess, and she appeared before me as a goddess. She was and is beautiful.

"Venus grabbed my hand and said to me, 'You are feeling grief and anger. You are feeling *furor*. But leave Helen and look for your father. Do you know whether your wife and your son are still alive? The Greeks are all around them.

"'While you have been gone, I have been protecting them. If I had not, they would be dead by now. Either the fires or the Greeks would have killed them.

"'Why is the city falling? Not because of Helen or Paris, but because of the gods, who are tearing apart your city.

"'I will give you special sight. Usually, the sight of mortal men is faulty. Mortal men are blinded by mist. I will sweep away the mist so that you can see the gods and you will learn that what I am saying is true.

"'The mist is gone. Now look and see clearly. Look at the foundation stones of Troy. Neptune himself is breaking them; he is destroying the foundation of Troy.

"'Now see Juno. She was the first god to reach the Scaean Gates. She led the Greek warriors inside Troy.

"'Look at the heights of Troy. There Minerva and Jupiter are putting courage into the hearts of the Greek warriors. They want the Greeks to kill the Trojans.

"'Run. Save your life. I will help you.'

"She vanished. I realized that she had spoken the truth. The gods themselves were destroying Troy. Neptune was tearing down Troy the way that woodsmen chop down and topple a proud, tall tree that has stood for ages, but conquered by the wounds the woodsmen inflict on it, it falls.

"My mother led the way, and I climbed down from the roof of Priam's palace, avoiding fire and enemy spears. I made my way to my home and my family.

"I found my father. I wanted to carry him to safety. If he stayed in Troy, he would die. But I had a chance to carry him out of Troy and to the safety of the mountains.

"But my father refused to go.

"My father said to me, 'You, your wife, and your son are young. Save yourselves. I am old. If the gods had wanted me to continue to live, they would not have allowed Troy to be destroyed. I would still have a home here. I have already witnessed one sack of Troy. I was alive when Hercules conquered Troy because its king, Laomedon, refused to give him the horses he had earned. I survived one sack of Troy. I need not survive another — I am too old to go into exile. Leave me here, and let me die. The Greeks will not allow me to live. My corpse will not be buried, but I prefer even that to exile. For many years now, I have been crippled. I boasted that Venus loved me. Jupiter heard me, grew angry that a mortal should make such a boast, and threw a thunderbolt at me to kill me. Venus pushed the thunderbolt aside so that it did not kill me, but it crippled me. My legs are useless, and I have lived long enough.'

"We pleaded with him — I, my wife, and my son — but he was determined to die. My duty was to my father, and I would not leave him. I prepared to die defending him.

"I told my father, 'Do you think that I would leave you? Never! If you are determined to die here, the rest of our family and I will also die here. Soon the son of Achilles, Pyrrhus, will arrive. He will be willing to kill all of us. Already, the blood of Priam is on his body, as is the blood of Priam's son Polites whom Pyrrhus slaughtered on an altar in front of his father, whom he also slaughtered on an altar.

"'My mother, your wife, told me to come back here. Why? So I could see my father, my wife, and my son slaughtered on an altar? So I could see their blood mingling on the floor?

"'At least I can kill some Greeks before I die. I will have Greek company as I go down to the Land of the Dead.'

"I strapped my sword to my hip again and took up my shield. I was leaving the house when my wife, Creusa, knelt with my son before me and grabbed my knees and supplicated me: 'If you are going away so that you can die, take us with you. Let us face death together. Don't leave us. Your duty is to defend us. You should not leave us alone and let the Greeks find us.'

"My wife cried. I had no good choice. My father refused to leave the house.

"Suddenly, the gods sent us an omen. My son's head appeared to be on fire. He wore a crown of fire. Afraid for our son, we tried to put out the fire — but the fire did not burn him. Our son was in no danger.

"My father interpreted the omen. It was a good omen. The omen meant that my son would become a king.

"My father raised his arms and prayed to the king of gods and men, 'Jupiter, send us another sign — one that will confirm this omen.'

"Immediately, thunder sounded on the right — the lucky sign. Also, a star fell from the sky and landed on Mount Ida — a sign that we should go there.

"My father changed his mind because of the omens. He said, 'Let us leave immediately. I am willing to go wherever the gods send me. Keep Ascanius, my grandson and your son, safe. You and he have a destiny.'

"My father was ready to leave. Just in time. The fires were growing stronger and closer.

"I told my father, 'I will carry you on my back. I will carry you to safety. Ascanius, my son, stay by my side. Creusa, my wife, follow me a little way behind. Servants, listen to me. Past the walls of Troy are a grave-mound and an old shrine to the goddess Ceres. The shrine has an old cypress tree growing by it. That will be our meeting place. Get to it by whatever route you can — we should not all take the same route. Father, carry the household gods. I am covered with blood, and it would be sacrilegious for me to touch them with bloody hands.'

"I put a lion's skin on my shoulders and then lifted my father and our household gods. I took my son by the hand, and my wife followed us. By taking my son by the hand and leading him, I was taking the future with me.

By taking my father and our household gods with me, I was taking part of the past with me. My wife did not make it out of Troy. Some of the past we cannot take with us.

"We walked along paths, seeking an escape from the city. I had not been afraid of Greek weapons. I had not been afraid to face death. But now I was terrified for my family. I wanted my family to stay alive. We got near the gates, and I thought that we were all safe, but suddenly I heard warriors approaching, and my father told me, 'Run! I see the warriors' weapons!'

"I ran. Blindly. I did not look back. At some time and some place, my wife was no longer behind me. She may have gotten lost in the darkness and the confusion. She may have been overcome by exhaustion. I made my way to the shrine dedicated to Ceres, and then I learned that my wife was not with me. I raved. I blamed the gods. I blamed every mortal, including myself. I hid my father and my son in a valley along with other Trojans who had escaped, and then I went back to Troy to look for my wife. Once again, I took the chance of losing my life.

"I went back to the walls and the rear gates through which we had exited Troy. I retraced the path we had taken out of the city. I went back to my home in case my wife had returned there. There I saw only Greeks and fire. I went to the palace of Priam, and in the courtyard I saw Phoenix and Ulysses standing guard over the loot they had taken — valuable religious items. Also in the courtyard were mothers and children who would soon be portioned out as slaves. I returned to the Trojan streets and risked calling aloud my wife's name: 'Creusa!' No reply. I called her name again. No reply.

"And then I saw my wife's ghost, larger than she had been while alive. I was afraid. She spoke to me, 'Aeneas, my husband and my love, do not grieve. My death and the fall of Troy occurred because of the will of the gods. The gods did not want you and me to be together after the fall of Troy. Jupiter will not allow that.

"'Let me prophesize to you. You will now have a long exile. You will sail the seas until you reach the land called Hesperia: the Land of the West. There you will see the Tiber River. It will be a land of rich soil and hardy people. You will find a kingdom there and a wife.

"'Don't mourn me. I will not be taken as a slave to serve a Greek master. Cybele, the Great Mother of Gods, has kept my body on Trojan soil.

"'Farewell, and take care of our son, whom we love.'

"Those were the last words she ever spoke to me. Three times I tried to hug her. Three times I hugged nothing. I was not able to touch her ghost — it dissipated each time I tried.

"Her ghost was gone. I went back to my father and son, and I saw many Trojans who had fled the city and come to the shrine of Ceres. They needed a leader, and they were ready to follow me. Dawn was approaching. The Greeks had taken the city — Troy was no more.

"I lifted up my father, and I led the Trojan exiles away from the city and toward the safety of the mountains.

Chapter 3: Wanderings

"Now that Troy was gone, we needed a new city, a new land, a new country. The gods sent us signs, and we attempted to follow them. At the bottom of Mount Ida, we built a fleet. We knew that we needed to set sail, although we did not know exactly where we were going.

"Summer had just arrived, and my father, Anchises, ordered us to set sail: 'Let us go and find our fate.' We left behind the land that had been our home. We journeyed on the water. I had my son, my fellow exiled Trojans, and my household gods.

"We arrived at Thrace, a land ruled by Lycurgus, a king without pity. He had supported us Trojans, as long as fate seemed to support us.

"Here we began building a city that I named after myself.

"I wanted to make a sacrifice to my mother, Venus, the daughter of Dione. I also was going to sacrifice a white bull to Jupiter. I needed to make a canopy for the altar. Seeing a thicket of dogwood and myrtle, I broke off a branch.

"But as soon as I broke off a branch, blood flowed from the broken wood and dripped to the ground. Of course, this was a bad omen. I was afraid, but I broke another branch, and more blood flowed. I prayed to the nymphs of Thrace and to the god Mars, 'Make this a good omen, not a bad one.' I broke a third branch — more blood flowed.

"And I heard a voice that came from the ground: 'Why, Aeneas, are you making me bleed? Spare me, and spare yourself. No good can come to you from fouling your hands with my blood. You know me. I am a Trojan, and the blood you see is Trojan. Escape from this guilty land. I am Polydorus, and I am one of the sons of Priam. Here I was murdered with spears. The spears stayed in my body after my death. They took root and grew.'

"I felt fear, and I could not speak to the voice.

"I had known Polydorus, who was a prince of Troy. Priam had sent him to the Thracian king along with a large quantity of gold. Priam wanted to ensure that at least one of his sons would survive the Trojan War. But when Troy fell, the king of Thrace was overcome by greed and murdered Polydorus and stole his gold. The lust for gold can motivate such evil.

"Soon, I regained my wits, and I carried news of the omen to my father and the other advisors. They all had the same opinion: We needed to leave Thrace immediately. This was not the land on which we should build our city. We set sail again.

"But first we built Polydorus a proper burial mound. We heaped great quantities of earth over his body. On the altar, we made offerings to all the gods. The Trojan women mourned with their hair unbound in accordance with the ancient custom. We poured out cups of milk and cups of blood. We mourned him, and we gave his soul rest.

"When dawn came, and a gentle South wind, we launched the ships and headed toward the island of Delos. Neptune and Doris, who is the mother of the sea-nymphs, love this island. Apollo was born there when it was a floating island, but later Apollo fastened it in between two other islands: Myconos and Gyaros. It no longer wandered; it stayed in one place.

"We landed at Delos, and we saw the city of Apollo that is ruled by Anius, who is both a king ruling men and a priest serving Apollo. Anius came to welcome us; he knew my father, Anchises, from long ago.

"We saw the shrine to Apollo, and I prayed to the god, 'Apollo, give us a home. We are weary. We want a permanent home of our own. We are the remnant of a once-proud city: Troy. Keep us safe, and tell us what path we should follow. Give us a sign, Apollo!'

"I had just finished my prayer when a sign revealed itself. An earthquake struck the island, and we fell to the ground. We heard a voice: 'Sons of Dardanus, an ancestor of the kings of Troy, seek your ancient homeland. From there, the descendants of Aeneas will rule the world for generations through all the years.'

"This prophecy by Apollo created joy and happiness among us Trojans, who asked ourselves, 'What is the land that Apollo wants us to sail to?'

"My father thought about our ancient history, and he said, 'I know the land that is meant. In the middle of the Mediterranean is an island: Crete. On Crete is the first Mount Ida, after which the Trojan Mount Ida was named. The Cretans have many cities and rich land. Teucer, one of our ancestors, came from Crete. He sailed to our shore and founded his kingdom there. When he arrived, Troy had not yet been founded. From Crete also came the goddess Cybele, whom her priests, the Corybantes, worship with dance and with cymbals. So let us follow the prophecy of Apollo and go to Crete to found our city. It is not far. Within three days, we can reach the island.'

"Anchises then sacrificed a bull to Neptune, a bull to Apollo, a black ram to the storms of winter, and a white ram to the warm West winds that are so helpful to sailors.

"We heard rumors about Idomeneus, the King of Crete who had fought against us during the Trojan War. We heard that he had left Crete. On the island, houses stood empty, ready for us to move into. Our enemies had left the island of Crete.

"We set sail, and we sailed past the islands of Naxos, Donusa, Olearos, and Paros — islands of the Cyclades near Delos.

"We sailed quickly, and our sailors encouraged each other: 'Forward to Crete. Forward to the land of our ancestor.' We landed in a harbor of Crete, and we began to build a city I called Pergamum — a Trojan name.

"Almost immediately, a plague struck us. We worked hard, but the plague attacked our bodies and our crops. People and plants died. For an entire year, the plague either killed Trojan men or weakened them. For an entire year, the plague blighted our crops.

"Clearly, the gods were against us. My father, Anchises, advised, 'Let's return to Delos and consult Apollo again. Let us pray for the god's help. Let us pray that the god will tell us our correct destination. Clearly, Crete is not where we should be.'

"Night fell, and Trojans slept. As I slept, the Penates — the Trojan household gods — stood before me. The Penates are the protecting spirits of the household, and Trojan families each have a shrine to these gods. Families give offerings to these gods — when the family members eat a meal, they throw a little food into a fire as an offering to these gods — hoping to keep them favorable to the family. However, Trojan families do not expect these gods to appear before them and speak to them.

"But the Penates appeared before me and gave me the help we Trojans needed. I had saved them from the fires of Troy when I had carried my father out of the burning city, and now they helped the Trojans.

"The Penates told me, 'You need not return to Delos to consult Apollo. All that he would tell you there, we will now tell you here. Apollo himself has sent us to you. We have stayed true to you Trojans, and in the future we will make your children famous and your city powerful. Your destiny is great, and it is worth the pain of exile and the labor of erecting huge walls. But your city will not be here. Apollo did not intend for you to settle on Crete.

"'Go to the country that the Greeks have named Hesperia: the Land of the West. It is a rich country, and its warriors are mighty. The people there call the land Italy — one of its founding fathers was Italus. It is there that you will find your and our true new home. Dardanus, one of the forefathers of the kings of Troy, was born there. So was Iasius, his brother. Go and tell your father what we have told you. You must go to the city of Corythus in Italy. You must not stay here in Crete — Jupiter forbids it.'

"This dream was not empty — I clearly saw the Penates and clearly heard them speak. This was a dream to take seriously. The Penates awed me, and a cold sweat came from my body. I woke up and prayed and poured a libation to the gods.

"I then told my father my dream. He remembered that the Trojans had two sets of forefathers. Dardanus had come from Crete, but Teucer had come from Italy. My father knew that he had erred when he advised setting sail for Crete.

"Anchises said to me, 'Cassandra prophesied to me, but I did not believe her. She told me that we would go to Hesperia. Often, she said that we would go to Italy. At that time, that seemed unlikely or impossible: Why would a Trojan fleet go there? At that time, no one believed Cassandra's prophecies — about Italy or anything else. But we must believe the words of Apollo sent to us by way of the Penates. Let us sail to Italy!'

"So Anchises advised us, and we rejoiced in his advice. We were eager to leave Crete and the plague, and we were eager to do what Apollo told us to do. A few Trojans stayed at Crete, but the rest of us set sail.

"Almost immediately, a storm made the sky black and the waves high. The light came from lightning, not from the sun. We could not tell the fleet's location. We could not tell daytime from nighttime. For three days and three nights, the storm continued. At dawn of the fourth day, we saw land — mountains, and smoke. We took down our sails, and we rowed to the land.

"We landed on one of the islands called the Strophades. On this island live the Harpies, creatures that are part girl and part bird. Celaeno was their leader. Their faces are those of girls, but their bodies are those of birds. Their hands are talons, they have wings, and they are ravenously hungry; from their bottom half arises a stench.

"When we landed, we did not see the Harpies and we did not know that they lived there. We did see cattle and goats. We killed some of them, and we cooked their meat. When the meal was ready to eat, the Harpies burst among us, tearing the food with their talons, eating some and fouling the rest, rendering it unsuitable to be eaten. Their cries deafened us, and their stench sickened us.

"Again, we tried to prepare a meal and eat. This time, we prepared our meal in a large hollow at the bottom of a cliff. Again, the Harpies arrived and ate or befouled the meal.

"We tried a third time to prepare a meal and eat, but this time we set a trap for the Harpies. I told my men, 'To arms! Let us fight them!' Some of my men hid their swords and shields in tall grass, Misenus worked as a lookout, and when he saw the Harpies coming, he blew a trumpet. My men armed themselves and fought the Harpies, but our weapons did not harm them. My men struck their feathers and backs with swords, but the swords did no damage. Again, the Harpies ate part of the meal and befouled the rest, and then they left.

"One Harpy stayed behind to prophesize. She shrieked to us, 'I am Celaeno. So you are making war against the Harpies on their own island after you have butchered their cattle and their goats? So you want the Harpies to leave their own island? Listen to the prophecy that Jupiter told to Apollo and then Apollo told to me and now I am telling to you: You will reach Italian shores, but you will not found a city until after ravenous hunger has made you eat your plates!'

"Celaeno then flew away. The Trojans were dejected after hearing the prophecy. They lost all morale. They wanted to hear a prayer to the gods.

"Anchises prayed, stretching out his arms to the gods, 'Keep us from bad things! Ward off the evil that Celaeno has prophesized!'

"We set sail, and we passed the islands of Zacynthos, Dulichium, Same, and Neritos. As we passed Ithaca, the home of cruel Ulysses, we cursed it. Finally, we landed at Actium in northwestern Greece. We walked to the small town there in order to sacrifice to Jupiter. We cleansed ourselves for the sacrifice, made our offerings to the gods, and then engaged in Trojan sports. My men stripped, oiled themselves, and wrestled naked in accordance with our ancient custom. We were happy because we had safely passed cities where our enemies, the Greeks, lived.

"Winter arrived while we were at Actium, and the North wind made the sea rough. At the temple I set up an offering: the bronze shield of Abas, which I had won in the Trojan War. On the shield I engraved these words: AENEAS DEDICATES THIS SHIELD SEIZED FROM THE GREEK VICTORS.

"We set sail again, and we passed Phaeacia and Epirus, and we sailed into the port of Chaonia, reaching the town of Buthrotum.

"At Buthrotum, we heard something incredible. The king of these lands was Helenus, who had been a priest of Apollo in Troy. He was now married to Andromache, the widow of Hector and the former concubine of Pyrrhus, son of Achilles.

"I wanted to see Helenus, my old friend, again and find out how these things had come to be. Walking away from the harbor, I saw Andromache. She was pouring out libations to Hector, her late husband. She had food and other offerings for Hector. His empty tomb was before the city, by a stream that was named Simois after one of the rivers of Troy.

"Andromache was at the tomb praying for the spirit of her late husband to visit the tomb erected for him. She saw me, recognized me, and wondered. She said to me, 'Is that really you? Are you really alive? If you are dead, why didn't the spirit of Hector come here with you?'

"Andromache cried, grieving for Hector. She could not be consoled.

"I said to her, 'Yes, I am still alive. I keep on living despite the many troubles I have encountered. Believe me when I say that I am real. You have suffered evil, too, in the death of your Hector. But have you also experienced good? Is Helenus still your husband?'

"Lowering her eyes, she said quietly, 'Polyxena, the youngest daughter of Priam, was the luckiest of all the women of Troy. She was a virgin, and she was sacrificed at the tomb of Achilles after the Trojan War. She did not become a sex-slave to a Greek master.

"'I did become a sex-slave to a Greek master. With Troy still burning, I was shipped to Greece in one of the ships of Pyrrhus, the son of Achilles, the Greek warrior who killed my husband: Hector. I was a slave, I was forced to serve Pyrrhus in bed, and I bore his child. But he wanted to marry Hermione, the daughter of Menelaus and Helen, and so he gave me to Helenus, another of his slaves. But Orestes, the son of Agamemnon and Clytemnestra, thought that Hermione had been promised to him, and while the Furies were pursuing him after he had murdered his mother, who had murdered his father, he killed Pyrrhus — he caught Pyrrhus off guard and murdered him at an altar. When Pyrrhus died, Helenus inherited part of his kingdom, and he created a little version of Troy.

"'But what is your story? How did you come here? Is your son, Ascanius, still alive? Does he still remember his mother, who died during the fall of Troy? Does he have your courage and the courage of his uncle, Hector? Hector was Creusa's brother.'

"Andromache, still crying, asked many questions. Her husband, Helenus, arrived and welcomed us. He showed us Buthrotum, a small version of Troy. Troy's towers were great; Buthrotum's towers were small. The Xanthus at Troy was a mighty river; the Xanthus at Buthrotum was a trickle of water. The Scaean Gates at Troy were great; the Scaean Gates at Buthrotum were small. Still, the king and queen of a Trojan city welcomed us. Their guests, we ate and drank.

"Time passed, and we were ready to sail again. I approached Helenus, whom I knew to be a prophet. I said to him, 'You are a seer, and you know the will of Apollo. You can interpret the signs of birds, and you can interpret omens. Give me information. The signs that we have received from the gods have all been favorable. Only the Harpy Celaeno prophesized something bad: terrible hunger. What are the dangers that we need to avoid? What is the course that we need to sail?'

"Helenus sacrificed many bulls, and he prayed for peace. He took me to the shrine of Apollo, and he began to prophesy, saying, 'Son of Venus, fate is on your side. You have a destiny. Jupiter, the king of gods and men, has a plan for you. I will reveal to you a few parts of your future so that you may more safely cross the sea and reach a harbor in Latium. The Fates will not reveal everything to me; Juno does not want me to tell you everything.

"'The eastern part of Italy lies near, but you must reach the western part of Italy and it does not lie near. You will have to undertake a long journey before you reach your destination. You will have to sail in the waters around Sicily, you will have to go past the lakes of the Land of the Dead, and you will have to go past the island of the goddess Circe before you can found your city.

"'Here is a sign for you to remember. It will tell you where to found your city. During a time of trouble, you will sail on a river in Latium. Under the trees you will run across a white sow nursing thirty white piglets. That is the place to found your city. After your city has been founded, you will no longer need to travel long distances.

"'Here is something to give you courage. You need not worry about the prophecy of Celaeno. The Harpy prophesied that you Trojans would be so ravenously hungry that you would eat your plates. Fear not. The Fates will find a way to make the prophecy harmless. Apollo is willing to help you.

"'Set sail away from Buthrotum, but on the eastern side of Italy, stay away from the coast. Every city on the eastern coast of Italy is Greek. The inhabitants are your enemies, including some who fought against you at Troy. Idomeneus, once King of Crete, has a city now in Italy. Philoctetes, a master Greek archer, has a city now in Italy.

"'Once you have sailed past the Greek cities and set up altars so you can sacrifice to the gods, wear purple and cover your heads during the rite. Make sure that no enemy can interrupt the rite. Remember this and make it a rite that you and your descendants perform in days to come. This rite is sacred.

"'When the winds take you to Sicily, sail to the left and go around the island the long way. If you sail to the right, you will see a narrow passage. Long ago, people say, Italy and Sicily were connected by land, but now there is a narrow passage of sea between them. A cataclysm separated them.

"'That narrow passage of sea is dangerous. Scylla is on the right, and Charybdis is on the left. Charybdis is a whirlpool; three times each day it sucks down the sea waters and then it vomits them into the sky. Scylla is a monster that lives in a cave. She thrusts her mouths out of the cave and grabs ships and wrecks them. From above the waist up, much of Scylla appears to be a beautiful woman, but her belly is that of a wolf and her body ends in the tails of dolphins. She is a sea monster. It is much wiser to take the long way around Sicily than to see Scylla.

"'The most important advice I can give you as a prophet and as a priest of Apollo is this: Respect Juno. Pray to Juno first of all the gods. Make vows to Juno. Give sacrifices to Juno. She is a powerful goddess. Only if you respect the goddess will you be able to leave Sicily and go to Italy.

"'Once you reach Italy, go to the city of Cumae. See the prophetess there — the Cumaean Sibyl. She will be in a forest by the lake of Avernus. The prophetess has visions in a cave, and she writes down the visions carefully on leaves and keeps them in the cave. As long as the leaves are undisturbed, they stay in the correct order. But if someone opens the door to the cave and the winds blow in, the leaves are blown out of order. The prophetess does not sort the leaves and does not restore them to their correct order. Such careless visitors who consult the Sibyl, she does not enlighten. Those visitors then hate her cave.

"'The time you spend with the Sibyl will be worthwhile. Your Trojans will be eager to sail onward; the winds will blow favorably. Although they press you to leave immediately, stay and see the Sibyl. Beg her to prophesy to you. She will tell you about the Italian tribes and about the battles you must fight. She will tell you what to do during your trials. Respect her; she can help you.

"'This is all that I am allowed to tell you. Sail to your destiny. Your actions can exalt the Trojans.'

"Helenus' words were very helpful, and after he had finished speaking, he gave us gifts: gold, ivory, silver, cauldrons, and the armor of Pyrrhus: his breastplate and helmet. He gave gifts of honor to my father. He also gave us horses, and he sent with us pilots who knew the Italian coast, Sicily, and the sea. He made sure my men were well armed.

"My father gave the order to set sail; the winds were favorable. Helenus said to my father, 'Anchises, the gods love you. You married Venus. Twice you have survived the fall of Troy. Italy is now the future of your family. But remember to sail quickly past the Greek cities on the eastern coast of Italy; your destination is the western coast of Italy. Apollo orders you and your pious son, "Set sail now." The winds are favorable. It is a good time to go.'

"Andromache was sorry to see us go. She gave my son clothing, including a cloak, saying, "Please take these gifts I made myself, and remember me,

Ascanius. You remind me of my son, Astyanax, whom the Greeks murdered after Troy fell. If he had survived, he would be your age.'

"With tears in my eyes, I said to our hosts, 'You have found your destiny. Your destiny is here. But I go forth still in search of my destiny. You have earned rest, but we still have dangers to face. You need not sail the seas. We do. You have created a little Troy here. I go to find the Tiber River and found a city. Let us hope that my people and your people may one day be one people. This is something that our descendants may one day accomplish.'

"They had created a city that looked to the past; I had yet to create a city that looked to the future.

"We sailed north, and when night came, we slept on the beach, but in the middle of the night, our pilot, Palinurus, woke up and scanned the sky. He saw the constellations, the sky was completely clear, and conditions for sailing were excellent. He blew his trumpet, we woke up and boarded our ships, and we took advantage of the excellent conditions for sailing.

"When dawn arrived, we had reached Italy — the western coasts that our enemies the Greeks inhabited. Achates first shouted, 'Italy!' Other Trojans echoed his shout.

"My father poured wine for the gods and prayed, 'Give us good winds for an easy and safe passage.'

"We saw a harbor and in the distance a temple built to Minerva. We headed for the harbor.

"On land, we saw our first omen: horses. My father interpreted the omen: 'Horses are used in war. We will fight a war in Italy. But horses are also used to plow during peacetime, so we have hope of finding peace. This country will bring us both war and peace.'

"We prayed to Minerva, and we stood at her altar, and remembering what Helenus had told us, we sacrificed to Juno.

"We did not stay there. We went to the ships. We were eager to sail past the dangerous Greek cities. We saw Tarentum, a bay, and we saw a city there that people believe that Hercules founded. We also saw a temple dedicated to Juno.

"We wanted to follow the advice of Helenus and avoid sailing in between Scylla and Charybdis — we wanted to sail the long way around Sicily.

"We saw Mount Etna on the east coast of Sicily, which was pounded by waves. Anchises saw the boiling water and said, 'That must be Charybdis — a death trap for ships and sailors! Row away, men! Row for your lives!'

"My men rowed hard, away from danger. Even so, three times our ships were raised high on the tops of waves and three times our ships fell deep in the troughs of waves. Three times we were raised up to the sky, and three times we were plunged deep in the pit of hell. Finally, we rowed out of this danger — and toward the coast of the Cyclopes.

"We sailed into a harbor near Mount Etna, which rumbled and poured forth smoke and lava. According to ancient stories, the giant Enceladus rebelled against Jupiter, who struck him with a thunderbolt and then placed him under Mount Etna. Whenever Enceladus moves, the volcano rumbles and pours forth smoke and lava. We stayed on the shore that night, and we could not see the stars — the smoke from Mount Etna blotted them out.

"In the morning, we saw a wild man — a hungry man, a man covered with dirt, a man wearing the rags of a Greek. He came out of the woods, saw us, and realized that we are Trojans, and he was afraid. He hesitated, but then he begged us, 'Please save me. Sail me away from this coast and the Cyclopes. I beg you by the stars, the gods, and the air we breathe! Sail me away from here and leave me anywhere else! I admit that I am a Greek. I admit that I fought to conquer Troy and your household gods. If you want to kill me because of that, do so. Death is preferable to staying here and being afraid of being captured and eaten by the Cyclopes! If I have to die, I prefer that humans kill me!'

"The Greek hugged my knees as he supplicated me for mercy: *clementia*. We asked him who he is and what is his story. How did he end up on the coast of the Cyclopes?

"He told us his story: 'I come from Ithaca. My name is Achaemenides, and my father was an impoverished man named Adamastus. I sailed to Troy with Ulysses hoping to make my fortune there. I did not.

"'Ulysses and my fellow Greeks left me here. We were fleeing from the Cyclops named Polyphemus. I fell behind, and Ulysses and my fellow Greeks forgot me. I thought that they were my friends. They were not. They were too concerned about saving themselves to worry about saving me.

"'We had been in the cave of the Cyclops. He is huge, and he eats human flesh when he can get it. His cave was gory with the blood of the Greeks he had eaten after he had trapped us in his cave. I have seen him grab two Greeks, knock their heads on the rocks of his cave, and then eat them while their arms and legs were still moving.

"'Ulysses found a way to pay the Cyclops back. Say what you will about him, he would not put up with that outrage. After the Cyclops lay drunk on the floor of his cave, vomiting human flesh and wine, we prayed to the gods and drew lots. Those chosen by lottery then used a huge sharpened stake to blind the Cyclops' one huge eye. It was as big as a Greek shield or the sun. We avenged our friends whom the Cyclops had killed.

"'But you Trojans need to flee! Now! Polyphemus is just one Cyclops, but a hundred Cyclopes just like him live here! They raise sheep, and they wander the land. For three months, I have lived here, if you can call it living. I have been on the lookout for the dangerous Cyclopes as I struggled to stay alive on berries and nuts and roots. Each day, I have watched the sea. Yours are the only ships I have seen, and I beg you to either take me with you as you set sail or kill me now.'

"Achaemenides the Greek finished speaking, and we immediately saw blind Polyphemus. He was with his sheep, and he made his way cautiously to the shore, feeling his way and using the trunk of a pine tree as a cane. Once on the shore, he went into the deep water and washed his eye socket, out of which still dribbled blood and pus.

"We ran to our ships, and despite our experience with Sinon the lying Greek, we took Achaemenides with us — we Trojans value *clementia*.

"We rowed away as quickly as we could, and Polyphemus heard our oars. He turned toward us, but he could not catch us, and so he howled. All the other Cyclopes heard him and came to the shore, but we were too far away for them to come into the water after us.

"We were still worried about Scylla and Charybdis, so we headed south and went around the cape of Pelorus and past the mouth of the Pantagias River, past the bay of Megara, and past the peninsula of Thapsis. Achaemenides knew the territory; he had sailed here with Ulysses.

"We landed on the island once named Ortygia and worshipped the local gods, and then we sailed past the town and river that are both named

Helorus, past the cape named Pachynus, past the town of Camerina, past the town and river that are both named Gela, past the city of Acragas, past the city of Selinus, and past the headland of Lilybaeum on the western coast of Sicily. We landed at the town of Drepanum on the northwest coast of Sicily.

"Drepanum did not bring joy to me because my father died there. He had helped me through many dangers, but he died and left me. Helenus had not prophesied his death. Not even Celaeno had prophesied his death. I was unprepared for the death of my father.

"We sailed from Drepanum, and a storm drove us to Carthage."

Aeneas had finished his story. He fell silent.

Chapter 4: The Passion of Dido

But the queen, Dido, was now seriously in love. Aeneas' story had been of the many dangers he had faced and survived. His story had also been of his heroism, including going back into a burning city filled with enemy warriors so he could search for his missing wife. His story was pleasing to unmarried Dido.

Dido's love for Aeneas gave her no rest, no peace. Her love burned.

As dawn arrived, Dido, who had not been able to sleep, said to Anna, her sister, "I am impressed by this stranger, this Aeneas. He is noble, he is courageous, and he is a mighty warrior. He must be the son of a god. A lowborn man would have shown fear amid the many dangers he has faced. The story he told us is impressive.

"When my husband died, I vowed to myself and to his ashes that I would not remarry. I had married one man, and my heart broke when he died. If not for this vow, I would be tempted to marry Aeneas. My own brother murdered my husband and spilled his blood and angered our household gods. Ever since then, Aeneas is the only man I have been interested in. For my husband, I felt the flame of love. When I think of Aeneas, and I think of him all the time, I feel again the flame of love.

"But I think it is best if I die before I break the vow that I have made not to remarry. I want to be true to my vow. I want to be true to my conscience. Queens and well-born women should not have affairs."

Dido stopped speaking. She cried.

Anna replied, "Why shouldn't you be remarried? Why shouldn't you know the joys of children of your own? Why shouldn't you know once more the joys of love? Will the ashes and ghosts of the dead care that you remarry? A city needs a king, not just a queen. The leader of a city must leave behind children who will grow up and assume power.

"You can do what you wish, but no one has tempted you to remarry before this. Back in Tyre, the city that we fled, and here in Libya, the land that we fled to, no one has tempted you to remarry before this. You have had suitors. Iarbas of Libya wanted to marry you, but you turned him down. Other suitors in Libya have courted you.

"But now that you are in love, why resist your love?

"Think of Carthage. What would be best for your people? Not all of our neighbors are friendly. On one side are dangerous peoples, including the wild Numidians. On the other side are a dangerous desert and a dangerous people: the raiders of Barce. Remember also that your brother is dangerous; he may make war on you from Tyre. Carthage needs a king who can lead troops into war when necessary.

"Juno has shown the Carthaginians great favor, I think, by sending the Trojan ships here.

"If you marry Aeneas, Carthage will have an impressive king. If the Carthaginian warriors and the Trojan warriors join together, think what an army we will have! We will have a mighty city and a mighty kingdom!

"As for the vow you made to yourself and to your late husband's ashes, pray to the gods. Sacrifice to them. Win them over.

"And keep our Trojan guests here. Winter is coming, and the Trojan ships are now too battered from the storm to sail. You have good reasons to use to convince Aeneas to stay here. Treat him and the Trojans like kings so that they will want to stay."

Anna's words helped convince Dido to hope for love, to break her vow, and to not worry about shame.

Dido and Anna visited several altars, and at each altar they sacrificed to the gods — to Ceres, Apollo, Bacchus, and Juno. They especially sacrificed to and prayed to Juno, the goddess of marriage.

Dido poured wine over the horns of a white cow and other sacrificial victims, and after the victims were killed, she examined their entrails for signs from the gods.

But Dido was in love, and her love was like a wound. She wandered the streets of the city. She was like a deer that an archer shoots in the forests of Crete. The archer is unaware that he has made a direct hit as the deer flees with the arrow in her side that will kill her.

Dido showed Aeneas the glories of Carthage. She wanted to tell him of her love for him, but her voice would not allow her to speak. She stopped in the middle of a sentence. Each night, she provided a feast for him and listened to his stories, wanting often to hear about the fall of Troy.

Whenever Aeneas and her guests left the feast, Dido sat in the chair he had vacated.

Dido was lost in love. She thought about Aeneas constantly, seeing and hearing him even when he was not present. Dido often held Ascanius in her lap, taking pleasure in his resemblance to his father.

Because Dido was in love, she no longer did her duty as ruler of Carthage. Before Aeneas came to Carthage, she had busied herself with the construction of her city. Only partially built, the city lay exposed to enemies. No longer did the Carthaginians build the walls and other fortifications. Work on the harbor was also only partially completed. Dido had given in to the *furor* of passionate love; she neglected her *pietas* of building and ruling a city.

Juno kept watch; she saw that Dido was in love. Dido was willing to sacrifice her pride and her reputation if she could have an affair with Aeneas.

Having formed a plot in her mind, Juno said to Venus, "You and your son Cupid have triumphed over Dido! You two have made her fall in love with Aeneas. You are the goddess of sexual passion, and Cupid is the god of love. Dido did not have a chance against you two.

"I know that you have not liked the rising walls of Carthage, a city I love, but why should you and I disagree? What good is it for we two goddesses to be opposed to each other?

"Here is a way for us to be at peace with each other. Why not allow Aeneas and Dido to be married? You are the one who made Dido fall in love with Aeneas, so I don't see why you would be opposed to their marriage. Aeneas, who is your favorite, and Dido can rule the Carthaginians together. Since Aeneas, your favorite, is the male, he will have the most power."

Venus knew that Juno had proposed a trick: a way for future Roman power to become future Carthaginian power. After all, if Aeneas never reached Latium and never founded his city, he could not found the Roman people and so the great power of the Roman people would never exist. Instead of Rome being the great power in the Mediterranean, Carthage would be the great power.

But Venus had her own secret plans. If Aeneas and Dido were to have an affair for a while, this would ensure that Aeneas would continue to receive the help he needed until he could set sail once more for Italy.

And so Venus said to Juno, "Your offer is a good offer, and I will not shun it. But will Jupiter agree that one city — Carthage — should be home to the exiles from Tyre *and* the exiles from Troy? I think that the Fates may forbid that. But you are the wife of Jupiter, and you have influence over him, so I will do what you say."

Juno replied, "I shall arrange everything. Let me tell you my plan. Tomorrow, Aeneas and Dido will go hunting together. I will create a storm. Everyone will scatter to seek shelter, and Aeneas and Dido will seek shelter in the same cave. I will be there. I will ensure that two will become one. This will be the marriage of Aeneas and Dido."

Venus nodded her consent to Juno's plan although she knew that the plan was meant to be a trap.

When dawn arrived, Carthaginians and Trojans prepared for the hunt. Huntsmen brought nets and spears. They brought horses and hunting dogs. Dido kept them waiting as she dressed. Finally, she appeared in rich clothing and with her hair neatly styled.

Now the Carthaginians and the Trojans were ready to hunt. Aeneas took the lead; his son, Ascanius, was with him. So were many, many hunters.

Following winter, Apollo visits the island of Delos to enjoy a festival, and around his altars dance people who worship him. Apollo swiftly goes to Delos as drums pound a welcome for him. As swiftly as Apollo goes to Delos, Aeneas went to the hunt.

The hunters found game: goats and deer. Ascanius rode his horse in the lead, but he longed for more dangerous game than goats and deer; he hoped to find a wild boar or a lion.

Before the hunters could find more dangerous game, a storm hurled hail at them. All scattered and sought shelter. Dido and Aeneas found and entered the same cave. Here the goddesses Earth and Juno lit what resembled wedding torches. Here nymphs sang what resembled a wedding song. Here the sky witnessed what resembled a wedding. But although Juno provided the trappings of a wedding, this was not a legal wedding. Aeneas did not hold the torch that a groom holds in a real marriage. Aeneas did not make the vows that a groom makes in a real marriage.

Dido called her relationship with Aeneas a marriage, but it was really an affair. Dido used the word "marriage" to lessen her feeling of guilt.

Rumors of the affair spread quickly to all the cities of Libya. Evil moves quickly, and of all evils, rumor moves the quickest. Rumor is the daughter of Mother Earth, who bore her after Jupiter had killed two of her sons: the Titan Coeus and the Giant Enceladus. Mother Earth gave birth to Rumor as a way to get revenge for the death of these sons.

Rumor has wings and many feathers. Her many eyes never sleep, and she has many tongues and many ears. By night she flies, and by day she watches and listens. She values lies as much as she values truths.

Now Rumor quickly travelled throughout Libya and filled the ears of Libyans. Rumor told all, "Aeneas, a Trojan, and Dido, Queen of Carthage, are having an affair. They neglect their duties because they are spending so much time having sex."

Rumor spread this gossip to many Libyans, and then she went to Iarbas, whom Dido had earlier declined to marry. Iarbas was the product of rape. Jupiter had raped a nymph in Libya, and she had given birth to a son: Iarbas. Jupiter suffered no punishment for his crime; as king of gods and men, he is too powerful to suffer punishment even for his many rapes. In contrast, mortals can be punished even for consensual love affairs.

Iarbas had built many temples and many altars to his father. He made sure that the sacred fires were kept burning. He made sure that the blood of many sacrificial animals reddened the ground. He made sure that wreathes of flowers decorated the doors of temples.

Maddened by rumor, Iarbas went to one of Jupiter's altars and prayed, "You are worshipped here. You are adored here. You are respected here. We make sacrifices to you here. And for what? What do we get in return for fearing your anger? Look at Dido. She came here, and she got at little price land on which to build her city. I proposed marriage to her; she turned me down. Instead, she is having an adulterous love affair with Aeneas, a womanizer like Paris, who ran away with Helen and started the Trojan War. Aeneas' Trojans are like eunuchs. Aeneas prettifies himself with oiled hair and with effeminate clothing. He gets Dido and Carthage, and we get nothing although we keep sacrificing to you. This is not fair."

Jupiter heard the prayer of Iarbas and so became aware of Aeneas' actions. Jupiter now paid attention to Carthage and to the adulterous love affair of Aeneas and Dido.

Jupiter ordered Mercury to come to him. He then gave Mercury orders to take to Aeneas: "Tell him that he is ignoring his destiny. He should not be in Carthage. He should be working to found his own city. This is not why his mother, Venus, saved him from the attack by Diomedes against him in the Trojan War. This is not why his mother saved him during the fall of Troy. Carthage is not his destiny.

"Italy is his destiny. He must go there and fight a war and establish a city and the Roman people. He must found a people who will bring law to the entire world.

"If Aeneas is not concerned about his own destiny, he ought to be concerned about the destiny of his son. Unless Aeneas goes to Italy, Ascanius will not have a glorious future. Ascanius is also supposed to have Italian offspring. His blood is also supposed to flow in the veins of Romans.

"Aeneas must not stay in Carthage: He must go to Italy. Give him this message from me: You must set sail!"

Mercury put on the winged golden sandals that sped him to his destinations. He grabbed the wand that can make ghosts exit the Land of the Dead or enter the Land of the Dead. Mercury's wand can also make men close their eyes in sleep or open their eyes in death.

Mercury flew through the air, and he saw Atlas, a Titan who used to hold up the sky, and who was transformed into north Africa's Mount Atlas, which holds up the sky. Clouds always surround the crown of Mount Atlas, ice is always in his beard, and snow always covers his shoulders.

Mercury landed on Mount Atlas first, and then he plunged down to the sea the way that a hawk flies above the water and hunts fish. Mercury flew in between the sky and the earth and went to Libya.

Landing at Carthage, Mercury immediately saw Aeneas, who had taken over the duties of Dido and was supervising the building of the city that in years to come would be Rome's greatest enemy. Dressed as a Carthaginian, Aeneas built the walls that Rome would fight against in three wars before finally destroying Carthage as a power in the Mediterranean.

Mercury scorned Aeneas: "Look at what you are doing! You are building the walls of a city that is not your own. You are sleeping with a woman who is your 'wife.' You are ignoring your fate, your destiny. Jupiter ordered me to come here and try to make you sane again. He wants you to stop ignoring your destiny. He wants you to leave Carthage — if not for your own destiny, then for the destiny of your son. Ascanius' destiny lies in Italy, not in Carthage. You owe him the land on which Rome will be built!"

Mercury vanished from Aeneas' sight.

Aeneas had clearly seen and clearly heard Mercury. The god had spoken clearly. Such direct messages from the gods are not to be ignored.

Instantly, Aeneas remembered his duty. He longed to go to Italy. He longed to leave Carthage, although this is a land he loves. He knew that he must obey the commands of Jupiter.

But what about Dido? What can he say to the queen that will have good consequences? How can he break up with a woman who loves him so? What should he do?

Aeneas gave orders to Mnestheus, Sergestus, and Serestus: "Get our ships ready to sail, but tell no one. Make sure that the Trojans are ready to sail. Keep everything secret from the Carthaginians."

Aeneas did not want to leave Dido without saying goodbye, but he did want to wait for a good time to talk to her. He hoped that time would quickly arrive.

Mnestheus, Sergestus, and Serestus quickly followed Aeneas' orders.

But the queen soon heard of a trick, a plot — the Trojans are planning to sail away in secret. She will be left behind without an explanation. Rumor was active, vicious, and destructive. Dido heard rumors that the Trojans were preparing their ships so that they could quickly sail away from Carthage.

Dido was like a Maenad, a wild follower of Bacchus, driven to frenzy by her worship of the god.

Dido spoke to Aeneas before he could speak to her and explain his actions: "Did you really think that you could keep your departure a secret from me? Why do you want to sneak away without even talking to me? Doesn't our love mean anything to you? Would my death mean anything to you?

"Why are you planning to leave now, in winter, a dangerous time to sail? Why would anyone attempt to set sail at this time when the sea is such a danger? The reason for your departure at this time must be me — you are running away because of me!

"Don't I deserve better from you? Aren't we married? Doesn't that mean anything to you? Don't my tears have any effect on you at all?

"If I in fact deserve better than this from you, stay here in Carthage!

"Because of my relationship to you, the tribes and kings that surround Carthage hate me — they are my enemies! Even the Carthaginians hate me because of my relationship with you!

"Because I so much wanted to have a relationship with you, I have broken my vow, I have lost my honor, I have lost my reputation.

"I thought that you would be my permanent husband, but apparently you are my temporary guest.

"What will happen to me now? Will Pygmalion, my brother, the King of Tyre, fight me and conquer the city of Carthage? Will Iarbas force me to become his sex-slave?

"I wish that you had made me pregnant. I wish that I could have your son. I wish that I could have a little Aeneas when you leave — at least, I could look at him and see your features in his face.

"If I could only give birth to your son, I would not feel so abandoned by you."

Dido stopped speaking, and Aeneas resolved to restrain his emotions as he replied to her. Jupiter had reminded him of his destiny and of the destiny of his son, and he thought it best to make a clean break with Dido and not give her a false hope.

Aeneas said, "You have been kind to my Trojans and me. I know this, and the gods know this. I shall always be thankful to you, and I shall always remember you throughout my life. I know that you deserve good things.

"Please let me say a few things.

"I never intended to leave you without saying goodbye. I did not ever intend to sail away from you in secret. Please do not believe that I ever intended such things.

"Also, remember that I am not your husband. We are not legally married. I have never held the torch of a bridegroom, and I have never said the vows of a bridegroom to you.

"If the Fates would have allowed me anything I wished for after the fall of Troy, I would not have come to Carthage. I would have stayed at Troy, and I would have rebuilt the city on its old site. I would have rebuilt the palace of

Priam, and I would have rebuilt the fortifications of Troy to keep its defeated citizens safe.

"But I was not allowed to rebuild Troy. The oracle of Apollo at the city of Gyrnia has stated my task, my destiny. I must go to Italy. That will be my new homeland, not Carthage.

"You, yourself, left Tyre and founded a new city — Carthage — in north Africa. I have left Troy and will found a new city in Italy. I want to do what you have done. If what you have done is the right thing to do, we Trojans should not be criticized for wanting to do the same thing.

"My father, Anchises, died in Sicily, but his ghost appears to me in dreams. He warns about things I ought not to do. I fear that I will do what I ought not to do: ignore my destiny.

"I think about my son, Ascanius. He, too, has a destiny. I must fulfill my destiny so that he can fulfill his destiny. I must not rob him of his future kingdom in Italy. Fate has decreed that his kingdom lies there, not in north Africa.

"I swear that a messenger of the gods who was sent by Jupiter appeared before me and brought me the commands of Jupiter himself. I saw and heard clearly Jupiter's messenger. He ordered me to achieve my destiny.

"Do not try to prevent me from sailing. You will be hurting both of us with your futile attempts.

"Yes, I will set sail for Italy — by the order of Jupiter, not of my own free will."

As Aeneas had spoken to her, Dido had glared at him. She had looked him over, as she silently stood. Now she shrieked at him, "Venus is not your mother! Dardanus is not your ancestor! Your parents are not immortal gods or mortal humans! Mount Caucasus with its rocks must be your father! The tigers of Hyrcania must have suckled you!

"How do I know this? Because you have no pity for me. Did you groan as you spoke to me? No. Did you even look at me? No. Did you cry as you ought to have done? No. Why do you not pity me — I love you!

"Why aren't Jupiter and Juno helping me? Why aren't they taking pity on me? Shouldn't the gods have a sense of fairness?

"You washed up on the shores of Carthage, and I gave you food, clothing, and shelter. I let you rule my kingdom. I saved your ships, and I saved your Trojans.

"The Furies are the gods who concern themselves with me. They madden me.

"The gods who concern themselves with you are Apollo and his oracles. They tell you what to do. So does Jupiter, who sends a messenger with orders for you. This is work for gods? Don't they have better things to do?

"So go to Italy. I won't stop you.

"But I hope that the gods do. I hope that you and your ships are wrecked on rocks in the middle of the sea. I hope that you die while crying out my name again and again. While I am alive, I will wish only evil for you.

"After I die, my ghost will follow you wherever you go. After I am dead, I will wish only evil for you. I will haunt you.

"Even when I am in the Land of the Dead, I will wish only evil for you. News of you will reach me even there, and bad news about you will comfort me."

Dido ran away from Aeneas, leaving him behind, unhappy. Once out of the room, she fainted and her serving women caught her and took her to her chamber and placed her on her bed.

Aeneas now pursued his duty. He felt bad about Dido, but he knew that he must pursue his destiny. Instead of going to Dido and talking to her, he went to his ships and worked to make them seaworthy.

He and his men worked hard. They brought timber with which to repair the ships and to make oars. They worked as hard as ants when they find a huge mound of wheat and pillage it and take it to their home. Some ants carry the grains of wheat, and some ants supervise the workers and punish the lazy. The Trojans repaired their ships and put them back in the water.

Dido witnessed the Trojans' labor. She looked out at all of the activity on the beach and mourned. Her lover was getting ready to leave her.

Love can be a cruel tyrant. It often treats people badly. Dido cried. She wanted Aeneas back. She tried to think of ways to get him back.

Dido said to Anna, her sister, "Look at the Trojan ships in the water. They are nearly ready to sail. I know that Aeneas wants to leave me, but go to him. You know him; he and you have been friends. Plead with him. Remind him that my ships did not join the Greek ships at Aulis where they sacrificed Agamemnon's daughter Iphigenia before sailing across the sea to attack Troy. Remind him that I never made a vow to make war against Troy. Remind him that I never sent ships to attack Troy. I have done nothing that would ever hurt his father, Anchises, either while Anchises was alive or after his death.

"Why should Aeneas be in such a hurry to leave? Make a request of him for me: Ask him to wait a while longer so that he will have safe sailing weather. He will need good winds and a smooth sea.

"I no longer request that he observe our marriage. I don't expect him to forget his destiny that lies in Latium.

"I do ask him to give me time — time to partially recover from the loss of his love.

"If he will give me time now, I will pay him back more than I owe when I die."

So Dido pleaded to her sister, who spoke to Aeneas and told him of Dido's tears. But Dido's tears did not turn Aeneas from his destiny. Fate had decreed that he go to Italy.

A huge tree can be blasted by the North wind, which tries to uproot it. The tree limbs move, but the tree stays firmly rooted. Aeneas was like that tree. He heard the appeals that Anna made, but he stayed true to his destiny.

Tears fell. In vain.

Consumed by *furor*, Dido resolved to die. She was tired of living. She laid gifts for the gods on an altar, and the omens were terrifying. She put holy water on the altar — the water turned black. She poured out wine for the gods — the wine turned to blood. She did not tell anyone — not even her sister — about the omens.

She went at night to a marble temple that held a shrine dedicated to her late husband: Sychaeus. She seemed to hear his voice calling her name from the Land of the Dead.

She heard an owl on a rooftop calling out what appeared to be a lament for the dead: a dirge.

She remembered the prophecies of seers of ancient times. The prophecies were terrifying, and they made her afraid.

She had nightmares about Aeneas: He was a savage hunter who wanted to kill her.

She had other nightmares: She wandered alone, looking for her people in a strange country.

She felt like Pentheus, who was driven insane by Bacchus because he did not respect the god. In his manic *furor*, his vision became double, and he saw two suns when only one existed, and he saw two cities of Thebes when only one existed.

She felt like Orestes, the son of Agamemnon. Consumed by *furor*, Orestes killed his mother, and so the Furies pursued him, driving him mad — he saw his dead mother threatening him with fire and snakes and he tried to run from her, but the Furies blocked his way.

Maddened with *furor*, Dido thought about her death. How should she die? When should she die?

Dido went to her sister, and putting on an act so Anna would not know what she was planning, she spoke to Anna calmly, "I have good news. I have found a way to do one of two things: make Aeneas love me again, or make me forget my love for him. In Ethiopia is a priestess who takes care of the temple of the daughters of the Evening Star. She takes care of the sacred grove, and she feeds honey and poppies to the dragon. The priestess knows spells for various purposes: how to end passionate love, how to cause pain, how to stop a river, how to make stars cross the sky in a different direction, how to bring the dead out of Hades, and how to cause an earthquake. She knows magic, and although I am reluctant to do it, I will use her magic now.

"Please do as I ask you. Build a funeral pyre in the inner courtyard in the open air. Don't let people know what you are doing. On the funeral pyre, put Aeneas' armor and weapons. He left them in our bedroom; he has not taken them. On the funeral pyre, put Aeneas' clothing and put the bed he and I slept in. The funeral pyre will burn every trace of Aeneas that remains in Carthage. So works the priestess' spell."

Dido fell silent, and her face grew pale.

Anna suspected nothing. She did not know that her sister was planning to commit suicide. She felt that Dido would grieve for Aeneas only as much she had grieved for her late husband.

But the queen took action when the funeral pyre was built under the sky in the inner courtyard. She placed funeral wreathes in her palace. She put an effigy of Aeneas on the bed on the funeral pyre, beside his armor and his sword.

Dido then performed rites of magic. At the altars by the funeral pyre, with her hair and robes unbound, in accordance with the rites of magic, she named three hundred gods, including Erebus, Chaos, and Hecate, goddess of the Land of the Dead, who was also Diana, a goddess huntress on earth, and Luna, the goddess of the moon.

Dido sprinkled water that represented the waters found in Hell. She found poisonous herbs by the light of the moon. She used the membrane that had covered a colt when it was born. With only one foot wearing a sandal, in accordance with the rites of magic, she prayed to gods who knew that she was about to commit suicide. She also prayed to any god — should one exist — who cares for lovers who love each other unequally, with only one lover greatly loving the other.

It was night, and everything and everyone but Dido was at rest. The woods were calm, the sea was calm, and the stars moved in their usual course.

Dido could not sleep; she could not stop thinking about her love for Aeneas and his refusal of her love.

She said to herself, "What should I do? What are my options? I have rejected proposals of marriage here in Libya. Should I make a fool of myself and urge kings to propose to me again?

"Or should I follow the Trojans as they sail away? I have helped them — oh, so recently — but will they remember? Will they welcome me? More likely, they will hate me. Haven't I realized yet that the Trojans are as untrustworthy as their early king, Laomedon, who cheated Poseidon and Apollo after they had worked for him for a year at the command of Jupiter? Haven't I realized yet that the Trojans are as untrustworthy as their early king, Laomedon, who tried to cheat Hercules of the horses that he had promised him after Hercules had rescued Laomedon's daughter?

"Should I follow Trojan ships by myself? Or should I follow Trojan ships with all my Carthaginians? Would my Carthaginians be willing to leave their new city? No. I found it hard enough to get them to leave Tyre and sail to north Africa. I will not be able to uproot them again.

"Therefore, it is best that I die.

"I deserve to die.

"I will end my life with the sword of Aeneas.

"I cried in front of Anna, and she advised me to seek love. She advised me to do what would be best for my new city. I gave in to her and to my love, and this is the result. Much better it would have been never to have felt love again, never to have been tempted to be married, never to have been tempted to break the vow I made to myself and the ashes of my late husband. I broke that vow!"

Dido agonized that night; Aeneas slept peacefully on one of his ships.

Mercury appeared to Aeneas in a dream. The blond god said to him, "Why are you asleep? Why aren't you sailing? The West wind is blowing, ready to take you away from Carthage.

"Dido, who is unhappy, is thinking about treachery, so leave now.

"Set sail now, while you still can. If you don't set sail now, tomorrow you will see your ships set on fire.

"Worry about your destiny, not about a woman. Women change; your destiny is unchanging."

Aeneas woke up. He took action, waking up his men and ordering them to set sail: "I have seen a god. He wants us to set sail — now!" He prayed to the god, "We will do as you say. Help us. Give us good sailing weather."

Aeneas used his sword to cut the rope that moored his ship. The crews of the other ships did the same. Soon, the harbor was empty of Trojan ships; they were at sea.

Dawn arrived, and Dido looked out at the harbor from her high tower. It was empty of Trojan ships, and she mourned. She beat her breasts and tore her hair in the ancient way of showing grief.

Dido lamented, "This stranger — Aeneas — has mocked Carthage. We Carthaginians should arm ourselves, set sail in our ships, and overtake the Trojans! We can fight the Trojans with weapons! We can set their ships on fire in the sea!

"But no. I am not making sense. I have already resolved to die.

"I am unhappy now, and I have been unhappy. I have acted the wrong way.

"Aeneas is supposed to be a good man. He carried his father out of burning Troy! He carried his household gods out of burning Troy! But is Aeneas a good man?

"I should have killed Aeneas when I first saw him. I should have killed his men. I should have killed Aeneas' son, cooked him, and served him to Aeneas.

"We Carthaginians should have fought a battle with the Trojans. The victory might have gone to the Trojans, but so what? Either way, win or lose, I, Dido, would have died. I should have set their camp on fire and burned their ships. I should have killed both Aeneas and Ascanius and then myself!

"Hear my prayers, sun, Juno, underworld goddess Hecate, and avenging Furies! Listen to me. I deserve that much. If Aeneas is fated to fulfill his destiny and found his city in Latium, let him and his descendants suffer from my curse! Let him fight a war in Italy. Let him beg for help and see his people die. Let him have a peace that is not just, that lacks *clementia*. Let him not enjoy his unjust peace. Let him die early. Let him lie unburied.

"I pray this with my words and with my blood. I also pray that my Carthaginians will forever be the enemies of his descendants. Let the Carthaginians' hatred for Aeneas' descendants be an offering made to my ghost. May the Carthaginians and Aeneas' descendants never love each other and never be at peace.

"I pray that a Carthaginian avenger, now unknown, will rise up in the future and battle the descendants of Aeneas. I curse Aeneas' descendants with war — unending war!"

Maddened by *furor*, Dido then turned her thoughts to suicide.

To Barce, the nurse of her late husband — her own nurse had died in Tyre — Dido said, "Ask Anna to come to me. Anna must sprinkle herself with river water in preparation for a sacrifice. She must bring the sacrificial animals here. You and she must wear the sacred headbands for the sacrifice. I am ready to set the rite in motion. I will end my love for Aeneas."

Barce set off on her errand.

Dido was frenzied by *furor*. Her eyes rolled, and her face paled. She climbed the funeral pyre and unsheathed a Trojan sword. The sword was a gift, but the giver had not intended that it be used for this purpose.

She looked at Aeneas' clothing and the bed that they had slept in. She wept, and she lay down on the funeral pyre and said her last words: "I am ready to die. I am ready to end my suffering. I am ready to be free of pain. I have lived my life. I have lived what I have been fated to live. I am ready to journey to the Land of the Dead. I have built a great city. I have avenged the death of my husband and punished my brother, who murdered my husband. I have been happy, and I would have continued to be happy if only the Trojans had not landed here."

Dido pressed her face into the bed that she had shared with Aeneas, and then she said, "I will die without a present avenger. So be it. I will die willingly, and I will make my way to the Land of the Dead. I much prefer that to continuing to live. I hope that Aeneas sees the smoke of my funeral pyre far out at sea. Let it be a bad omen for him."

Maddened by *furor*, Dido fell on the sword. Blood reddened the sword; blood reddened her hands. Female servants screamed.

Rumor ran like a maddened follower of Bacchus throughout Carthage. The Carthaginians mourned; the women cried and shrieked. It sounded as if a city — Tyre or Carthage — were falling to enemy soldiers, and waves of fire were destroying the city.

Anna heard the cries of grief and despair. Terrified, and mourning, she scratched her face and beat her breasts and cried, "Dido, is this what you wanted? Is this why you wanted the funeral pyre? You have deceived me. You have hurt me. You should have told me what you planned to do — we could have died together. I built this funeral pyre at your request. I did not know what you planned to do. You have destroyed so much: your life, my life, and your people and city.

"Come, women of Carthage, and help me to bathe my sister's wounds. Let me be with my sister in her final moments of life."

Anna climbed to the top of the funeral pyre and held her dying sister in her arms. Anna cried. She used her gown to try to stop Dido's bleeding.

The wound had penetrated one of Dido's lungs. As she labored to breathe, her wound hissed.

Three times Dido tried to raise herself on one of her elbows. Three times she failed.

Dido looked at the sky and sought the sun. When she saw it, it hurt her eyes and she moaned.

Dido was dying hard.

Juno saw her and pitied her. Dido was dying at the wrong time, too early a time. Because Dido's death was a suicide, Proserpina, the Queen of the

Land of the Dead, refused to come and cut the lock of hair that would free Dido from life and from an agonizing death. Juno sent Iris down to free Dido. Iris flew to Dido, held a lock of her hair, and said, "As commanded by Juno, I cut this lock of hair — an offering to the god of Death — and I release you from life and from your body."

Iris cut the lock of hair, and the warmth left Dido's body and her breath fled with the wind.

Chapter 5: Funeral Games and Fire

Aeneas and his ships were underway, but the sky darkened. He looked back at Carthage, and he saw the glow of a fire. He did not know it, but the glow came from Dido's funeral pyre, which the Carthaginians had lit. Although he did not know the source of the glow, it made him uneasy. The Trojans and he knew how much a woman can feel passion, and how much *furor* a woman can feel when a love affair ends.

The Trojans reached open water; they were out of sight of land. A thunderstorm reared in the sky and made the waters high and the day as dark as night. Even Palinurus, an experienced pilot, was concerned. He asked, "What trouble have you, Neptune, god of the sea, planned for us?" Palinurus then gave the Trojans orders: "Trim the sails! Row!"

He called to Aeneas, "With the sky and the sea like this, we can't sail for Italy — not even with the help of Jupiter! The winds are unfavorable for that destination. We can't fight the winds; we can't fight the storm and the waves. Our best course of action is to sail for Sicily. There we will find friends. We are close to the part of Sicily where your half- brother, Eryx, lived. I remember the way to Sicily, and I remember the location of the stars before the storm arose."

Aeneas replied, "Good thinking, Palinurus. I have watched you try to fight the wind. It is better to go with the wind, when possible, than to fight it. The wind is driving us to Sicily, and to Sicily we shall go. It is a good place for our ships and us. Our friend Acestes lives there, and the bones of Anchises, my father, rest there."

A West wind blew them to Sicily. High on a mountain, Acestes saw and recognized the sails of the Trojan fleet. Carrying spears and wearing the fur of a she-bear from Libya, he went to the harbor and welcomed his friends. Acestes' parents were a woman of Troy and the god of the Crinisus River in Sicily. Acestes gave the Trojans food and shelter.

The following day, Aeneas spoke to his Trojans: "It has been one year since my father died, one year since we buried his bones, one year since we cried for him.

"It is time for us to perform the anniversary rites. We need to have a funeral procession, and we need to give gifts to the gods. This is a vow that I would keep even if I were an exile at Carthage in north Africa or a prisoner on the Greek island of Mycenae. But we are on the friendly island of Sicily. Let us hold rites to honor my father. I will always honor my father. After I build my city, I will hold rites to honor him year after year.

"Acestes, who was born in Troy, is our friend. He has agreed to give us two head of cattle for each ship. We will sacrifice them, and we will invite to the feast the household gods of Troy and the gods of Sicily that Acestes worships.

"In nine days, if the weather is good, we will hold funeral games to honor my father. We will hold contests of racing ships and racing men, as well as contests of throwing javelins or shooting arrows and a contest of boxing with gauntlets made of rawhide. All of you are welcome to attend. Now crown your heads with wreathes."

Aeneas put on his own head a wreath made of myrtle, a plant sacred to his mother, Venus. The Sicilian Helymus, old Acestes, Ascanius, and the young men also put wreathes on their heads.

Aeneas and the others went to the tomb of Anchises, and Aeneas poured the proper libations: two bowls of wine, two bowls of milk, and two bowls of blood. He scattered red flowers around the tomb, and then he prayed, "Father, I honor your ashes and your spirit. I rescued you from Troy, but I regret that I was unable to take you to Latium and the Tiber River in Italy."

As Aeneas said the final words of his prayer to his father, a snake slithered up from under the tomb and made its way among the altars. It shimmered in the sun like a rainbow, and it tasted the feast that Aeneas had provided. It then slithered away under the tomb. The snake was a good omen.

Aeneas wondered whether the snake was a local god, or whether it was a spirit associated with his father. He continued the rites. He sacrificed two sheep, two pigs, and two steers. He then poured out wine, and he called out his father's name. The others also brought sacrifices for the gods, and they cooked the meat.

On the ninth day, the weather was good. Many people gathered for the funeral games in honor of Anchises. Some wanted to compete; most wanted to watch. Aeneas set out prizes: tripods, crowns made of leaves for victors, armor, purple clothing, gold, and silver. A trumpet blew to announce the beginning of the games.

The first event was a race with ships. The crews of four ships readied themselves to compete. Mnestheus commanded the *Dragon*; he would give rise to the Memmian clan. Gyas commanded the *Chimaera*; it was a huge ship, with three tiers of oars. Sergestus commanded the *Centaur*; he would give rise to the Sergian clan. Cloanthus commanded the *Scylla*; he would give rise to the Cluentius clan.

Far out in the water was a rock; it would be the midpoint for the race. In bad weather, the rock was washed over by high waves; in good weather, it rose above the sea and was a favorite resting place for cormorants. Aeneas marked this rock; ship crews knew to circle the rock and race for home.

The ship captains drew lots to determine their starting place, and the crews oiled their bodies and wore on their heads wreathes made of poplar leaves.

The trumpet sounded, and the oarsmen began rowing. At first, all four ships stayed together as they raced faster than chariots drawn by two horses that the charioteer whips to make them run faster.

The spectators shouted, and their shouts echoed back to them.

Gyas' *Chimaera* took the lead, and Cloanthus' *Scylla* followed close behind. Cloanthus had the better oarsmen, but Gyas' *Chimaera* was better constructed for speed — Cloanthus' *Scylla* had a hull made of pine.

Mnestheus' *Dragon* and Sergestus' *Centaur* fought for third place. The *Dragon* surged ahead, and then the *Centaur* surged ahead and they were tied.

The ships reached the rock that was the turning point. Gyas' *Chimaera* was still in the lead, but his pilot, Menoetes, was cautious — wary of hidden rocks — and he made a wide turn.

Eager for victory, Gyas yelled at him, "What are you doing? Stay close to the rock! Let the other ships make their turns in deeper water!"

Still cautious, Menoetes headed for deeper water, and Gyas shouted, "No! Hug the rock as you turn!"

Cloanthus' *Scylla* took advantage of the wide turn being made by the *Chimaera*. It took the inside track, stayed close to the rock, and raced into first place.

Humiliated, Gyas, a young man, cried. He wanted to win so badly that he was willing to risk the safety of his crew and of his ship. He seized Menoetes and threw him overboard, and then he became his own pilot.

Menoetes was weighed down by his clothing, but he struggled to the surface of the water and swam to the rock, climbed it, and sat there. The race's spectators laughed when Gyas threw Menoetes overboard, they laughed again as Menoetes struggled in the water, and they laughed again as he spit up salty sea water.

Mnestheus and Sergestus hoped to pass Gyas' *Chimaera*, which Gyas, a young, inexperienced helmsman, now piloted.

Sergestus' *Centaur* took the lead as it and the *Dragon* neared the turning point, but not by much — not even the whole length of the ship. Mnestheus ordered the oarsmen of his *Dragon*, "Row harder! We are not rowing for first place. Cloanthus' *Scylla* is too fast for us. But we must not finish last — that would be a disgrace! You are the oarsmen I picked. You are the best of my men. You have shown what you can do on the sea during storms; now show what you can do in a race! Spare us disgrace! Don't allow us to finish last!"

Mnestheus' oarsmen rowed hard in the *Dragon*. Sweat streamed from their bodies, they gasped for breath as they rowed, and their mouths were dry. But an accident by another ship allowed them to avoid a last-place finish.

Sergestus chose to turn close to the rock — too close! His *Centaur* struck some rocks. Oars broke, and the *Centaur* hit the rocks so hard that part of it was lifted out of the water. The oarsmen tried to get the ship off the rocks. The crew used pikes and poles and oars to push the ship off the rocks.

Mnestheus' oarsmen took advantage. They rowed hard, and a favorable wind gave their *Dragon* speed. Their ship sped like a terrified dove flies. Meanwhile, Sergestus had to figure out how to get his ship to shore when so many of the ship's oars had shattered.

Mnestheus' oarsmen passed Gyas' *Chimaera* — the ship now lacked an experienced helmsman. Then Mnestheus' *Dragon* tried to overtake Cloanthus' *Scylla*. Mnestheus' oarsmen rowed as swiftly as they could.

The crowd was excited as Cloanthus' *Scylla* and Mnestheus' *Dragon* arrived at the finish line. Cloanthus' crew would be embarrassed to lose now after leading the race for so long. Mnestheus' crew would love to achieve a last-second victory after trailing for so long.

Mnestheus and his men might have achieved the victory if Cloanthus had not prayed to the gods of the sea: "I will sacrifice a white bull to you, and I will pour out wine for you."

The gods of the sea — the sea-nymphs known as the Nereids, the old sea-god named Phorcus, the virgin sea-nymph named Panopea, and the god of harbors named Portunus — heard and answered his prayer. Portunus used his hand to shove Cloanthus' *Scylla* quicker than Mnestheus' *Dragon* toward the finish line.

A herald announced that Cloanthus' ship had won the race, and Aeneas crowned Cloanthus' head with a wreath made of green laurel. Aeneas gave the crew of each ship wine, three bulls, and a bar of silver. The captains of the ships got prizes of honor.

Aeneas gave Cloanthus, whose ship finished first, a gold and red cloak decorated with an eagle sent by Jupiter grabbing Ganymede as he hunted and taking him to Mount Olympus to be Jupiter's cupbearer and paramour.

Aeneas gave Mnestheus, whose ship finished second, armor that he had stripped from the Greek Demoleos, who died at Troy by the Simois River. Two of Aeneas' aides, Phegeus and Sagaris, could barely hold up the armor, yet Demoleos had worn it as he chased after Trojans and tried to kill them.

Aeneas gave Gyas, whose ship finished third, two cauldrons and two silver cups.

Finally, Sergestus arrived with his crippled ship. Many of the ship's oars were missing; many of the ship's oars were in splinters. His ship was like a snake that has been run over by a wheel on a road or injured by a rock thrown at it. Its head is still dangerous and eager to bite. Its tail is damaged and useless. Sergestus' ship slowly sailed to the finish line.

Aeneas, happy that the ship had been salvaged, gave Sergestus the last-place prize: a Cretan slave-girl named Pholoë, and her twins who nurse at her breasts.

The next event was the footrace. Aeneas set out the prizes. The competitors included Nisus and Euryalus; Nisus was a man who loved the younger Euryalus, who loved him back. Other competitors were Diores, who was related to Priam; Patron, who was from Acarnania; Salius, who was from Arcadia; the Sicilians Helymus and Panopes, who were hunters; some friends of Acestes; and many others.

Aeneas told the racers, "Every competitor here will win a prize: two Cretan arrows and a double-headed axe, but the first three finishers will win special prizes and crowns made from olive leaves. The first-place finisher will win a horse and its trappings. The second-place finisher will win an Amazon's quiver and arrows and a belt decorated with gold and a jewel. The third-place finisher will win a Greek helmet."

The race started, and Nisus quickly ran ahead of everyone else. In second place was Salius, and in third place, far behind the two leaders, was Euryalus. Following him was Helymus, and close behind him and coming closer was Diores.

The racers neared the finish line, and Nisus — with the victory practically assured — slipped on some blood from a sacrifice and fell headlong into manure. But if Nisus couldn't be the winner of the footrace, he wanted his best friend, Euryalus, to be the winner, so Nisus threw himself into the path of Salius, deliberately held him back, and Euryalus raced past Salius and took first place. Helymas finished second, and Diores finished third.

But Salius protested — loudly. If not for Nisus' foul, Salius would have finished first, not Euryalus. But many Trojans and Sicilians took the side of young and handsome Euryalus — they wanted him to win. Diores, who finished third, also wanted Euryalus to win — if Salius were to be awarded first place, Diores would be fourth and would lack a special prize.

Aeneas handled the situation well. He said, "I will not alter the order of the finishers, but I will give an additional prize to Salius: the giant hide of an African lion."

Nisus said, "If Salius gets such a prize, what about me? I clearly would have won if I had not had the bad luck to slip on the bloody ground." He displayed the blood and manure that covered his face and body because he had slipped and fallen down.

Generous Aeneas smiled and awarded Nisus a shield that the Greeks had taken from a temple of Neptune. The shield was the work of the metal-smith Didymaon.

The next event was the boxing match; the boxers would use rawhide gauntlets. Aeneas announced, "Who wishes to compete in the boxing match? Who are the two volunteers?" He set out the prizes for the match.

The victor would win a bull with gilded horns, and the other boxer would win a sword and helmet.

Dares, a huge man, stepped forward. He had boxed Paris, and at the funeral games held to honor Hector, he had boxed the braggart Butes, another huge man — and killed him. Dares was a strong man, and he intimidated almost everyone as he shadow-boxed.

Was anyone willing to box Dares? It seemed not. It looked as if Dares would win the bull by default. Dares grabbed one of the bull's horns and said to Aeneas, "It looks as if I have already won."

The Trojans were willing for Dares to lead away the bull, but Acestes said to his fellow Sicilian Entellus, "You were a boxer once — are you still a boxer? Should we allow Dares to take away the first prize without a fight? The famous boxer Eryx was your teacher. You have fame as a boxer, and you have won many boxing prizes."

Entellus replied, "I still love glory and fame, but I am older than I used to be. My blood is colder, and it moves sluggishly. If I were younger, like Dares, I would not hesitate to fight him. I would not even need the promise of a prize."

Entellus then threw into the boxing area the heavy gauntlets that he had used as a boxer. They had belonged to Eryx, who would first wrap his fists with rawhide and then put on the gauntlets, which were made of layers of oxhide and pieces of metal. Dares looked at the gauntlets and did not want to box anyone wearing them. Aeneas lifted the gauntlets and examined them closely.

Entellus said, "These are the gauntlets of Eryx, but all of you should have seen the gauntlets of Hercules. The two fought here, and Eryx used these gauntlets, as I did later. If you examine the gauntlets, you will see traces of blood and brain.

"Now, I challenge Dares. I will not use these gauntlets. I do not want to have that advantage over Dares. He and I can use gauntlets that are matched in style and weight."

Entellus took off his shirt and revealed his muscles. He may have been older than Dares, but no one could question his strength.

Aeneas gave the two boxers gauntlets that were matched in style and weight, and the two put them on and squared off. They began to trade punches, looking for an opening and testing each other. Dares relied on speed and footwork; Entellus, whose knees creaked, relied on strength. Soon, the testing was over, and the real fight began. The two traded heavier blows and sought a way to win.

Entellus tried for a knockout with one blow, but Dares saw the blow coming and dodged it. Entellus had put so much force into the blow that he fell to the ground like a pine tree struck by lightning falls to the ground on a mountain. This excited the crowd, and Acestes helped his friend regain his footing.

Entellus was unshaken by the fall; instead, he was angry and redoubled his efforts to knock out Dares. Now, his blows came fast and furious and repeatedly hit Dares, who was driven back and was clearly defeated.

Aeneas stopped the fight and declared Entellus the victor. He said to Dares, "This is not your day to win. Entellus has superhuman strength. The gods support Entellus today, not you."

Dares could barely stand up; as his friends led him away, he spit out blood and teeth. His friends also took away for him the runner-up prizes: the sword and helmet.

Entellus was proud of his victory and of his prize: the bull. He said to Aeneas, "Let me show you an example of the power I have now — that will help show you the power I had when I was young. It will also show you that you did the right thing when you stopped the fight — you saved Dares' life."

Entellus put on his own, heavy gauntlets, drew back his fist, and then hit the bull right between the eyes, crushing bone and brain and killing it.

Entellus said, "Here is a sacrifice for you, Eryx. It is more suitable to sacrifice the life of a bull than the life of a human being such as Dares. And now, I retire from boxing with my final victory."

The next event was the archery contest, and Aeneas tied a live dove to the mast of Sergestus' crippled ship. Four archers put their lots in a helmet, which was shaken to determine the order in which they would compete. Hippocoön's lot fell out first, so he shot first. The next lot belonged to Mnestheus, and the third lot belonged to Eurytion, the brother of the Trojan archer Pandarus, who at Troy had broken a truce by attempting to assassinate Menelaus. The final lot belonged to Acestes, an older man competing with younger men.

The archers warmed up by flexing their bows, and then Hippocoön shot first — his arrow missed the dove and stuck in the mast. Mnestheus shot next. He also missed the dove, but his arrow severed the cord that tied the dove to the mast. The dove, sensing freedom, started to fly away, but Eurytion prayed to Pandarus, his late archer brother, and shot the dove, which fell to the earth with the arrow in its body.

Only Acestes remained to compete, but the competition was over. To show his skill, he shot an arrow high into the air. The arrow burst into flames — an omen — and it vanished the way that a falling star or a comet vanishes after trailing flames or a tail behind it.

Omens, whether good or bad, are important. This omen foretold fire and a loss.

The Trojans and the Sicilians prayed to the gods, and Aeneas declared Acestes the winner of the archery contest, giving him gifts and telling him, "Jupiter wants you to have these gifts, including an engraved bowl that Cisseus of Thrace gave to my father, Anchises."

Although Eurytion had shot the dove, he agreed that Acestes should be declared the victor.

Before the archery contest had been concluded, Aeneas had told Epytides, who looked after the safety of Ascanius, "Make sure that Ascanius and the other boys are ready to perform their parts in the honor of Anchises."

Ascanius and the other boys rode up on horseback. First, they paraded in front of their parents. The boys wore their hair bound tight, and they each carried two lances. Some carried the gear of archers. Three captains each commanded twelve boys.

The first captain was Priam, who bore his famous late grandfather's name. He rode a stallion from Thrace. The second captain was Atys, a close friend of Ascanius. From Atys came the Latin line of the Atians. The final captain was Ascanius, who rode a stallion that was a gift from Dido and that came from Sidon in Phoenicia. The other boys rode Sicilian horses.

Once the parade was finished, Epytides ordered the boys, "Get ready." He cracked a whip, and the boys enacted a little battle. They charged, they retreated, they charged again. They wheeled and circled and rode in a pattern as complex as the labyrinth at Crete. The boys rode as swiftly as dolphins at play. Sometimes, the groups of boys made peace, and then they rode side by side.

Ascanius later made this mock battle a tradition in Italy. When he built the city of Alba Longa, he taught this mock battle of the Trojan boys to his Italian citizens. From generation to generation, this tradition was passed down, and it — the Trojan Games — became a tradition of great Rome.

The funeral games for Anchises ended with the end of the Trojan Games.

But now a bad thing happened. Juno had been watching, and she sent Iris, goddess of the rainbow, down to the Trojan women to cause trouble. Iris went to the harbor, where the Trojan ships had been left without guards. At burning altars on the shore, the Trojan women mourned Anchises.

They also mourned their long journey. For the seven years since the fall of Troy, they had not had a real — a permanent — home. They lamented, "How much longer must we travel? How many more sea-miles must we go?"

The Trojan women wanted a permanent home — a permanent city. They did not want to sail on the sea.

Iris assumed the form of Beroë, an aged woman of Troy. Iris cried to the Trojan women, "It would have been better if we had died at Troy. Even after seven years of wandering, we do not have a home. Why should we sail to Italy? We could have a home here. This is the land where Eryx, the half-brother of Aeneas, lived. Here is a king, Acestes, who is friendly to us. Why don't we build walls and a city right here? That is better than more journeying. We will never see the Simois and Xanthus rivers again. We will never see Troy again. So let us make our home here! Let us burn these ships and force the men to settle here! I have seen the ghost of the prophetess Cassandra in a dream. She gave me flaming torches and told me, 'This is your new home, your new Troy.' She wants us to burn the ships. So let us do it. Fires are burning at the altars; we have what we need to set the ships on fire! The altars are dedicated to Neptune — Neptune must want us to set the ships on fire!"

Iris, disguised as the mortal Beroë, took fire from an altar and threw it on a ship.

The Trojan women, shocked, did not move. The oldest Trojan woman, Pyrgo, who had been the nurse to Priam's sons, said, "This is not Beroë! Look at her! Look at her beauty and her bearing! Listen to her voice! This is a goddess. Beroë is not here. I just left her — she is too ill to attend these rites!"

The Trojan women still hesitated. They hated the ships, they loved Sicily, but they remembered the promise of Italy. Iris then revealed herself and rose in the air and created a rainbow. Now the Trojan women were convinced that they should burn the ships. They screamed, and they grabbed fire and threw it onto the ships.

The fire caught quickly. All of the ships were on fire. Eumelus carried the news to the Trojan and Sicilian men, who now saw the smoke rising from the ships.

On horseback, Ascanius raced to the ships and shouted at the Trojan women, "What are you doing? You are not burning the camp of the Greeks! In your *furor*, you are burning our own ships!" In frustration, he threw his helmet on the ground.

Aeneas and the Trojan men arrived, and the Trojan women fled and hid in woods and caves — wherever they could. They now regretted what they had done, and they feared the consequences.

The ships burned, despite the attempts by the men to put the fires out. Aeneas ripped his clothing in the ancient way of showing grief. He prayed, "Jupiter, if you still have some sense of concern for Trojans, save our ships! Or, if you prefer, kill me now with a thunderbolt! Kill all of us Trojans with thunderbolts!"

Immediately, a rainstorm arose. Thunder sounded, and rain fell on the ships until all the fires were put out. All of the ships — except for four — were saved.

The fires disheartened Aeneas although he still had fifteen ships left. He wondered whether he should stay in Sicily and give up the hope of settling in Italy.

Old Nautes, whom Minerva had taught and had made renowned for his intelligence and prophecies, advised Aeneas, "Let us follow our destiny despite whatever challenges we face. This is a new challenge, but we shall meet it. Acestes is the king here, and he is a friendly king. Let him be the king of some of the Trojans — our ships can no longer carry all of us Trojans. All Trojans who are exhausted by the long journey, all the old men, all the women who hate the sea, all who are weak and feeble, and all who wish to avoid danger can stay here and build a city and name it Acesta after Acestes."

Aeneas listened carefully to the words of Nautes, but he did not immediately make a decision.

That night, the ghost of Anchises came to Aeneas in a dream and told him, "Son, when I was alive, I loved you more than my own life. I know that you are disheartened now. Jupiter is taking pity on you and so the god sent me to advise you. Take Nautes' advice — he advised you well and truly. Take the best troops with you to Italy. In Latium, you will fight a war, and you will need soldiers who are not afraid of war.

"But before you fight the war, go down to the Land of the Dead. The entrance is near the lake of Avernus. See me there. I am not in Tartarus, where the wicked are punished. Instead, I am in the Elysium Fields, where the good are rewarded. The Cumaean Sibyl will be your guide to and in the Land of the Dead. She will take you there after you have sacrificed many black sheep to the gods. In the Land of the Dead, I will teach you about your future descendants and about your future city. But now I must go — morning is coming."

The ghost of Anchises vanished. Disappointed and isolated, Aeneas called after it, "Why are you going so quickly? Are you fleeing? Why can't we hug each other?"

Awake, Aeneas worshipped his Trojan household gods and Vesta, the goddess of the hearth.

Aeneas first talked to Acestus, and then he talked to other leading Trojans. He reported what the ghost of his father had told him in the dream, and he told them that he had decided to follow the advice of Nautes and Anchises.

Aeneas decided who would stay in Sicily and who would journey to Italy. The Trojans then set about repairing the fire-damaged ships. The Trojans who were ready and willing to fight in war were the ones who would go to Italy.

As some Trojans repaired the ships, Aeneas and the other Trojans planned the new city on Sicily. Aeneas determined the city limits and assigned homes by lot. One neighborhood of the city he named Troy; another neighborhood he named Ilium. Acestes was pleased with the new city, and he determined its laws and system of justice. Acestes also founded a temple to Venus and appointed a priest to take care of the tomb of Anchises.

After nine days of feasting and sacrificing, the Trojans and Sicilians recognized that the time had come for Aeneas and the best of the Trojans to depart. The weather was good for sailing. Now all the Trojans wanted to journey to Italy, even those who had most wanted to stay in Sicily, but it was impossible for all to sail to Italy. Aeneas comforted those who would stay in Sicily.

Aeneas ordered that three calves be sacrificed to Eryx and a ewe be sacrificed to the gods of the winds and storms, and then the Trojans set sail.

Venus, who was worried about Aeneas and his Trojans, went to Neptune to ask for help. She complained, "Juno's hatred for Troy and the Trojans never stops. Even now that the Greeks have destroyed Troy, she continues to hate the Trojans despite the will of Jupiter and despite fate. You have witnessed her hatred — not long ago she even caused a storm in your own realm, the sea, to drive the Trojans to Carthage, not Italy! She even caused the Trojan women to set fire to their own ships in Sicily!

"I have a favor to ask you. I want you to give the surviving Trojans safe passage in their ships over your sea to Italy. Let them reach the Tiber River safely."

Neptune replied, "You can trust me to keep Aeneas safe, Venus. You were born in the sea, which is my realm. I have often calmed the sea, and I have even saved Aeneas on land — the Xanthus and Simois rivers witnessed that.

"Achilles was slaughtering the Trojans and threw so many Trojan corpses into the Xanthus River that its waters were dammed and could not reach the sea. Aeneas challenged Achilles, although Achilles was the more powerful warrior and had the help of powerful gods. I saved the life of Aeneas although I wanted to see Troy destroyed — I supported the Greeks during the war because an early king of Troy, Laomedon, refused to pay me after I had built the walls of Troy.

"Even now, I want to protect Aeneas, so don't worry about him. He will reach Italy safely. Only one Trojan will die as they cross my waters."

Venus was happy to hear that Aeneas would cross the sea and reach Italy safely.

Neptune hitched his horses to his chariot, and then he drove them over the sea and calmed the waves. Storm clouds moved away. Following Neptune's chariot were whales, the monsters of the sea; the followers of the minor sea-god Glaucus, who was the father of the Cumaean Sibyl; Palaemon, the son of Ino, both of whom were once mortal but are now immortal; some minor sea-gods known as the Tritons; the old minor sea-god Phorcus and his Nereids, including Thetis, who had given birth to Achilles, and Melite and Panopea, as well as Cymodocea, Spio, and Thalia.

The weather was good, and Aeneas was in a good mood. All seemed to be going well.

That night, nearly everyone was asleep except for the pilots of the ships. Palinurus was awake and working, and the god of Sleep came down to him to make him die. The god of Sleep assumed the form of Phorbas and said to Palinurus, "All is going well. The sea is calm, and the winds are blowing in the right direction. It is night, so sleep for a while — I will take over as pilot."

Palinurus wanted to do his duty, so he replied, "No, thank you. The sky and sea are calm — now. But I have enough experience to know that they can quickly change. I want to make sure that I keep Aeneas and his ships safe."

Palinurus wanted to do his duty, but the god of Sleep took a branch from which dripped dew from the Lethe, a river in the Land of the Dead that makes its drinkers forget, and shook it over Palinurus.

Palinurus fell asleep, and instantly the god of Sleep heaved him overboard. Palinurus had a tight grip on the steering oar — it broke and Palinurus took a part of it into the water. He called for help, but no one heard him, and the ship left him behind.

The ship kept sailing — safely. It sailed close to the island of the Sirens and the shore on which so many bones lay bleached by the sun. Aeneas felt the ship moving strangely. He investigated, discovered that Palinurus was gone, and took over as pilot, mourning to himself, "Palinurus, you fell overboard and you will die. Your naked corpse will wash up on a shore somewhere."

Chapter 6: The Land of the Dead

As the ships sailed, Aeneas continued to mourn for Palinurus.

Eventually, the ships safely arrived at Cumae in Italy. The Trojans moored the ships, and then they disembarked. Finally, they were on Italian soil and they began exploring the immediate vicinity.

Aeneas went to visit the Cumaean Sibyl, the prophetess of Apollo. She lived in a temple and a cave sacred to Apollo, and there she made prophecies that he inspired in her. Outside her cave was a grove sacred to Diana, Apollo's twin sister.

Daedalus had built the temple in front of a cave. He was the first man ever to fly, and he used his wings to escape from Crete. Flying to Cumae, he built the temple and created works of art for it.

On one panel, he told the story of Androgeos, the son of King Minos and Queen Pasiphaë of Crete. Androgeos had competed in athletic games and was victorious, but some of his competitors, jealous Athenians, murdered him. Because of that, King Minos demanded tribute in the form of human beings from Athens, which sent seven young men and seven young women to Crete each year to be killed.

On another panel, Daedalus told the story of the Minotaur. Queen Pasiphaë felt lust for a bull, and she made Daedalus create a replica of a cow for her to hide in. When the bull had sex with the replica of the cow, it had sex with the queen, who became pregnant and gave birth to a creature that was half-man and half-bull. Daedalus built a labyrinth at Crete to house the creature, which was called the Minotaur. Each year, the seven Athenian young men and seven Athenian young women were put in the labyrinth, and the Minotaur feasted on their flesh.

One year, one of the seven Athenian young men was Theseus, with whom Ariadne, daughter of King Minos and Queen Pasiphaë, fell in love. Daedalus sympathized with Ariadne, and he told her how Theseus could find his way out of the labyrinth: He should carry a ball of string, tie one end of the string to the entrance of the labyrinth, and unwind the ball of string as he walked the labyrinth.

Because Daedalus had helped Ariadne and Theseus, he and Icarus, his son, were put in prison in Crete. Daedalus conceived the idea of making wings out of feathers and wax so he and his son could escape from prison. He warned Icarus not to fly too high because the sun would melt the wax and the feathers would fall out, but Icarus was so excited by his flight that he ignored the words of his father. The feathers fell out of Icarus' wings, and he fell into the sea and drowned.

Daedalus attempted to create a work of art depicting the death of his son. He tried twice to create the work of art, but each time grief forced him to stop. He never completed the work of art.

The gods had given Daedalus great gifts, but he did not always use his great gifts in an ethical manner. Building the replica of the cow and building the labyrinth were misuses of his great gifts.

Aeneas looked at the works of art as Achates went ahead to talk to the Sibyl, whose name was Deiphobe. She was the daughter of Glaucus, a minor sea-god. This priestess of Apollo and Diana arrived with Achates and told Aeneas, "Don't spend your time looking at the works of art. Instead, now is the time to sacrifice seven bulls and seven sheep." This was quickly done.

Aeneas and the Sibyl then entered the temple. Inside the temple an enormous cavern had been carved into rock. The cavern had a hundred tunnels that echoed the prophecies of the Sibyl when she spoke. The Sibyl said to Aeneas, "Apollo is coming here now — I see him! Now is the time for you to learn your fate!"

Before Aeneas' eyes, the Sibyl changed as the god began to possess her. Her chest heaved, her face changed, her braided hair became loose, she became taller, and her voice changed. She shouted, "Aeneas, you must pray. Until you do, you will hear no prophecies."

Aeneas prayed, "Apollo, you have always helped the Trojans. When Paris shot Achilles with an arrow, you guided the arrow to a mortal spot. You have been with the remaining Trojans and me as we have sailed the seas, making our way at last to Italy.

"Let the bad luck of the Trojans stop now, please, Apollo and all you gods and goddesses who opposed Troy. Sibyl, I hope that you will also grant my prayer. I ask no more than my destiny requires: I request that the Trojans and their household gods be allowed to find a new home in Latium. If you grant that, Apollo, I will build a temple of marble for you and your twin sister, Diana. I will set aside sacred days for festivals for you. And Sibyl, for you I will build a magnificent shrine in which to safely keep your prophecies and to ordain your priests.

"Now, Sibyl, I ask you to say your prophecies out loud. Don't write them on leaves that are quickly scattered by the wind!"

The Sibyl resisted being possessed by Apollo. The god was like a breaker of horses as he worked to possess the Sibyl and prophesy through her. The Sibyl tried to buck off Apollo, but the god won and the hundred tunnels of the cave echoed with her frenzied prophetic words: "You Trojans have endured bad things at sea, but you will endure worse things on land. You will reach the land where you will found a city, but war and a bloody Tiber River await you. The horrors of the Trojan War will be renewed in Italy. I see a new Achilles, another warrior son of a goddess, arising to fight you. Juno will continue to be your enemy, and you will be forced to ask cities for help. What will be the cause of this new war? The same cause as that of the old war. The Trojan War was fought over who would be the husband of Helen. This new war will be fought over who will be the husband of an Italian princess. But fight the war. You will find help from an unexpected source — a city that Greeks have built!"

So the frenzied Sibyl prophesized, and the hundred tunnels echoed with her words. She stopped speaking.

Aeneas said to her, "I am used to dangers. Whatever I will face in a new war, I have already experienced in the old war.

"But I have a request. Here at Avernus is an entrance to the Land of the Dead. Please allow me to enter it and consult the ghost of my late father, Anchises. Show me how to enter the Land of the Dead, how to get past its gates. I saved my father during the fall of Troy by carrying him on my shoulders out of a city on fire. He shared my travels until his death. He appeared to me in a dream and told me to consult you. Now help me, please — you have the power! Hecate, the goddess of the Land of the Dead, gave you power when she made you the guardian of the forest and lake and cave of Avernus!

"Others have traveled to and back from the Land of the Dead. Orpheus traveled to the Land of the Dead in an attempt to bring his wife back to the Land of the Living. Pollux traveled to the Land of the Dead to be with Castor, his late brother, and to share his life with him: They alternate being alive and being dead together. I do not need to tell you that Theseus and Hercules also visited the Land of the Dead. Other heroes also visited the Land of the Dead and returned. Like these heroes, I also have an immortal as a parent, and Jupiter is one of my ancestors."

The Sibyl replied with grim humor, "Entering the Land of the Dead is easy; the hard part is returning to the Land of the Living. Only a few have ever returned, and they have been the children of gods.

"You are correct: An entrance to the Land of the Dead is here. If you really want to enter the Land of the Dead twice — now and then again after you die — I will tell you what you have to do.

"Hidden in the forest of Avernus is a tree that has a golden bough — the stem and the leaves are gold. This is the gift that you must offer to Proserpina, the goddess of the Land of the Dead. The golden bough is well hidden, and without it you cannot enter the Land of the Dead. Each time the golden bough is plucked — which rarely happens — another golden bough appears in its place.

"If you are fated to enter the Land of the Dead while you are still alive, you will be able to easily pluck the golden bough. If you are not fated to enter the Land of the Dead, no matter how hard you try you will not be able to pluck the golden bough.

"Listen to one more thing because it is important. Unknown to you, one of your friends is dead. Before you can enter the Land of the Dead while you are still alive, you must bury your friend."

Aeneas left the Sibyl and the cave and thought about all that he had heard. Achates walked with him, and they talked about whom the dead friend might be.

They arrived at the Trojan camp, and they saw the corpse of Misenus, their trumpeter who rallied the Trojan troops in times of battle. Misenus had fought beside Hector at Troy. After Achilles had killed Hector, Misenus fought beside Aeneas. Proud of his ability with the trumpet, Misenus challenged the gods to a competition. The sea-god Triton was angered by such presumption and drowned Misenus.

The gods had given Misenus the great gift of blowing the trumpet, but Misenus became overly proud. Challenging the gods to a competition was a misuse of his great gift.

Aeneas and the Trojans mourned the death of Misenus. They searched for wood to build a funeral pyre for his corpse.

In the forest, Aeneas thought about the words of the Sibyl. He said to himself, "I wish that I could see the golden bough shining. What the Sibyl told me about it must be true since what she said about the death of one of my friends is true."

Two doves — the sacred birds of Venus, Aeneas' mother — flew to the ground at his feet. He recognized the birds and prayed, "Let the doves be my guides to the golden bough. Mother, help me now to find the golden bough."

The birds led him to the golden bough. They flew ahead a little, let Aeneas catch up, and then flew ahead a little more. Eventually, they flew to a tree that had many boughs of green — and one bough of gold.

Aeneas grabbed the golden bough and pulled. He had to pull hard to pluck it, but it eventually came away in his hand. Founding the Roman people was difficult in many ways. Aeneas carried the golden bough to the Sibyl.

The Trojans built the funeral pyre for Misenus. They bathed his corpse in warm water, they clothed his corpse, and they mourned for him. They burned his corpse along with offerings to the gods: frankincense and oil. After the fire burned down, they put it out with wine.

The Trojan priest Corynaeus gathered Misenus' bones and sealed them in an urn, then said the final prayer. Aeneas built a mound over the cremation site. At the top he placed Misenus' oar and trumpet. The cape that is the site where the Trojans cremated Misenus' corpse was thereafter named Misenum.

Aeneas then went to meet the Sibyl at a cave by a lake and woods. From the cave came poisonous fumes; no bird could fly above the cave and live. The Sibyl sacrificed four black calves to Hecate, goddess of the Underworld. Aeneas sacrificed a black lamb to honor the goddess Night, who is the mother of the Furies, and the goddess Earth. He also sacrificed a black heifer to Proserpina, Queen of the Underworld. To Hades, the god of the Land of the Dead, he sacrificed many cattle.

The earth shook and the dogs of hell approached, and the Sibyl shouted, "All unhallowed ones, stay away. But you, Aeneas, are ready to go to the Land of the Dead. Unsheathe your sword — you will need courage!"

The Sibyl went into the cave; Aeneas followed her.

Please, gods of the Land of the Dead, of Chaos, and of the River of Fire, give me permission to reveal the secrets of the Land of the Dead.

The Sibyl and Aeneas walked a dark path like that dimly lit by the Moon when night has taken all color from the world.

The entrance to the Land of the Dead was densely populated with Grief, Cares, Diseases, Old Age, Fear, Hunger, Poverty, Death, Hard Labor, Restless Sleep, Evil Joys, Hallucinations, and War. Here lived the Furies and Discord.

A tree grew at the entrance to the Land of the Dead — a tree whose fruit was False Dreams.

Also living at the entrance to the Land of the Dead were monsters: Centaurs, Scyllas, Briareus and his hundred hands, the Hydra, the Chimera, Gorgons, Harpies, and Geryon and his three bodies.

Terrified, Aeneas held his naked sword in front of him. He was ready to fight, but the Sibyl told him that the forms he saw were ghostly and without physical substance.

Aeneas and the Sibyl passed through the entrance and followed a road that led to Acheron and Cocytus, two rivers of the Underworld.

Aeneas and the Sibyl saw Charon, the ferryman of Hell, who took souls to the Land of the Dead. He is an old god, bearded, with staring eyes, and he wears rags.

The ghosts of the dead — mothers, adult men, heroes, boys, unmarried girls, and young sons — came to Charon. They were as numerous as the leaves that fall in autumn and as numerous as the birds that migrate when winter arrives. They begged Charon to ferry them across the river to the Land of the Dead. He sorted them. Some he would take across the water; some he would leave behind.

Aeneas asked the Sibyl, "What is the reason for what I am seeing here? What makes Charon divide the souls into two groups?"

The Sibyl replied, "Here you see the water of Cocytus and the marsh of the Styx. Charon is determining who shall be taken across the water to the Land of the Dead. Only those souls whose bones have been buried are allowed to cross the water. Any soul whose corpse did not receive a proper funeral will not be allowed to cross the water until a hundred years have passed following his or her death. Until that time, the soul unhappily wanders these shores."

Aeneas recognized two men whom Charon refused to ferry across the water: Leucaspis and Orontes. They had drowned in the storm that had sunk one of Aeneas' ships and driven the remaining ships to Carthage. They had been dead for one year.

Aeneas also saw Palinurus, his pilot, who came toward him. He was very recently dead, having fallen off Aeneas' ship after the god of Sleep drugged him with dew from the Lethe River.

Aeneas spoke first: "Palinurus, Apollo has never lied to me but once. Apollo told me that you would not drown. That is the only lie he has told me."

Palinurus replied, "Apollo did not lie to you. I did not drown. True, I fell into the water. I was piloting your ship, and the steering oar broke and flung me into the water. I swear that I worried more about the safety of you and your ship than about the safety of my own life. For three days and three nights, I stayed afloat, and finally I reached shore. But barbarians killed me there and robbed my corpse. I have not been buried — my corpse rolls in the waves.

"I beg you to help me somehow to cross the water and reach the Land of the Dead. Find my corpse and throw soil on it. Or if Venus will allow you, take me with you — make Charon ferry me across the water!"

The Sibyl knew the rules of the Land of the Dead. She said, "Palinurus, talk sense. Your corpse is not yet buried, and so you cannot cross the water. The gods have set the rules here, and no one can break them.

"But listen to me, and I shall comfort you. The gods will send signs to the people who live where you died. The signs will convince those people to give your corpse a proper burial, and then you can pass over the water and enter the Land of the Dead. What's more, your burial site will become known as Cape Palinuro."

The Sibyl was right: This information greatly comforted Palinurus.

Charon was now close to the shore. He saw Aeneas and knew that he was a still-living man. He shouted at Aeneas, "Stop! Do not come closer!

I am forbidden to carry the living across the water. The living should stay out of the Land of the Dead. Whenever living men have come here, they have brought trouble. Hercules came here, and he carried away Cerberus, the three-headed watchdog of the Underworld. Theseus and Pirithous came here and tried to kidnap Proserpina, the Queen of the Underworld. Their attempt failed. I have had bad experiences with the living!"

The Sibyl replied to Charon, "Aeneas will not cause you trouble. Cerberus will stay here. Aeneas will not try to kidnap either Cerberus or Persephone. Aeneas is renowned for his *pietas* — he knows how to behave both in the Land of the Living and in the Land of the Dead. Aeneas has come here to consult his late father, a good reason for visiting the Land of the Dead. He also brings the golden bough."

The Sibyl showed Charon the golden bough, something that he had not seen for a very long time. Charon no longer objected to the presence of Aeneas, a still-living man.

Charon brought his ferry to shore and allowed Aeneas and the Sibyl to board. Aeneas' weight made the ferry groan as Charon took them to the Land of the Dead.

Here they saw Cerberus — snakes wrapped themselves around his three heads. The Sibyl gave him grain sweetened with honey and drugged with a sleeping potion. The three-headed dog slept as Aeneas and the Sibyl passed him.

They heard cries and wails. Here were the ghosts of babies who had died before they had experienced much of life. Also here were people who had been incorrectly judged guilty and then executed. In the Land of the Dead, Minos, the judge of the Underworld, judged them again — correctly, this time. Also here were the suicides who had treated their lives as if they were disposable. Now they wanted their lives back, even if living meant poverty and hard labor. They will never get their lives back.

The Sibyl then pointed out to Aeneas the Fields of Mourning, where reside those who died because of love. Even here, in death, they suffer because of love.

Aeneas saw Phaedra, who had married Theseus and then had fallen in love with Hippolytus, Theseus' son by a previous wife. She committed suicide after Hippolytus died.

Aeneas saw Procris, who became falsely jealous of her husband, Cephalus. He accidentally shot her with an arrow when she hid and spied on him.

Aeneas saw Eriphyle, who accepted the bribe of a necklace in return for making her husband participate in a war against Thebes. Her son killed her in revenge.

Aeneas saw Evadne. When her husband died in a war against Thebes, she burned herself alive at his funeral pyre.

Aeneas saw Pasiphaë. She fell in love with a bull, copulated with it, and gave birth to the Minotaur. She was unable to prevent the death of the Minotaur.

Aeneas saw Laodamia, the wife of the Greek Protesilaus who fought at Troy. When he died in the war — he died as the Greeks landed their ships at Troy as the Trojans opposed them — Laodamia committed suicide.

Aeneas saw Caeneus, who was born female. After Neptune raped her, he gave her a wish that he would grant. She requested to be changed into a man so that men would never again rape her. After Caeneus died, he became a woman again in the Land of the Dead.

Aeneas also saw Dido in the shadows of the woods. Her ghost was dim and misty, like a new moon seen through clouds, but Aeneas could see her self-inflicted sword wound. Aeneas cried and said to her, "Dido, I heard that you died. I have heard that you committed suicide with a sword. Did you die because of me? I swear by the stars, by the gods, and by whatever one swears by in the Land of the Dead that when I left you I did so unwillingly — I left you against my will. My gods and my destiny forced me to leave. I did not know that you would commit suicide because of me. Please stay, Dido. This is the last time that I will see you while I am alive — these are the last words that I will say to you while I am alive."

Crying, Aeneas tried to convince Dido to stay, but stony-faced, she turned away from him and would not speak to him. She walked away and met her dead husband, Sychaeus, a man who returned her love.

Aeneas and the Sibyl continued their journey. They walked along the path and came to the part of the Underworld where great heroes of war resided.

They saw Tydeus, the father of the Greek warrior Diomedes. Tydeus had fought against the city of Thebes — he was one of the famous Seven Against Thebes.

They saw Parthenopaeus, another of the famous Seven Against Thebes. Both he and Tydeus had died at Thebes.

They saw Adrastus, the leader of the Seven Against Thebes and a warrior who had survived the war.

They saw Trojans who had died during the Trojan War: Polyboetes, Idaeus, and three sons of Antenor — Glaucus, Medon, and Thersilochus. These ghosts crowded around Aeneas and asked him why he was visiting the Land of the Dead.

Also present here were the ghosts of Greeks who had died during the Trojan War. Many of these ghosts were afraid and ran away from Aeneas, as during the war at times they had ran back to their ships. Some of the Greeks tried to shout a war-cry, but they could manage to produce only a whisper.

Aeneas saw here Deiphobus, a son of Priam. After the death of Paris, Deiphobus had married Helen. He had been tortured and mutilated. His hands, his ears, and his nose had been cut off. Even in death, these wounds remained. Aeneas barely recognized Deiphobus, who tried to hide his wounds.

Aeneas said, "Deiphobus, who mutilated you? Who is capable of such cruelty? I heard that you died at Troy after killing many Greek warriors. I built a tomb — empty — for you on Cape Rhoeteum north of Troy, and I called on your spirit three times. I was unable to find your bones and bury them."

Deiphobus replied, "You did for me everything that you ought to have done and were capable of doing. I am in the Land of the Dead and am not wailing on a distant shore and waiting for Charon to ferry me across the river.

"You remember the last night of Troy. We had brought the Horse into Troy. We thought that the Greeks had left Troy. We thought that we had won the war. We celebrated that night.

"Helen led the women of Troy in a dance, supposedly to celebrate our victory. In reality, she used a torch to signal the troops of Agamemnon to come to the Scaean Gates, where the Greek warriors who had been hidden inside the Horse came to let them into the city to sack it.

"I was home asleep. Helen crept into our house, and she removed every weapon, including the sword I kept under my pillow. Then she let Menelaus, her husband at Sparta, in. With him came cruel Ulysses. By turning me over to her husband of long ago, Helen hoped to win his forgiveness.

"Menelaus and Ulysses gave me the wounds you see now. They tortured me, and they killed me. I pray that the gods will avenge me.

"But why have you come here? Did the gods send you here? Does your destiny bring you here?"

They talked, noon arrived, and then the Sibyl said to Aeneas, "You have much more to see, Aeneas. Let us continue our journey. The path now divides in two. The right fork leads to our destination: the Elysium Fields, where the truly good are rewarded. The left fork leads to Tartarus, where the truly evil are punished."

Deiphobus said, "Sibyl, you are correct. You two should leave and accomplish your goal. Aeneas, may you have a better fate than mine." He departed.

Aeneas looked to the left and saw a fortress with three walls. Outside the three walls was a river of molten lava, a river of fire. Tisiphone, one of the Furies, guards the gate to Tartarus. Aeneas heard the groans and wails of sinners, the cracks of whips, and the sound of metal against metal.

Aeneas asked the Sibyl, "Who is punished there? What kinds of crimes have they committed?"

The aged Sibyl said to Aeneas, "You cannot go there, even for a visit — no pure soul can. But Hecate has told me about Tartarus and what goes on there. The judge is Rhadamanthus of Crete, who hands out punishments to souls who while they were alive enjoyed committing secret crimes. That is, they were secret in the Land of the Living — they are not secret in the Land of the Dead. When a guilty soul comes here, the Fury Tisiphone whips them and sends them through the gate — a gate from which they will not exit. Inside the gate is another monster: the Hydra with its fifty heads and fifty mouths.

"Tartarus is a pit. It plunges down into darkness twice as far as our gaze goes upward to Olympus, home of the gods. At the bottom of Tartarus lie the Titans, who rebelled against Jupiter and whom Jupiter subdued with his thunderbolts.

"Also in Tartarus are the giant brothers Otus and Ephialtes, who also rebelled against Jupiter.

"Also in Tartarus is Salmoneus, who impersonated Jupiter and faked his thunder and lightning. He faked thunder by having his horses run over a bridge made of metal. Because of Salmoneus' excessive pride, Jupiter hurled a thunderbolt at him that knocked him down into the agonies of Tartarus.

"Also in Tartarus is Tityus, whose giant body lies across nine acres. A vulture feeds on his internal organs, which, once eaten, grow back so the vulture can eat them again and eternally torment Tityus.

"Also in Tartarus are sinners over whom a rock is balanced and always about to fall, terrifying the sinners below.

"Also in Tartarus are sinners before whom a table is set with food, but whenever the sinners reach out to get food to eat, a Fury forces them back with terrifying shrieks and a flaming torch. The sinners are always hungry.

"Also in Tartarus are Ixion and Pirithous, Ixion's son, both of whom are Lapiths. Ixion tried to rape the goddess Juno, and Pirithous tried to kidnap the goddess Persephone. Ixion is bound on a flaming wheel that constantly spins. Pirithous is chained for eternity.

"So many sinners are punished in Tartarus, including sinners who hated their brothers or killed their fathers. In Tartarus are sinners who defrauded their clients. In Tartarus are sinners who piled up gold they never used although they could have helped family members with it — multitudes are in Tartarus because of that sin. In Tartarus are sinners who committed adultery. In Tartarus are sinners who waged civil war against their rightful rulers.

"Many sinners are in Tartarus, waiting to learn what will be their punishment.

"Do not try to learn all the punishments in Tartarus — they are too numerous. Some sinners push boulders. Some sinners are tormented on spinning wheels. Theseus sits forever and cannot leave. While alive, Phlegyas set fire to a temple of Apollo. Too late, and in torment in Tartarus, he warns others, 'Don't try to fight the gods — they are too strong!'

"In Tartarus are sinners who betrayed their country for money. In return for money, they set up a tyrant to rule the country. In return for money, they made bad laws. In return for money, they repealed good laws.

"In Tartarus are sinners who committed incest with their daughters.

"It is impossible for me to tell you about all the sinners in Tartarus and about all their punishments. I could not do that even if I could speak with a hundred voices.

"But let us continue our journey. You have not yet accomplished what you set out to do. We must hurry. Ahead of us I see a gate guarded by Centaurs. There you must place the golden bough, your gift to Persephone."

They reached the gate, Aeneas purified himself with water, and he placed the golden bough at the gate.

They passed through the gate and entered the Elysium Fields that are the reward for especially good souls. Here are air, stars, and sun. Here is land for roaming and for sports. Here are singing and dancing. Here Orpheus plays his lyre.

Here are the descendants of Teucer: famous Trojans, including Ilus, Assaracus, and Dardanus, who founded Troy.

Aeneas, awed, looked around. The things that give joy in the Land of the Living are here in the Elysium Fields: weapons, horses, chariots, and more.

Aeneas saw several souls feasting and singing a song in praise of Apollo.

Among the souls here are many warriors who died fighting for their country. Among the souls here are priests who truly served their god. Among the souls here are talented poets. Among the souls here are talented artists. Among the souls here are those who did much good for Humankind.

All of the souls here wear white headbands. Many souls crowd around the Sibyl, including the famous Greek singer Musaeus. The Sibyl asked them, "Tell me, please, where can we find Anchises? We have come here to consult him."

Musaeus replied, "Here in the Elysium Fields, souls are free to wander where they please. No one has a permanent home in one particular place. But I can show you where you need to go to meet Anchises."

Musaeus showed them a valley. Aeneas and the Sibyl climbed down from the heights and into the valley.

They found Anchises passing his time in a review of heroes who would be reborn into the Land of the Living. The heroes he was at this time reviewing were his own descendants and the descendants of Aeneas. Anchises knew the souls' future histories and future fates. He knew which values they held and which heroic acts they would perform.

When Anchises saw Aeneas walking toward him, he started to cry and he said, "So at last you have come! I have waited for you. The love you have for me outweighed the difficulty of your journey here. Let me look at you, let me talk to you, let me hear your voice. I have dreamed about you, and I knew that you would come. I was afraid for you when you went to Carthage. You have traveled in dangerous lands to come here."

Aeneas replied, "You appeared in my dreams and told me to come here. Let me hug you, father."

Aeneas tried three times to hug his father, but three times his arms closed on air. Aeneas, a living man, was unable to touch the soul of his father.

Knowing that he could not hug his father, Aeneas then looked around him. He saw a river. He also saw many, many souls around the river. They were like the numerous bees that flit from flower to flower in a meadow.

He asked his father, "What river is this? And who are these souls?"

Anchises replied, "These souls will be given a second body. This is the Lethe River; whoever drinks from it loses all memory. These souls will drink from the river and then be reborn in the Land of the Living.

"I have long wanted to show you these souls. They are our descendants. They are the reason for your coming to Italy. This is the people you will found."

Aeneas said, "Do souls here return to the Land of the Living? Will a physical body again burden these souls? Why would souls want that?"

Anchises replied, "Let me explain the universal spirit, purgation, and reincarnation to you.

"Understand first that spirit permeates all things: sky, earth, sea, moon, sun, and stars. Nothing is untouched by spirit. Spirit and matter joined together and formed the universe first and formed human beings and other living things later. Spirit is pure, but matter is not pure. The matter that makes up the bodies of human beings weighs down their spirits. Human beings have fears and desires and joys and sorrows. Because of the impurity of their bodies, human beings are unable to clearly see the spiritual things that are real.

"Even when human beings die and their spirits are separated from their bodies, the spirit remains tainted by its earthly contact with the physical body it used to have. The sins of the body taint the spirit. Therefore, the spirit undergoes a process of purgation that varies for each spirit. Some spirits are exposed to the winds, some spirits are exposed to flooding waters, some spirits are burned by fire — the spirits undergo whatever is needed to purge their old sins.

"Reincarnation is part of God's plans for most spirits. After their sins have been purged, the spirits are sent to the Elysium Fields. A few are completely purified and remain here forever, but most are not completely purified and they stay in the Elysium Fields for a thousand years. They then drink from the Lethe River and are reincarnated in the Land of the Living — they live again, burdened with physical bodies."

The Sibyl thought, *This means that living human beings are, to some extent, tarnished. All living human beings, if they live long enough, sin. Some living human beings are slightly tainted by the sins of a past life. Romans, like all other peoples, will be tainted by sins although Romans are also capable of great things. Individual Romans can give in to* furor, *or they can be renowned for* pietas *and for* clementia. *If enough individual Romans are renowned for one or the other quality, that will result in the Romans as a whole acquiring a reputation for that quality.*

Anchises watched the spirits in front of him. They were spirits who would be reincarnated as Romans.

Anchises said to Aeneas, "Let me show you our descendants. These are your descendants and the descendants of your Italian wife. These descendants are your reward for fulfilling your destiny.

"Here is Silvius, who will be the last-born son of you and your Italian wife — her name will be Lavinia. Silvius will become a king of the city of Alba Longa — your son Ascanius will be the founder of Alba Longa.

"Here are Procas, Capys, Numitor, and Silvius Aeneas. All will play important roles in Italy before Rome is founded. The men you see here will build the cities of Nomentum, Gabii, Fidena, Collatia, Pometia, Inuis, Bola, and Cora.

"Here is Romulus, a son of the god Mars. A king of Alba Longa will be Amulius, who will be an evil man who will exile Numitor, his brother, and will force his brother's daughter, Rhea Silvia, to become a Vestal Virgin. The god of Mars will see Rhea Silvia, desire her, and sleep with her.

"The unions of gods with mortal women are fertile. Rhea Silvia will give birth to twins: Romulus and Remus. Because Vestal Virgins are supposed to be virgins, King Amulius will order the twin boys to be thrown into the river. Instead, the man responsible for throwing them into the river will put them in their cradle and let it float down the river. A she-wolf will find the twin boys and suckle them.

"A shepherd by the name of Faustulus will find them by the banks of the Tiber River and will take care of the boys and raise them. Eventually, as grown men, Romulus and Remus will build a city on the bank of the Tiber River where they had been discovered. You, Aeneas, will found the Roman people. Romulus will found the city of Rome. Romulus and Remus will quarrel. Romulus will kill Remus, and so the city will be known as Rome rather than Reme. Romulus will be the first king of Rome.

"Rome will become a great empire. Much glory will be in its future. Rome will be happy with its hero sons just as the goddess Cybele is happy with her hundred grandsons.

"Let me skip ahead hundreds of years and show you Caesar Augustus, the first emperor of Rome. Before his time, Rome will be a republic.

"Caesar Augustus will fight a civil war to become the first Roman emperor. He will be born with the name Octavian. He will live from 63 B.C.E. to 14 C.E. He will defeat Mark Antony and Cleopatra at the naval Battle of Actium in 31 B.C.E.

"Many stories will be told about Caesar Augustus.

"Before the Battle of Actium, Octavian will set up a camp that will overlook his fleet and the fleet of Mark Antony. He will meet a peasant with a donkey, and he will ask the peasant what is his name and what is the donkey's name. The peasant will reply that his name is *Eutyches*, which means 'Good Fortune,' and the donkey's name is *Nikon*, which means 'Victor.' Such positive omens will go a long way toward motivating his superstitious soldiers.

"Caesar Augustus will fire a young soldier, who will plead with him not to be fired, saying, 'How am I to go home? What shall I tell my father?' Caesar Augustus will reply, 'Tell your father that you didn't find me to your liking.'

"After a Roman nobleman dies, leaving behind enormous debts, Caesar Augustus will order that the nobleman's pillow be bought at an auction, saying, 'That pillow must be particularly conducive to sleep if its late owner, in spite of his debts, could sleep on it.'

"A retired Roman commander who will have fought for Caesar Augustus will have to appear at court, and he will ask Caesar Augustus to appear at the court and testify for him. Caesar Augustus will reply that he will not appear in court himself but will send an agent instead. The retired Roman commander will show Caesar Augustus several scars and say, 'When you were in danger at the Battle of Actium, I didn't choose a substitute; instead, I fought for you in person.' Caesar Augustus will appear in person in court and will testify for the retired Roman commander.

"Caesar Augustus will bring another Age of Gold to Rome. He will stop the civil wars that will have ravaged Rome for decades. He will greatly extend the power of Rome. Not even Hercules and Bacchus have traveled over as much territory as the territory over which Rome will hold power.

"Let us now see some of the early future kings of Rome and other early Romans. Romulus, of course, will be Rome's first king.

"Here is Numa Pompilius, the white-haired second king of Rome, who will give laws to Rome.

"Here is Tullus Hostilius, the third king of Rome, who will make the Romans fight again in war after they have grown stagnant in peace. He will be a warrior king.

"Here is Ancus Martius, the fourth king of Rome, who will desire too much to be popular with the people.

"Here is Brutus the Avenger, who will expel the last of the Roman kings: Lucius Tarquinius Superbus, whose son will rape Lucretia, who will then commit suicide. Brutus will found the Roman Republic, and as consul he will protect it. When his own two sons rebel against the republic, he will allow them to be executed.

"Here are the Decii, who will be an important family who will win victories in war for the Roman Republic.

"Here are the Drusi, who will be another important family who will provide many generals for Rome.

"Here is Titus Manlius Torquatus, who will be a consul and who is carrying an axe, who will execute his son when his son disobeys orders.

"Here is Camillus, who will recover the Roman standards that the Gauls will take from Rome when they occupy the city. The standards will be tall poles topped with various insignia and symbols, including the Roman eagle. The loss of standards in battle will be taken very seriously.

"Now let us see some spirits who will be Romans further in the future than the spirits we just looked at.

"Here are Pompey and Julius Caesar. They are friends here and now, but they will fight a civil war as they attempt to gain power. Civil war is evil; peace is better.

"Eventually, Julius Caesar will be victorious over Pompey, but after Julius Caesar is assassinated, a new round of civil wars will break out. Mark Antony and Octavian will fight for supreme power. Eventually, Octavian will defeat Mark Antony and Cleopatra, Mark Antony's ally, and then Octavian will become Caesar Augustus.

"Julius Caesar will be a Roman general and politician who will help turn the Roman Republic into the Roman Empire. In 55 B.C.E., he will invade Britain. In 48 B.C.E., he will defeat Pompey at Pharsalus. On the Ides of March, 15 March 44 B.C.E., a group of republicans led by Cassius and Brutus will assassinate him.

"Many stories will be told about Julius Caesar.

"When Julius Caesar is a young man, he will sail for the island of Rhodes, where he will wish to study rhetoric and persuasive speaking. Pirates will capture him and will hold him for ransom. Julius Caesar will tell the pirates that after he is ransomed he will hunt them down and crucify them — something that the pirates will think is funny. After Julius Caesar is ransomed, he will get some ships, hunt down the pirates, and crucify them.

"Among his other accomplishments, Julius Caesar will be a good writer. In 47 B.C.E. after he defeats the king of Pontus, Pharnaces II, near Zela in Asia Minor, he will send this message to Rome: '*Veni, vidi, vici*,' which means, 'I came, I saw, I conquered.'

"In 49 B.C.E., against orders, Julius Caesar will take an army of soldiers to Rome, precipitating civil war. To reach Italian soil after traveling from Gaul, he will have to cross the Rubicon River. This will be a big step. Once he crosses the Rubicon River, he will have defied the orders of the Roman Senate, and he will not be able to turn back. He and his army did cross the Rubicon River, and he said, '*Alea iacta est*,' which means 'The die is cast.'

"During the Roman civil wars when Julius Caesar will be fighting Gnaeus Pompeius Magnus — Pompey the Great — for power, Julius Caesar will land on the coast of north Africa. As he jumps from his ship into the shallow water, he will stumble and fall. Knowing that his superstitious Roman troops regard accidental stumbling as an unlucky omen, Julius Caesar will pretend that he did not stumble. He will grab two fistfuls of sand, stand up, and raise his hands so his troops can see the sand. He will then yell, 'Africa, I hold you in my hands!' Hearing these inspiring words, his troops will charge upon the beach with high morale.

"During a dinner that Julius Caesar will have with friends, conversation will turn to the subject of death. Someone will ask Julius Caesar what kind of death is best, and he will reply, 'A sudden one.' The next day, 15 March 44 B.C.E., a group of republicans led by Cassius and Brutus will assassinate him.

"Early in March of 44 B.C.E., an augur named Spurinna will warn Julius Caesar that the Ides of March — that is, March 15 — would bring danger to him. On March 15, Julius Caesar will walk to the Senate. He will see Spurinna and say to him, 'The Ides of March have come.' Spurinna will reply, 'Yes, they have come, but they have not yet gone.' Shortly afterward, Julius Caesar will be assassinated.

"One of the people who will assassinate Julius Caesar will be Marcus Junius Brutus, whom Julius Caesar trusted. When Julius Caesar sees Brutus among the assassins, he will cry out, '*Et tu, Brute*?' This means, 'You, too, Brutus?'

"Now let us see some spirits who will be generals involved in the wars against Greeks and in the wars against Carthage. These wars will occur long before the time of Julius Caesar.

"Here is Lucius Mummius, who will help avenge the fall of Troy by sacking the Greek city of Corinth in 146 B.C.E.

"Here is Lucius Aemilius Paullus, who will help avenge the fall of Troy by defeating Perseus, the king of Macedon, in the Battle of Pydna in 168 B.C.E. Perseus will claim to be the descendant of Achilles.

"Here is Cato the Censor, who will recognize that Carthage is the great enemy of Rome. He will end every speech he makes, whatever its topic, by saying, '*Carthago delenda est*,' which means 'Carthage must be destroyed.'

"Here is Aulus Cornelius Cossus, who will be only the second Roman general to win the *spolia opima*, which means 'rich spoils,' which is given to a Roman general who has killed the enemy general in single combat. Romulus will be the first Roman to win the *spolia opima*.

"Here are the Gracchi, who will be a famous Roman family who will produce two tribunes who will be reformers, but who will be killed.

"Here are the Scipios, a family who will produce two famous generals who will fight the Carthaginians.

"The elder Scipio will be Africanus the Elder, or Publius Cornelius Scipio Africanus Major. Hannibal will be a great Carthaginian general — the unknown avenger called up by Dido before she committed suicide. He will be a great enemy of Rome and will cross the Alps into Italy with war elephants. For fifteen years, he will terrify the Roman people in Italy. The elder Scipio will take the war away from Italian soil and move it to north Africa by taking an army to Carthage. He will decisively defeat Hannibal at the Battle of Zama in 202 B.C.E. This will be the end of the second of three Punic, or Carthaginian, wars that Rome will fight with Carthage.

"The younger Scipio will be Africanus the Younger, or Publius Cornelius Scipio Africanus Minor. He will defeat Carthage in the third and final Punic War. He will crush Carthage, and it will no longer challenge Roman power.

"Here is Caius Fabricius Luscinus, who will defeat the Greek general Pyrrhus, who will win a victory at heavy cost, leading him to say that one more victory like that and he would lose the war. This will lead to the term 'Pyrrhic victory.' Fabricius will be renowned for his incorruptibility — he will not accept bribes.

"Here is Marcus Atilius Regulus, also known as Serranus the Sower, who will be a hero of the First Punic War, or the first war between Rome and Carthage. He will have a farm, but he will leave it at the request of his country so that he can lead the Romans.

"Here are the Fabii, who will be an important Roman family. Quintus Fabius Maximus will be a hero of the Second Punic War, or the second war against Carthage. Hannibal will achieve a great early victory at Cannae against the Romans, after which he will collect bushels of gold rings taken from the fingers of dead upper-class Roman warriors. Hannibal's army will be greater than Fabius' army, so Fabius will harass Hannibal's army but will not fight it in open battle. Fabius will be known as *Cunctator*, which means 'The Delayer.'

"Listen, Aeneas, because this is important. Other peoples, no doubt, will be better than the Romans in many endeavors. Others will be better at creating sculptures, whether of bronze or of marble. Others will be better at public speaking. Others will be better at astronomy. But Romans must remember to rule well the peoples of the world, including their own people. Romans must remember to rule while encouraging peace. Romans must remember to spare the defeated, just as Romans must remember to defeat the proud. Good government and good laws will be the arts of the Romans."

Anchises then pointed out another famous Roman of the future: "Here is Marcus Claudius Marcellus, who will be a Roman general who will win the *spolia opima* in 222 B.C.E. by killing the general of the rebelling Insubrian Gauls. He will do this following the end of the First Punic War, in which he fought. Marcellus will be the third Roman to win the *spolia opima*."

Aeneas now saw a young, handsome Roman walking by the side of Marcellus the Roman general. His armor shone, but his face was sad.

Aeneas asked his father, "Who is this by the side of the Roman general Marcellus? Are they related? He is handsome, yet so sad."

With tears in his eyes, Anchises replied, "This young man will only briefly have a second body in the Land of the Living. His death will rob the Romans of a man who would have been a great hero. If he would live longer, the Romans would be too powerful, so the Fates will cut short his life.

"When he dies, the Romans will grieve mightily. The Romans' hopes for him will be high, but his death will dash those hopes.

"He will be an honorable man, and he will be undefeated in arms. If only his fate could be changed and he could live a normal span of years!

"He will be Marcus Claudius Marcellus, the son of Octavia, Caesar Augustus' sister. He will be born in 42 B.C.E. and he will die in 23 B.C.E. He will marry Julia, Caesar Augustus' daughter. If he would not die so young, he would be the second Roman emperor.

"Let me scatter lilies to honor Marcellus, although it is a vain tribute."

The Pageant of Heroes ended with Marcus Claudius Marcellus.

Aeneas, Anchises, and the Sibyl stayed longer in the Elysian Fields. Anchises showed them many parts of the Elysian Fields, and he made his son happy about the future glory of the Romans. Anchises also told his son about the battles that he would fight in Italy. He also told him about Italian people and about the city of Latinus, and he advised him about how to handle each ordeal that he would face.

The time came for Aeneas and the Sibyl to exit. Two gates lead out of the Elysian Fields. Both are gates of sleep. The gate of transparent horn is the gate through which true visions pass easily from the shadows. The gate of polished ivory is the gate of false dreams.

Anchises showed Aeneas and the Sibyl to the gate of polished ivory: the gate of false dreams.

The Sibyl wondered, *Why are we exiting the Elysian Fields through the gate of false dreams? Is it because the Pageants of Heroes that Anchises showed us is in some sense a false dream? Roman history will have much glory, but it will also have much human suffering and human misery. Roman history will have good parts and bad parts. And what about Anchises' exhortation to future Romans to rule with* pietas *and* clementia *and not with* furor? *To what extent will that happen? To what extent will Anchises' exhortation be ignored? Anchises has set an ideal for future Romans. That ideal can be a goal that future Romans will strive for, or it can be something that future Romans will ignore. That Aeneas and I left the Elysian Fields by way of the gate of false dreams may be a bad omen for future Romans.*

Chapter 7: A Fury and Warriors

Caieta, who had been Aeneas' nurse when he was young, now died in Italy. To honor her, he gave her name to a port and promontory on the western coast of Italy.

After Caieta had received a proper funeral and the Trojans had piled earth over her bones, Aeneas and the Trojans set sail again on a calm sea under a full moon. They passed by the home of Circe, a sorceress who turned men into beasts. As they passed by her land, they heard the growls of lions, boars, bears, and wolves — all of these animals used to be human men. Neptune wanted to spare the Trojans an encounter with Circe, so he gave them favorable winds and so they passed by her home without incident.

At dawn, the wind died and the Trojans began to row. Aeneas saw a river — soon the Trojans would know that it is the Tiber River — and he ordered his men to row into the river's mouth and land on the bank of the river.

Erato, Muse of love, help me to tell the tale of Aeneas in Italy, of how he sought an Italian wife and of how he fought a war to gain her. Erato, who were the kings in Italy when the Trojans landed on Italy's western shores? Inspire me as I tell how things were and how they changed. I must tell of a war and warriors and death. I must tell of many people fighting. This is a greater mission than the one I have already undertaken.

Latinus was an Italian king. He was old, and for many years he had ruled a people at peace. His father was the horned god Faunus, and another of his ancestors was the nymph Marica. Faunus' father was Picus. Latinus had no living son, but he did have a daughter named Lavinia. His only son had died young, so he needed to find someone who would rule after he died; that someone would be whoever married his daughter. Lavinia was single and of an age to be married, and she had many suitors. Of all her suitors, Turnus was the handsomest and the most eligible. His birth and breeding were impressive, and Amata, the wife of Latinus, wanted Turnus to marry her daughter. However, omens warned against such a marriage.

In a courtyard of Latinus' palace was a sacred laurel tree. When Latinus was a young ruler and building his city, he had found the laurel and dedicated it to Apollo. Latinus also named his followers Laurentes and his city

Laurentum after the laurel tree, but they were also known as Latins. One day, an omen occurred. A swarm of bees went to the laurel tree and covered it in a mass. So many bees clung to the laurel tree that its branches bent. A prophet interpreted the omen: "An army of strangers will come here. They will want to rule our city."

Another omen occurred as Lavinia lit an altar with torches. A non-burning fire lit her hair, and she seemed to wear a fiery crown. Prophets predicted fame for Lavinia and war for the Laurentes.

Troubled by the two omens, Latinus consulted the spirit of his father, Faunus, in a sacred grove where lived an oracle whom the Italians consulted in times of need. The priest would first sacrifice a hundred sheep and then sleep by the sacred spring and wood and communicate with swarms of spirits and gods and learn from the dead and the immortals.

Latinus sacrificed a hundred sheep and then slept by the sacred stream and wood. As Latinus slept, Faunus, whose voice came from the sacred grove of trees, told him, "Do not allow Lavinia to marry a Latin. Do not go through with the previously arranged marriage. Strangers will arrive, and they will become your relatives. Their and your descendants will have fame that reaches the sky, and the sun will never set on their empire."

Latinus did not keep the words of his father secret. Rumor spread the prophecy throughout western Italy even before Aeneas' ships reached the Tiber River.

Aeneas and his men prepared a meal on the banks of the Tiber River. They prepared flatbread, and using the flatbread as plates, they put food on top of the bread. Having eaten the food on top of the flatbread, and still hungry, they began to eat the flatbread.

Ascanius joked, "We are so hungry that we are even eating our plates."

Aeneas recognized the sign: A prophecy had been fulfilled.

Aeneas said to all the Trojans, "This is our home. This is the home promised to us by Fate. My father once told me, 'When you reach a strange shore and your hunger drives you to eat your plates, that is your new home. That is where you must build your houses.' This is the land my father meant! This is where our exile ends. Let us explore the land and see what people live here and where their towns are. But first let us pour wine to Jupiter and pray to my father."

Aeneas put a wreath on his head and prayed to many spirits and many gods: the spirit of the shore, the goddess Earth, nearby nymphs and rivers, Night, stars, Jupiter, Cybele, and his immortal parent and his mortal parent. Jupiter heard his prayer and answered it with thunder in a mostly clear sky with one cloud that Jupiter made blaze with light.

The Trojans now knew from the omen that this is the land where they were to build their city — they had arrived at their new home.

The next day, the Trojans explored the country, locating towns and rivers. Aeneas picked a hundred envoys to go to Latinus, king of the Laurentes, to ensure peace between the Trojans and the Laurentes. Aeneas' envoys carried an olive branch of peace, and they carried gifts for King Latinus.

As the envoys set off on their mission, Aeneas and the other Trojans began to build their first settlement in Italy. They built a defensive trench and walls; the settlement was an armed camp.

Aeneas' envoys reached Latinus' city. Boys and young men were busy training in the arts of war. They practiced riding horses, shooting arrows, throwing javelins, running, and boxing. A Latin herald told Latinus, "Powerful men — strangers — have arrived and are coming this way."

King Latinus invited the Trojans into his impressive palace and temple of the gods. The palace had one hundred columns; his ancestor Picus had ruled here. Kings ruled here, senators met here, feasts and sacrifices were held here, and here were many statues, carved from the wood of cedar trees, of gods and men: Italus, after whom Italy was named; Sabinus, a vintner and founder of the Sabine people; Saturn, god of agriculture; two-faced Janus, a god who looks at both the past and the future; and many kings and many warriors. Many trophies of past wars were here: armor, chariots, axes, helmets, javelins, and shields. Even the beaks of captured ships were here. A statue of Picus when he was human was here. The sorceress Circe had in his later life changed him into a colorful woodpecker when he refused her love.

King Latinus greeted the Trojans with friendly words: "We know your history. We know that you come from Troy. Tell me what you want. Why have you come to Italy? Are you lost? Have storms blown you away from your destination?

"We welcome you. We Latins are a fair and just people. We obey the laws, and we are fair and just.

"We remember the old stories of your ancestor Dardanus, who was born in Italy but who traveled to eastern lands, the land from which you came. Dardanus is now a god with a palace in heaven."

Ilioneus, the head of the Trojan envoys, replied, "Son of Faunus and king of the Laurentes, we have not been blown off course by storms or faulty navigation. We have come here on purpose. Once we were driven from Troy, we sought the home of our great ancestor Dardanus, whose father is Jupiter. Aeneas sent us here to meet you. Everyone knows the story of Troy and the destruction that came to it from the city of Mycenae, home of Agamemnon.

"Now we seek a safe home here. We want water and air. We will not disrespect you or your kingdom. We will always be grateful to you for any kindness you show us. You should have no regrets for making us your friends. We come to you bearing the olive branch of peace, but that does not mean that we are not warriors. Many people have wanted us to ally ourselves with them. But this is the place where the gods and our fate have wanted us to come. Dardanus was born here, and the gods have told us to seek the birthplace of our ancestor. Apollo wanted us to seek the Tiber River.

"Aeneas offers you these gifts in friendship: These are items taken from burning Troy. Aeneas gives you this gold goblet that his father used to pour wine to the gods. Here are more gifts for you: the scepter that Priam held and the coronet and robes that he wore when making laws for the people of Troy."

King Latinus looked down at the ground and concentrated, thinking about the recent omens. He was impressed by the gifts of the Trojans and by their wish for peace, but he was much more concerned about whom his daughter should marry.

Latinus thought, *Aeneas is the man whom the omens say should marry my daughter. He comes from a foreign land, and he shall be my son-in-law. He and my daughter shall have famous descendants with much power.*

Latinus' thoughts made him joyful, and he said to the Trojan envoys, "I make you my friends and the friends of my family. The omens are in favor of our friendship. I accept your gifts, and you shall have land on which to build a city and to farm.

"Please tell Aeneas to come here in person and make an alliance with us. Let he and I shake hands in peace. Tell Aeneas that I have a daughter whom omens have told me to marry to a man from a foreign land. The descendants of that foreign man and my daughter will be famous and powerful. Aeneas is the man whom the Fates want to marry my daughter. I want him to become my son-in-law."

Latinus then gave the Trojans horses, blankets, and golden bridles and bits. For Aeneas he picked out two stallions and a chariot. The stallions came from immortal stock — Circe had stolen an immortal stallion from her father the Sun-god to breed with her mares.

The Trojans returned to Aeneas with the gifts and with news of peace.

But Juno saw Aeneas happy with news of peace. She saw the Trojan ships safely at anchor, and she saw the Trojans building homes. Unhappy, Juno said, "I hate the Trojans. Why couldn't all of them have died at Troy? Why couldn't they stay defeated after the fall of Troy? Despite their troubles, they are building a future glory! Am I now a goddess with no power? When the Trojans were at sea, I tried to harm them — to little effect. The dangerous coastal reefs called the Syrtes did not stop the Trojans, nor did Scylla and Charybdis. The Trojans are now building a camp on the bank of the Tiber River. They are now safe from the sea — and apparently they are safe from me!

"Why should that be? Mars was angry at the Lapiths, and he destroyed the Lapiths. When Pirithous, the king of the Lapiths, married Hippodamia, he did not invite Mars to the wedding, but he did invite the Centaurs. Mars tempted the Centaur Eurytus to attempt to rape Hippodamia, and a battle broke out between the Lapiths and the Centaurs.

"And when Oeneus, the king of Calydon, insulted Diana, Jupiter allowed Diana to send a boar to ravage the countryside of Calydon. Eventually, the hero Meleager, who was the son of Oeneus, killed the boar, but first the boar caused much damage.

"I, Juno, hate the Trojans more than Mars hated the Lapiths and more than Diana hated the king of Calydon. Yet, even though I am a powerful goddess, Aeneas and his destiny defeat me! But even if I am not powerful enough to defeat the Trojans by myself, I will enlist the help of others, even if I have to go to Hell to find that help.

"Is Aeneas fated to marry Lavinia? Then let him marry Lavinia. I cannot go against fate. But I can make fulfilling his fate difficult for Aeneas. I can delay the marriage. I can kill many Trojans and many Laurentes. I have no intention of making things easy for Aeneas. Both he and King Latinus will pay for their alliance. Lavinia, the dowry I will give you will be Trojan blood and Italian blood. I will choose your maid of honor: Bellona, the goddess of war.

"When Hecuba was pregnant with Paris, she dreamed that she was pregnant with a flaming torch. This was an omen of future war. Aeneas, Venus' son, will be another flaming torch, another Paris. In his search for a foreign bride, he will find war!"

Juno then brought Allecto, one of the three Furies, out of Hell. The Furies are winged avenging goddesses with snakes in their hair. They bring misery to the human beings whom they target. War, anger, premeditated evil, and bloody crimes bring joy to Allecto. She causes so much misery that even her father, Pluto, god of the Land of the Dead, hates her. She brings so much sorrow that even her sisters, the other two Furies, hate her. She can assume many shapes in order to cause her many sorrows.

Juno requested, "Allecto, do something hateful for me. Let Aeneas and his Trojans know what kind of goddess I am. Let Aeneas and his Trojans know how powerful a goddess I am. You are capable of making loving brothers fight each other in war. You are capable of destroying a loving family by making the members hate each other. You are capable of destroying a loving family by filling its house with funerals. You have a thousand ways of bringing sorrow to human beings.

"Now bring war to western Italy! Make the young men desire weapons and blood!"

Allecto flew to Latium and the palace of King Latinus. She sought the queen, Amata, who was already angry. Amata had wanted Turnus to marry her daughter, Lavinia, but the omens of the gods and the arrival of Aeneas had changed all that. Now her husband, the king, wanted Lavinia to marry Aeneas and not marry Turnus.

Allecto took a snake from her hair and flung it at Queen Amata. The snake glided between Amata's clothing and her breasts, but Amata felt nothing except a desire to resist her husband's plans and to keep her daughter from marrying Aeneas. The snake changed its form and became a golden necklace hanging around Queen Amata's neck.

The snake inflamed Queen Amata's smoldering resentment. Before the snake did its evil work, Amata was unhappy, but she could still speak and make arguments to her husband, King Latinus: "So you want our daughter to marry a Trojan. Do you really think that is best for her, for you, for me? Aeneas is a pirate. When the wind blows in the right direction, he will sail away like the pirate he is. The treasure he steals will be our daughter!

"Aeneas is another Paris. Paris visited Sparta, the home of Menelaus and Helen, and he ran away with Helen, Menelaus' lawfully wedded wife. Aeneas will run away with Lavinia, who is engaged to Turnus.

"You have allies in western Italy. One of them is Turnus, with whom you have pledged peace many times. The omens say that Lavinia must marry someone who is a foreigner. Anyone not ruled by you in this land is a foreigner. The person whom the omens want Lavinia to marry is Turnus. His ancestors include Inachus and Acrisius, both of whom were kings of Argos, the land where is the city of Mycenae."

So Amata spoke, but her words did not change her husband's mind. The snake bit Amata, and its venom went through her body and brain. She raved. She was frenzied. Her heart was filled with *furor*. She was like a top spun as quickly as possible by boys at play. Amata raved through the city, and then she went to the woods. She pretended to have been driven insane by the god Bacchus, whose female followers, the Maenads, lived without men in the woods and mountains. She hid her daughter, Lavinia, in the woods with her, so that Aeneas could not marry her.

Putting on a performance, Queen Amata yelled, "You alone, Bacchus, deserve to have my daughter! She will become a Maenad. She will dance in your honor."

Rumors of Amata's actions travelled quickly, and mothers joined her in the woods. They deserted their homes, they wore clothing that left their necks uncovered, and they unbound their hair. Many of the women cried aloud to the god Bacchus. Many of the women wore the skins of fawns, and they carried the thyrsus: a stick around which vines were wrapped.

Amata, in the midst of the Maenads, sang a wedding hymn for Turnus and Lavinia, and she said to the Maenads, "If you care for me and my rights as a mother, then carry out the religious rites due to Bacchus."

Allecto whipped Amata and the Maenads into a frenzy.

Having succeeded in her first goal, Allecto flew to Turnus, commander-in-chief of the Italian people known as the Rutulians. Their chief city was called Ardea, and according to tradition, a woman had founded it. Danaë, made pregnant by Jupiter, gave birth to the Greek hero Perseus. An oracle had told Danaë's father, King Acrisius of Argos, that her son would kill him. Therefore, he put Danaë and Perseus, her son, into a chest and threw it into the sea. Neptune provided a calm sea, and the chest washed up on the western coast of Italy, where Danaë founded the city of Ardea. Perseus grew up, learned about the prophecy that he would kill his father, and resolved never to go to Argos. Unfortunately, he competed in athletic games elsewhere, his aged father watched the games, and Perseus accidentally killed him with a discus.

Turnus was asleep when Allecto came to him. She transformed herself and took on the shape of an old woman named Calybe, a priestess of Juno. In a dream, she said to Turnus, "How can you do nothing? You are sitting back and watching as your hopes disappear! You should become the king of Latinus' country, but now the kingship is being handed to a Trojan! You were promised Lavinia as your bride, but King Latinus is giving her to another man. And yet you have kept his people from danger — you have fought battles for them.

"Juno has told me that you must go to war. Stop sleeping! Get up! Fight the Trojans and burn their ships! The gods order you to do that. If King Latinus will not remember his promise and give you Lavinia, then you must marry her by force!"

In his dream, Turnus laughed at the Fury, whom he thought to be merely an old woman. He told her, "I already know that a fleet of ships has sailed into the mouth of the Tiber River. Don't try to make me panic. I have faith in Juno; she wants me to marry Lavinia. Old woman, you must be in your dotage — you are overreacting and you are getting yourself worked up about nothing. Don't try to raise the alarm. Don't try to be a prophet. Don't try to make troops go to war. Do your womanly chores, worship the gods, and leave war and battles to the men."

Allecto became angry. She reverted to her own form. Her snakes hissed at Turnus. He was terrified. She pushed him back and said, "So you think that I'm in my dotage? You think that I do not know what is reality? You think that I cannot prophesy? You think that I am raising false alarms? Look at me now! I am a Fury, and I have come to you from Hell!"

She threw a burning torch at Turnus, and it buried itself in his chest and made him eager for war. Sweat pouring from his body, he woke up and shouted for his weapons and armor. Now he wanted war and blood. He was like burning brush under a cauldron filled with water. The water boils and overflows from the cauldron, and steam shoots into the air. Turnus was overheated just like that. Turnus' heart was filled with *furor*.

Despite the pact of peace between the Rutulians and the Laurentes, Turnus ordered, "Get ready for war! We will march against King Latinus and his Laurentes! We will drive the Trojans away from Italy!" He prayed to the gods for help in battle.

The Rutulians were eager for war. They were eager to follow Turnus because of his strength and his youth, because of his royal heritage, and because of his prowess as a warrior.

Allecto's work completed here, she flew to the Trojan camp. She must find a way to start the war. Ascanius was hunting with other Trojans and with his dogs, and Allecto made sure that the dogs picked up the scent of a tame stag. The war would start over a trivial cause — the death of a pet stag would result in the death of many, many people.

The dogs chased the stag, which had been taken from its mother when it was a fawn. Tyrrhus, the keeper of King Latinus' herds, and his sons had raised the stag. Tyrrhus' family and especially his daughter, Silvia, made it a member of the family. Silvia loved the stag and tamed it and put garlands in its horns. She bathed it and combed it. It roamed the woods during the day, and it returned to its human home at night.

Ascanius' dogs scented this stag and chased it. Ascanius sighted it and drew an arrow. Allecto steadied his hands, and the arrow hit the stag, driving deep into its body. The stag ran back to its human home and filled it with cries of pain.

Mourning, Silvia called for help, and help arrived from the surrounding area. Country folk came with charred torches, heavy clubs, and other weapons that can be found on a farm. Tyrrhus himself carried an axe; he had been splitting wood.

Eager to cause more misery, Allecto flew to the roof of the stable and blew on a horn — this was the signal for country folk to assemble for emergencies. The horn sounded throughout the woods and valleys, traveling far away. Mothers heard the emergency signal and held their babies close.

Herdsmen heard the signal, grabbed whatever would serve as a weapon, and came running to Tyrrhus. Young Trojans also came running; they were eager to defend Ascanius.

The lines of battle formed. The Trojans had real weapons: swords that gleamed in the sunlight. The battle grew just like waves grow; small waves sometimes grow into huge waves.

People fought and died. The oldest son of Tyrrhus, Almo, took an arrow in his throat that cut off his breath. Amid the heaps of dead was Galaesus, an old man who went into the middle of the battle to plead with both sides to stop fighting. Galaesus was a just man; he was a good man. He was also rich; he owned five flocks of sheep and five herds of cattle, and a hundred plows tilled his cropland.

The two sides fought, and neither side achieved victory. Allecto was happy; she had performed well the task that Juno had given to her.

Allecto flew away and found Juno. Allecto said, "I have done what you asked me to do. I have started a war. Now let the Trojans and the Latins try to achieve peace! The Trojans now wear the blood of the Latins!

"With your permission, I shall do worse things than I have already done. I can start rumors, and I can draw other Italian peoples into the war. I can make everyone willing to go to war. Instead of the seeds they plant in their fields, I will plant swords!"

Juno replied, "You have done enough already. The war has started. The Trojans are fighting the Latins, and weapons are red with blood. An alliance will not now happen between Aeneas and King Latinus. I am afraid that Jupiter, my husband, will not allow you to cause any more trouble than you have already caused. I myself will handle the rest of the war."

Allecto obeyed Juno. The Fury flew away, and she and her snakes went back to Hell, which has many entrances. One such entrance is a cave in a wood on a hillside in the valley of the sulfurous lake named Amsanctus. Allecto went there to re-enter Hell and relieve the Land of the Living of her presence.

Juno had more work to do. Now that the battle had ended, the Latins carried their dead, including the young Almo and the elderly Galaesus, home. The Latins prayed to the gods, and they complained to King Latinus. Turnus was present, and he asked the angry Latins, "Do we want the Trojans to conquer the Latins? Do we want Trojan blood to mingle with and corrupt our blood? Do you want Aeneas, and not me, to marry Lavinia?"

Amata and the mothers who had been worshipping Bacchus arrived, and they also called for war. Now everyone — the Latin men, the Latin mothers, Turnus and the Rutulians — were calling for war against the Trojans. The only advocate for peace was King Latinus. All others opposed the omens, and they opposed fate. They surrounded King Latinus and begged for war, but he resisted them the way that a rock at sea resists a huge wave.

But the mass of people wanted war — the war that Juno is causing. King Latinus told them, "We are doing the wrong thing by wanting war. Our emotions and not our reason are in control. We ought to oppose war. We will bleed, and many of us will die. Turnus, you are wrong when you call for war. I prophesy that you will die in the war — by the time you pray to the gods for mercy, it will be too late. I myself will not call for war, but I see that I am powerless to keep all of you from going to war. I am an old man, I will not live much longer, and now that war has come, I will not be able to die the good death I could have had if my country were at peace."

King Latinus said no more. He stayed in his palace, and he no longer attempted to keep his people from going to war.

Latium had a custom that was later adopted by Alba Longa and then by Rome. Whenever men went to war anywhere, they would open the doors of the temple of Janus. They called these doors the Twin Gates of War. In times of peace, the gates were kept closed; in times of war, they were kept open. Now the Latins opened the twin doors. In Roman times, a consul would wear the clothing of Romulus and open the doors. When the doors are opened, the trumpets sound and the soldiers go off to war.

The Latins wanted King Latinus to open the gates of the temple of Janus, but he refused to touch them. He stayed in his palace. Therefore, Juno herself flew down from the sky and hit the gates with her hand. The Gates of War swung open. Some Latins prepared to go to war on foot, others planned to ride horses, and all shouted, "To war!" They polished their shields and the heads of their spears, and they sharpened their axes.

Five cities readied themselves for war: Atina, Tibur, Ardea, Crustumerium, and Antemnae. The blacksmiths forged new weapons and armor. Previously, the cities had taken pride in the arts of peace: They grew life-giving food. Now, they took pride in the arts of war: They got ready to kill. Instead of plows, they preferred swords.

Muses, you remember the warriors and you can help me to sing a song that tells what you know. Which Italian kings went to war? Who were the Italian warriors? Who opposed Aeneas and the Trojans? Who marched to war against the Trojans?

At the front of the line, Mezentius marched to war against the Trojans. A former king of the Etruscans, he was renowned for his cruelty. He did not worship the gods. Lausus, his son, rode with him. Turnus was the only Italian warrior who was more handsome and had a better build than Lausus. A person with many good qualities, Lausus deserved to have a better father than Mezentius. Lausus led a thousand warriors to war, but they would not be able to save his life. Lausus would die in battle.

Next came Aventinus, a son of Hercules. His shield depicted the Hydra with its hundred heads — each time one head was cut off, the Hydra grew two more in its place. Hercules had succeeded in killing the Hydra of Lerna by having a nephew cauterize each neck after Hercules had cut its head off — this was the second of his twelve famous labors. Hercules had come to Italy, where he slept with the princess Rhea, who gave birth to Aventinus. Hercules had previously killed the monster Geryon of the three bodies, and he had watered in the Tiber River the cattle he had taken from Geryon. Aventinus' warriors carried spears and pikes and swords to battle. Aventinus himself wore the hide of a huge lion — its shaggy head hooded Aventinus' head.

Twin brothers — Catillus and Coras — marched next in the line to war. Their brother was Tiburtus, after whom the city of Tibur was named. The twins were fearless — they charged into battle as quickly as two Centaurs would run down a mountain, crashing through the thickets.

Next came Caeculus, whose father was the god Vulcan. Caeculus was born among sheep in a field but was found lying in front of a fire. He founded the city of Praeneste, and he brought many of its citizens and many of the people who lived near the city to fight for Turnus. Some had chariots, armor, and shields. Many of them carried slingshots to use as weapons. They wore caps made of wolfskin. Their left feet were bare; their right feet were covered with boots made of rawhide.

Messapus, the son of Neptune, also allied himself with Turnus and marched to war. He and his people had long been at peace, but now he and they held swords again. They sang as they marched. Their songs were like the songs of swans. If you were to hear the men singing, you would think not of warriors, but of birds.

Next in the line marched Clausus, who led mighty warriors and who himself was a mighty warrior. He was a Sabine, and he led men of Sabine blood. From them would arise the Claudian tribe after the Romans and the Sabines had united. He led many warriors. They seemed to be as numerous as waves rolling to shore from the sea in winter or as numerous as ears of corn in a field. As they marched, their shields clanged and the earth shook under their pounding feet.

Next in the line was a man who hated Troy and all Trojans: Halaesus, who was once the companion of Agamemnon. His warriors used long stakes that they hurled with a thong, they used shields to protect their left side, and they used scimitars to cut the enemy.

Oebalus marched next in the line. According to tradition, his parents were the mortal Telon and the river-nymph Sebethis. Oebalus expanded the territory that his father had ruled. His warriors threw barbed lances, and they used the bark they stripped from corkwood trees to make their helmets. They carried bronze shields and swords.

Ufens marched next in the line. His warriors were accustomed to hunting. They farmed, but they wore armor even as they plowed. They enjoyed going on raids and seizing booty.

Next in the line marched a warrior-priest named Umbro, whom King Archippus sent. Umbro knew the ways of snakes, and he could cure their venomous bites with herbs. But when he was speared in battle, he could not cure his mortal wound.

Virbius, the son of Hippolytus, rode next in the line. His mother, Aricia, sent him to battle. Hippolytus' stepmother, Phaedra, fell in love with him, he resisted her advances, and she told his father, Theseus, that Hippolytus had raped her. Hippolytus died while riding in a chariot; sea-monsters spooked his horses, which upset his chariot and killed him. The healer Aesculapius and the goddess Diana brought Hippolytus to life again. Jupiter was angry that a dead man had been restored to life, and so he killed Aesculapius and sent him to the Land of the Dead. Diana, however, took Hippolytus away to the water-nymph Egeria, who lived in a healing wood that is sacred to Diana. Hippolytus took a new name: Virbius, which means "twice a man." He also named his son Virbius. Because of the way that Hippolytus had died, no horses were allowed in the grove. His son, Virbius the younger, however, rode a chariot drawn by horses into battle.

Next in the line was Turnus, the commander-in-chief. He was taller than any other warrior by a head. His build was impressive, and he was well armed. His helmet was decorated with the figure of a fire-breathing Chimaera — the fires of the volcano Etna seemed to blast from its throat. As a battle grew fiercer and more blood spilled, the fire of the Chimaera on Turnus' shield grew redder. His shield also depicted Io in the form of a cow. Jupiter had fallen in love with the beautiful girl named Io, and so Juno, a jealous wife, had turned Io into a cow and sent Argus, who has a hundred eyes, to keep her away from Jupiter. His shield also depicted Io's father, Inachus, a river-god, who was pouring water from an urn. Turnus brought many, many warriors with him.

Coming at the end of the line was Camilla, a woman who knew the ways of war. She led men into battle. Camilla's education did not include weaving; instead, it consisted of the arts of war. She ran quickly and lightly. It seemed that she could run on the tops of wheat stalks with hurting the kernels or on the tops of waves without getting her feet wet. Young males and mothers travelled just to see her: a woman who was going to war. They stared at her purple clothing, the gold brooch that bound her hair, and her arrows and spear.

Chapter 8: Allies and a Shield

Now that Turnus was armed and leading armies to battle, all of western Italy wanted to go to war. His allies Messapus, Ufens, and Mezentius took men from farms and enrolled them among the soldiers.

Turnus and his commanders also sent the Latin Venulus as leader of some envoys to Diomedes, a great Greek hero of the Trojan War who had founded the city of Argyripa in southern Italy. The envoys carried a message asking Diomedes to fight with them against Aeneas and the Trojans: "Aeneas has arrived in western Italy with his ships and with the household gods that he carried away from conquered Troy. He claims that his destiny led him to western Italy to become a king here. Many Italian tribes support him — there is much talk about him in western Italy. Come help us to fight against him."

The envoys also hoped to get information from Diomedes about what Aeneas would want and what would happen if fortune favored the Trojans in war. Chances are, they thought, Diomedes would know that better than King Latinus or King Turnus.

Aeneas was aware of the armies being raised and marching against him. He thought over his options. His thoughts moved from option to option as quickly as sunlight or moonlight reflected from a bowl of water rises to a ceiling.

Late at night, Aeneas, worried about war, lay down on the bank of the Tiber River and slept. The river-god, wearing a crown made of reeds, came to him in a dream and said, "We here in western Italy have long waited for you to come. This is now your home; this is now the home of your household gods. Do not be afraid that you will be conquered in war — you and your Trojans will be triumphant. Most of the gods who have been angry at you have ceased their anger.

"I will tell you something so you will know that what I say is true. Soon, you will find on the bank of my river a white sow nursing thirty white piglets. This is a sign. In thirty years, Ascanius, your son, will found the city of Alba Longa. All of this is fated to happen.

"Now let me give you advice about the upcoming war — the war that you will win. Listen — this is important. On the shores of my river is a city that was founded by the Greeks. Its king, Evander, was born in Arcadia in the Peloponnese of Greece. His grandfather was Pallas, a king of Arcadia. King Evander named his city in Italy Pallanteum after him. He also named his son Pallas. These Greeks are at war against your enemy, and they will be your allies. Go to them and make a pact. I will help you to reach Pallanteum. Your men will have to row upstream, but I will make my current gentle so that you can go faster.

"Get up now, Aeneas. Pray to Juno and seek to end her anger at you. Ask her for help. When you are successful in forming a pact with King Evander, you can sacrifice to me: I am the river-god of the Tiber River. The gods love my river and its clear blue water. Noble cities lie along my banks."

The river-god disappeared, and Aeneas woke up. He cupped his hands and held up water from the Tiber River, and he prayed, "Water-nymphs and the river-god of the Tiber, help me and shield me from danger. Help the Trojans. I will sacrifice to you often. Please help the Trojans."

Aeneas then took two ships and filled them with men wearing armor. As he was outfitting the ships, he saw a white sow and thirty white piglets lying on the riverbank. Aeneas sacrificed all thirty-one of the pigs to Juno at her altar.

The two ships made good speed. The men rowed, but the river-god kept the river's current gentle, as he had promised. They rowed all that night, and the next day at noon they saw a city. Aeneas did not know it, but this city was built on the future site of Rome. Rome would be a mighty city, but this city was humble. As the river-god had told Aeneas, the city's name was Pallanteum, and its king was Evander, whose son was Pallas. Evander had come to Italy from Arcadia, which is in Greece. Evander's grandfather had been named Pallas; he was a noted king of Arcadia.

The day that the Trojans arrived at Pallanteum was a day devoted to honoring Hercules, a hero of the past who had slain the half-human, half-beast, fire-breathing monster named Cacus that had terrorized the citizens of Pallanteum.

Evander, Pallas, and the city's other citizens were honoring Hercules with incense and with sacrifices. The city's citizens were feasting. When Aeneas' ships arrived, the city's citizens were startled and would have fled, but Pallas forbid them. Fearless, he grabbed a spear and went to the ships and shouted at Aeneas and his armed men, "Who are you? What do you want? Do you bring war or peace?"

Aeneas held up a branch of an olive tree: a sign of peace. He lifted it high so that Pallas could see it. Aeneas then replied, "We are Trojans. The weapons that we carry we intend to use not against you, but against the Latins, our common enemy. We wanted peace, but they want war. We are looking for King Evander. Please tell him that Trojans have arrived and want to form a pact with him and his city."

Pallas had heard of the Trojans; he was impressed. He said to Aeneas, "Disembark and talk to my father. You are welcome here." He took Aeneas' right hand and led him to his father.

Aeneas said to King Evander, "I have come to you in peace. You are the best of the Greeks, and although I am a Trojan, and the Greeks and the Trojans fought a war, I can approach you without fear although you are related to Agamemnon and Menelaus, the two leaders of the Greek forces against Troy.

"We have ties, and we have good reasons to form a pact. The Trojans and I are strong, and we will make a good ally for you. The river-god Tiber sent me here. We have a common ancestry. Also, your fame is worldwide — we would be proud to form a pact with you.

"Let me explain our common ancestry. Atlas had many daughters, including Electra and Maia. Electra gave birth to Dardanus, ancestor of the Trojans. Maia gave birth to Mercury, the god who is your father. Therefore, you and I have the blood of Atlas flowing in our veins; the same is true of many of our people.

"Knowing our common ancestry, I came to you in person instead of sending envoys to you. I am a suppliant to you. The Trojans and I need help. Your enemy is also our enemy. Turnus, your enemy, is leading his Rutulians against us. If Turnus succeeds in driving us from Italy, he is likely to keep making war until he rules all of western Italy. Form a pact with us. We are brave soldiers, and we will fight well as your allies."

While Aeneas spoke, King Evander looked him over carefully. When Aeneas stopped speaking, Evander replied, "You are welcome here. I recognize in your features the features of your father, Anchises. I remember well Anchises' face, words, and voice.

"Priam, the son of Laomedon, the king of Troy, once visited the island of Salamis, where Hesione, his sister, was queen, in Greece. He also visited Arcadia, where I was born. I was young then, and I rejoiced to see the leading men of Troy, including one who was taller than the rest: Anchises, your father.

"A young boy, I went to Anchises and showed him around the city. When Anchises left with the other Trojans, he gave me gifts: a quiver and arrows, a cloak, and golden bridles. Now that I am old, I have given these gifts to Pallas, my son, who loves them.

"You and I, your people and my people, are allies. Tomorrow, you can leave along with soldiers that I will send with you. Today, you and your men can participate in the festival honoring Hercules."

Evander ordered cups and food to be brought, and most of the Trojans sat on the grass. Aeneas, the guest of honor, sat on a wooden chair with a lion's hide serving as a cushion. The priests and young men brought meat and bread and wine. Aeneas and the Trojans feasted.

After the meal, Evander said, "This annual festival has been held for many years and for good reasons. Hercules saved us from a monster. Look at this hill. It has a long-abandoned lair: a cave that has been filled in with rocks. A half-human, half-beast monster lived there. Its name was Cacus. In front of its lair was much human blood, and nailed to his doors were the rotting, bloodless, pale faces of human men. The father of Cacus was Vulcan, and Cacus breathed fire.

"We prayed to the gods for deliverance from the monster, and the answer to our prayers came in the form of Hercules, who had recently slaughtered another monster: the triple-bodied Geryon. Now Hercules was driving the herd of cattle that had belonged to Geryon to pasture near here. Cacus, greedy as always, stole four bulls and four heifers from the herd. Wanting to keep his crime secret from Hercules, he grabbed the cattle by their tails and pulled them to his lair so that the prints of their hoofs led away from his lair. Cacus dragged them inside his cave and waited for Hercules to leave.

"As Hercules prepared to drive his cattle away, they mooed, and one of the heifers in Cacus' cave mooed back. Realizing that some of his cattle had been rustled, Hercules came running to the cave. Terrified, Cacus let down a boulder — using an apparatus created by Vulcan, his father — to seal the cave.

"Furious, Hercules circled the hill three times, looking for a way inside the cave. He could not find a way in. Finally, he went to the top of the hill and used his great strength to push over a crag and send it tumbling down the side of the hill. This exposed the cave within the hill. It was as if an earthquake had torn open the earth and exposed the Land of the Dead and the ghosts of the dead.

"The light flooded into the cave and exposed Cacus, who howled with fear and terror. Hercules threw down on him whatever he could find: enormous tree branches and enormous rocks the size of millstones. Cacus had no way out of his home, which was now a deathtrap.

"Cacus used the fire inside his body to spit great bursts of fire up at Hercules. All this did was to make Hercules angry, and he jumped into the cave and strangled Cacus. Hercules gripped Cacus' neck so hard that his eyes bulged and no blood was left in his neck.

"Hercules then burst out of the cave. He dragged out Cacus' carcass and left with the cattle that he had recovered. All the people of this area stared at the corpse of Cacus and rejoiced at the death of the monster that had terrorized us.

"Since that time, we have celebrated his death with this annual festival. The priest Potitius founded the festival, and ever since we have observed these rites. Potitius built this altar in this grove. We call the altar the *Ara Maxima*, or the Greatest Altar, and we dedicate it to Hercules *Invictus* — the Unconquered Hercules.

"So let us wear garlands and pour out wine as an offering to the gods."

Evander put on his head a wreath that Hercules had once worn, and all poured out wine and prayed to the gods.

Evening was coming, and the priests — Potitius was in the front — continued the rites. They brought more food for another round of feasting. The Salii — priests of Mars — danced in honor of Mars, and a chorus of young boys and a chorus of old men sang in honor of Hercules. They sang of how he had exhibited his strength as a baby. Juno had hated Hercules, and now she hated Aeneas. Juno had hated Hercules because her husband, Jupiter, was his father, but she was not his mother. Juno sent two huge snakes to kill the infant Hercules, but he strangled the snakes. The two choruses also sang of two notable victories of the adult Hercules: how he had conquered the city of Troy and how he had conquered the city of Oechalia on the island of Euboea in Greece. They also sang of the Twelve Labors that Hercules had performed for Eurystheus.

The two choruses sang, "Hercules, you are unconquered. Your victories are many. You have defeated Hylaeus and Pholus, two half-man, half-horse Centaurs. Ixion, the king of the Lapiths, tried to rape Juno. Jupiter made a cloud in the shape of Juno. Ixion coupled with it, and from this union came the Centaurs, most of whom were wild.

"Hercules, you also conquered many beasts in your famous Twelve Labors. You defeated the Cretan bull by roping it and taking it to Eurystheus. You defeated the Nemean lion that was impervious to weapons by choking it to death. You defeated Cerberus, the three-headed watchdog of the Land of the Dead by fearlessly going down into Hell and dragging Cerberus to the Land of the Living. Cerberus trembled in fear of you as he stood over half-eaten bones. You were not afraid of even the giant Typhoeus, who was armed with many weapons. You also killed the Lernean Hydra that had seven heads. Hercules, you are the son of Jupiter, and you are now a god. Come to your festival and bless it and us!"

Then the two choruses sang about how Hercules had killed Cacus.

Now that the festival was over, all turned away from the altar and went back to the city. King Evander, who was old, told many stories as he walked with his friends, his son, and Aeneas, who eagerly listened to the stories of heroes of long ago.

King Evander showed Aeneas around the city and its environs as he told stories of the past.

Evander told Aeneas about the early history of the area: "Here lived immortal fauns and nymphs. Mortal humans also lived here, but they were wild. They ate berries and nuts and the fare of hunters. They were not civilized, and they did not farm. They were hunters and gatherers.

Saturn had been the king of gods, but Jupiter, his son, overthrew him. Saturn then came here and made the wild people civilized. He gave the wild people laws, and he named the country Latium. Saturn's age was the Age of

Gold, but it was slowly succeeded by a worse age, an age of war, an age of desire for possessions.

"In this age were present the Ausonian peoples and the Sicanian tribes. In this age were kings and a giant named Thybris, after whom the Tiber River was named, replacing its mostly forgotten old name of Albula.

"Driven by exile, I came here from Arcadia. Fate and Fortune brought me here. So did the prophecies of my mother, the nymph Carmentis, and so did the power of Apollo."

Pallanteum was built on the future site of Rome, and so as Evander showed Aeneas Pallanteum, he was — without knowing it — showing him some of the sites of future Rome. For example, Cacus' cave was in the Aventine Hill of Rome.

Evander also pointed out the Altar of Carmentis and the Carmental Gate, both of which honored his mother: the nymph Carmentis, who was a true seer and who was the first to foretell the greatness of future Rome. The Carmental Gate would later be an entrance to Rome at the western base of what would later be known as the Capitoline Hill.

Evander then showed Aeneas a grove between the two summits of what would later be known as the Capitoline Hill. This grove was later the site of the Asylum, a temple that Romulus would establish where refugees from other cities could find asylum.

Evander then showed Aeneas a cave at the foot of what would be known as the Palatine Hill. The cave would later be called the Lupercal because a female wolf suckled Romulus and Remus in this cave until Faustulus, a shepherd, found them.

Evander then showed Aeneas the grove of Argiletum, the site of which would later be a main road leading between the Roman Forum and the Esquiline and Viminal hills.

Evander told Aeneas a story about Argus, who had been a guest of Evander's, but Argus had plotted against Evander and so Argus had been killed.

Evander then showed Aeneas the Tarpeian Rock on what would later be known as the Capitoline Hill and, all unknowingly, showed him the site of the future Roman Capitol.

Although neither Evander nor Aeneas could know it, one of the most sacred sites in Rome would be the temple of Jupiter Optimus Maximus: Jupiter the Best and Greatest. It would stand at the top of the Capitoline Hill. Because Pallanteum had been built on the future site of Rome, Evander and Aeneas were now looking at the site where the temple would later be built. In Roman times, it would be an urban site. Now, it was a wooded area, but Evander and his people knew that it was sacred.

Evander said to Aeneas, "This wooded area is sacred to a god, but we don't know which god. Some of my town's citizens, however, believe that they have seen Jupiter here."

Evander also showed Aeneas two other important sites. One site was called Janiculum, and on this site — a hilly ridge along the Tiber River — the god Janus had built a fortress in the days of old. The other site — on the Capitoline Hill — was called Saturnia, and the god Saturn had built a settlement there in the days of old.

They drew close to Evander's home, passing a herd of cattle grazing in what would later be known as the Roman Forum. Cattle also grazed in what would later be known as the Carinae — an elegant area of future Rome.

King Evander's home was humble. He said to Aeneas, "Hercules once passed through these doors. He had to stoop as he entered this home. This is a humble home, but it was good enough for Hercules, and I hope that it will be good enough for you. Hercules humbled himself here, and after he died as a mortal, he became a god. Be like Hercules — scorn luxury. Come into my home, and please be kind."

Aeneas entered King Evander's home. That night, Aeneas slept there on a pile of leaves, and he used the hide of a Libyan bear as a blanket.

As Aeneas slept, his mother, Venus, went to her husband, Vulcan. The war-cries of the Latins alarmed her, and she wanted to protect her son. In the bedroom that she and her husband shared, Venus said to Vulcan, "When the Greeks were warring against doomed Troy, which was fated to fall, I did not ask you to create armor and weapons for the Trojans although I loved Priam and the Trojans and although I wept because of the dangers that Aeneas faced in the war. Now Aeneas is facing a new danger. He is in western Italy, and he will be fighting a new enemy. This time, I beg you to create armor for my son. You have done this for other mothers. Aurora wept and asked you to make armor for Memnon, her son. You made the armor. Thetis wept and asked you to make armor for Achilles, her son. You made the armor. Please make armor for my son Aeneas. In western Italy, armies are massing — they are filled with warriors who want to kill my son."

Venus, the goddess of sexual passion, threw her arms around her husband, and he reacted exactly the way she knew he would. He was filled with the ancient flame that he knew very well. The ancient flame went through him the way that lightning goes through a cloud. Venus rejoiced in her power.

Vulcan said to Venus, his wife, "You can count on me. If you had asked me to arm the Trojans, I would have done so. Troy was fated to fall, and it would still have fallen, but Priam would have been able to live inside the as-yet-unconquered city for ten additional years. But now, since you ask me, I will create divine armor for Aeneas using all my skill. You need not beg me any more. You know that you have much power over me!"

Venus and Vulcan made love — something they both desired — and he fell asleep with his head resting on her breast.

Very early in the morning, he woke up. So did many faithful, hard-working mortal women who work some hours of the night as well as all hours of the day. They work at weaving, and they supervise female servants who work at chores. They are good wives and good mothers.

Vulcan's workshop is in a cave on Vulcania, an island off the northern coast of Sicily. Here Cyclopes work as blacksmiths. Vulcan flew there and found the Cyclopes already hard at work. Brontes, Steropes, and Pyracmon were creating a thunderbolt for Jupiter to hurl. They had yet to add the sound of thunder to the thunderbolt. Other Cyclopes were creating wheels for the chariot of Mars, god of war, which he would use to fight mortal warriors and their towns. Yet other Cyclopes were creating a shield — an aegis — for Minerva. The shield was decorated with the image of the severed head of a Gorgon — a female monster that had living snakes for hair. Anyone who looked at a Gorgon would be turned to stone.

Vulcan said, "Cyclopes, whatever creations you are working on now, put them away. We have another, different task to perform. We must create divine armor for a mortal warrior. We will need strength, quick hands, and skill! Let's get started!"

Vulcan and the Cyclopes worked well together. Soon different kinds of metal — bronze and steel and gold — had been melted, and they were forging a huge shield. Some Cyclopes worked the bellows, some plunged hot metal into water, and some beat the hot metal on anvils.

As Vulcan and his Cyclopes created the divine armor, dawn arrived and Evander woke up. He dressed himself in simple clothing: a tunic and sandals. He wore a sword in a belt over his right shoulder and the skin of a panther over his left shoulder. He and two watchdogs went to visit Aeneas, who was already up. Evander and Pallas met Aeneas and Achates, and all greeted each other as friends.

King Evander remembered his promise to provide military aid to Aeneas and the Trojans. Evander said to Aeneas, "You are a great warrior, and I cannot regard the Trojans as a defeated people because you are leading them. I have promised to help you, and I will keep my promise to the extent that I am able. I wish that I could do more. The Tiber River hems us in on one side, and hostile people sometimes harass us on the other side.

"I, however, know of a population with great armies who will become your allies. I believe that fate brought you here to become their leader.

"Close by here is Agylla, an Etruscan city. Agylla was a happy and prosperous city until Mezentius became its king. Mezentius is a cruel man who has committed many murders and many savage crimes. He was a tyrant to his people. He used to tie a living person to a corpse. Living head was tied to deceased head, and living hand was tied to deceased hand. The living person, locked in a putrid embrace, died — slowly. Finally, the Etruscans rebelled and drove Mezentius out of the city. They attacked his palace, they killed his guards, and they threw fire on the roof of his palace. Mezentius escaped and went to the country of the Rutulians. Turnus, King of the Rutulians, is his friend and shields him.

"The Etruscans want to punish Mezentius for all of his crimes. They are eager to attack the Rutulians and to capture Mezentius. They have thousands of soldiers and many ships. They are eager to fight, but an old prophet is stopping them, telling them, 'Etruscans, you are courageous and your cause is righteous. Mezentius deserves to be punished for his murders and his other crimes. But the gods forbid you to go into battle with an Italian as your commander. You must chose a commander who comes from overseas!'

"The Etruscans are trying to find that commander. Tarchon, an Etruscan leader, even sent envoys to me, asking me to lead their troops into battle. I come from overseas, having been born in Greece. But I am old. My blood is sluggish and cold. I am no longer strong. Pallas, my son, cannot be the commander because his blood is mixed. I married an Italian woman, and so Pallas is part Italian.

"You, Aeneas, will be their commander. You are a mighty warrior, and you come from overseas. The gods want you to lead the Etruscans to war.

"I will send Pallas, my beloved son, with you. Watch after him. Teach him to be a soldier. Be a role model for him.

"In my name, I will give you two hundred horsemen now — they are our best warriors. In addition, you will get two hundred more warriors in Pallas' name."

Aeneas and Achates thought about what Evander had said, and Venus sent all a sign: A thunderbolt flashed from a sky without clouds. They seemed to hear trumpets. Another thunderbolt flashed and rumbled, and the sky grew blood-red.

Some of Evander's people were frightened, but Aeneas knew that the omen had come from his mother. He said, "I know what this sign means. My mother, the goddess Venus, promised to send me this sign when war broke out. She also promised to bring me armor forged by Vulcan, her husband: the blacksmith god.

"War will be bad for the Laurentes and for Turnus. Much blood will flow, including the blood of Turnus. Under the water of the Tiber River will be many shields and helmets and corpses of brave warriors. But the Rutulians want war, not peace, and they will get what they want!"

Aeneas prayed to Hercules and to the gods of the household, and all sacrificed sheep to the gods.

Aeneas went to his ships and picked out the best Trojans to go with him to the Etruscans. The other men he sent back to the Trojan camp downriver at the mouth of the Tiber. The river current carried the ships home — Ascanius would soon hear news about his father.

Evander gave horses to the Trojans. Aeneas' horse was the best and had a lion's skin as a blanket. In the town of Pallanteum, citizens knew that Aeneas was going to visit the Etruscans to seek their help in the war. Afraid of war, mothers prayed.

Evander held his son's hand and cried. He said, "I wish that Jupiter would make me young again. I once was a mighty warrior. I once fought before the city of Praeneste in Latium in Italy. I killed the city's king, Erulus. Feronia, his goddess mother, had given him three lives, so I had to kill him three times. He also had three suits of armor — one for each life. I took all three of his lives — and all three of his suits of armor.

"If I could be young again, I would not leave you, Pallas, my son. I would stay with you and watch over you. If I were young, cruel Mezentius would not have been able to kill so many men and make so many women widows.

"Gods, please listen to my prayer! Jupiter, grant me my wish! Protect my son, if the Fates permit it. As long as I can see my son alive again, I can endure any pain. But if my son is going to die in the war, then let me die now! I love you and hug you, my son, and I pray that I will never learn of your death!"

Evander collapsed, and his servants helped the old man back into his home.

Aeneas and the others then rode away from Pallanteum and toward the Etruscans. Aeneas rode in the lead, with Achates and other Trojans behind him. Wearing armor, Pallas rode in the center of the line. Pallas was as bright as the morning star.

Mothers, trembling, watched them ride away from the city.

Aeneas and his horsemen reached a sacred grove by the river that flowed by the Etruscan city of Caere. People of long ago held a festival there for Silvanus, the god of woods and fields. Close by the grove were Tarchon and his Etruscans. At the grove Aeneas and his horsemen dismounted, watered their horses, and rested.

Venus saw Aeneas resting alone on a bank of the river. She flew to him, bearing the armor created by Vulcan, and said to him, "Here is the divine armor that I promised to give to you. Vulcan, my husband, created it for you. It will protect you from all the enemy warriors, including Turnus!"

Venus hugged her son and put down the armor under a tree.

Aeneas loved the gifts of his mother and her husband. He stared at them. He held them. He looked at them from all sides. He looked at the helmet and the sword and the breastplate and the spear. And he looked at the shield.

The shield was special. It told the history of Italy and of Rome. As a god, Vulcan knew the future history of Rome, although Aeneas did not. Vulcan knew the achievements of the descendants of Aeneas, and he knew of the future wars of Rome.

Vulcan put on the shield a depiction of Romulus and Remus, who will be suckled by a she-wolf in the cave known as the Lupercal. The baby boys will not be afraid of the she-wolf that licks them with her tongue — the tongue of a mother.

Vulcan also put on the shield a depiction of the abduction of the Sabine women. Rome will need citizens, and the citizens whom Romulus will gather around him will be young men. Romulus' city will need female citizens as well as male citizens — the young men who will gather around Romulus will need wives. Romulus and the early citizens of Rome will get wives by violating a religious festival. The Roman men will invite their neighbors, the Sabines, to a religious festival. Someone will give a signal, and the Romans will abduct the Sabine women. These women will become their wives. The Romans will later make peace again with Tatius, the king of the Sabines, and they will sacrifice to Jupiter together.

Vulcan also put on the shield a depiction of the death of Mettus, King of Alba Longa, who will not keep his word to Tullus Hostilius, the third king of Rome. Tullus will want the army of Alba Longa to fight alongside the Roman army. Mettus will promise that his warriors will fight, but he will keep them out of the battle. Tullus will then tear Mettus apart with horses.

Vulcan also put on the shield a depiction of Horatius Cocles, a famous Roman soldier. Lars Porsenna, an Etruscan king, will attack Rome in the 6th century B.C.E. The Romans, who will have recently overthrown their king, will gather behind the walls of the city. Porsenna will want to force the Romans to let the deposed king, Tarquin, rule them again. A vulnerable spot will be the wooden Sublician bridge over the Tiber River. Horatius will be guarding this bridge when the Etruscans appear. Horatius' soldiers will want to run to safety behind the walls of Rome, but he will convince them to stay and destroy the bridge so that the Etruscans will not be able to use it. Horatius will guard the bridge as his soldiers destroy it. Two soldiers will join him, but when the bridge is almost destroyed, Horatius will tell them to cross the bridge to safety. This will mean that Horatius alone will face the Etruscan army. The Etruscans will have held back, impressed by the bravery of Horatius, but now they will attack Horatius just as the bridge falls. Horatius will jump into the river while wearing armor and swim to safety.

Vulcan also put on the shield a depiction of Cloelia, who will have been taken hostage by Lars Porsenna, but who will escape and also swim across the Tiber River to safety. Cloelia will be a Roman girl at a time when Rome will be having difficulties with the Etruscans. At one point, the Etruscan king Lars Porsenna will make a treaty of peace with Rome. To ensure that the peace will be kept, he will receive a number of Roman hostages: both boys and girls. The Etruscan camp will be close to Rome, and Cloelia will lead an escape of some of the Roman girls back to Rome. Porsenna will be angry at first, but then he will respect her courage. He will ask that she return to be his hostage, and he will promise to keep her safe. She will return, and Porsenna will even allow her to choose some hostages to be returned to Rome. She will choose the little boy hostages. Because of Cloelia's great bravery, the Romans will put up an equestrian statue of her in the Via Sacra.

Vulcan also put on the shield a depiction of the cackling geese on the Capitoline Hill. In 396 B.C.E. the Romans will make Marcus Furius Camillus dictator. He will fight and conquer the Etruscans and become a hero. Camillus, however, will be accused of taking booty from the Etruscan stronghold named Veii. It will be against the law for him to take the booty for his own personal gain. He will say that he is innocent, but he will be thought to be guilty. Camillus will go into voluntary exile, along with some supporters. An army from Gaul will arrive and win a battle 11 miles north of Rome. The Roman general Marcus Manlius and a few supporters will defend the temples of Jupiter, Minerva, and Juno on the Capitoline Hill. Manlius will send a messenger to Camillus, asking him to return and fight the Gauls. Camillus will agree to return — as long as the troops of Manlius formally approve his return. A messenger will take Camillus' message to Manlius, using a hidden trail up the Capitoline Hill. The Gauls will observe the messenger and discover the hidden trail. At night, the Gauls will use the hidden trail, hoping to spring a surprise attack upon Manlius. Geese that are sacred to Juno will be on the Capitoline Hill. The geese will hear the Gauls, and the geese will begin to cackle. The Romans will hear the geese, and they will successfully repel the Gauls. Camillus and an army of 40,000 soldiers will arrive at exactly the right time. Manlius and his men will be exhausted, and so they will be trying to use gold taken from Juno's temple to buy peace for the Romans. Camillus will say, 'Rome buys its peace with iron, not gold,' and then he and his army will attack the Gauls and drive them north, away from Rome. Camillus will be given the title of Second Founder of the City and stay in Rome.

Vulcan also put on the shield a depiction of the Dancing Priests who are and will be known as the Mars-worshipping Salii, the priests of the god Lupercus, and the chaste women who will lead sacred marches through Rome.

Vulcan also put on the shield a depiction of Hades and its sinners. He depicted the sinner Catiline, who will try but fail to overthrow the Roman government. Catiline's eternal punishment will be to dangle from a mountain crag and be tormented by the Furies.

Vulcan also put on the shield a depiction of Hades and its heroes. Marcus Porcius Cato Uticensis — the grandson of Cato the Elder, who will also be known as Cato the Censor — appeared on the shield giving laws to the just souls in the Land of the Dead. Cato the Elder will be a Roman politician, general, and writer who will live in the 2nd century B.C.E. Cato the Elder will have ethical principles that he will strictly observe, and he will have an austere way of life.

Marcus Porcius Cato Uticensis — often called Cato the Younger — will also live according to strict ethical principles. He will fight against Julius Caesar, whom he will believe would like to do away with the Roman Republic and make himself king of Rome. After Julius Caesar will defeat the army of Cato the Younger at Utica in Africa, Cato the Younger will commit suicide after reading the *Phaedo*, a dialogue by Plato in which appear arguments for the immortality of the soul. Julius Caesar will be noted for his *clementia* — for his clemency. Julius Caesar will be very unlikely to order Cato the Younger to be killed; most likely, he would forgive him. Cato the Younger will kill himself because he will love freedom and will not want to live in what he will think would become a kingdom rather than a republic.

Vulcan also put on the shield a depiction of the Battle of Actium. After the death of Julius Caesar, people will jockey for power in Rome. The main contenders for power will be Octavian, who will later take the name of

Caesar Augustus, and Mark Antony. Mark Antony will marry Octavian's sister, Octavia, but he will start an affair with Cleopatra, Queen of Egypt. Mark Antony and Cleopatra will become enemies of Rome. The Battle of Actium will take place on 2 September 31 B.C.E. Actium will be a Roman colony in Greece. In the naval battle of Actium, Octavian's forces will defeat the forces of Mark Antony and Cleopatra. Cleopatra and her 60 ships will leave the battle and flee back to Egypt in the late afternoon, and Mark Antony will follow her with 40 of his own ships. With the opposing leaders gone, Octavian's forces will win a massive battle. They will kill 5,000 of Mark Antony's men. Mark Antony's land soldiers will also surrender. One year later, Octavian will take the war to Egypt. Both Mark Antony and Cleopatra will commit suicide. Octavian will capture Cleopatra, but rather than be seen in a Roman triumph, she will order that a poisonous snake be smuggled in to her. She will allow the poisonous asp to bite her, and she will die from the poison. Within three years after the Battle of Actium, Octavian will become emperor and take the name of Caesar Augustus.

Vulcan's depiction of the Battle of Actium showed Egyptian gods such as the dog-headed Anubis battling the Roman gods Neptune, Venus, and Minerva. The Egyptian gods will be defeated along with the Egyptian mortal forces.

Vulcan also put on the shield a depiction of Caesar Augustus' triple triumph that Rome will celebrate in 29 B.C.E. All Romans will celebrate Caesar Augustus' conquest of the country of Illyricum, victory in the Battle of Actium, and annexation of Egypt. All Rome will celebrate for three days. Caesar Augustus will parade through the city with enemy captives and booty and his troops, he will sacrifice to Jupiter, and people will eat at a public feast.

Many heroes have walked on the site of Rome, including Hercules, Aeneas, and Caesar Augustus. Although Aeneas did not know what the scenes depicted on the shield meant, he gloried in them.

Aeneas lifted his shield. When he lifted his shield, he lifted the history of Rome: depictions of important events in Roman history. When he lifted his shield, he lifted the history of his future descendants.

Chapter 9: Battles by Night and by Day

Because Aeneas was traveling to seek help from the Etruscans, he was away from the Trojan camp on the bank of the Tiber River. Seizing the opportunity, Juno sent the goddess Iris to take a message to Turnus.

Iris said, "Turnus, I have good news for you. Aeneas has left the Trojan camp. He has been visiting Evander and Pallanteum, and now he is going to the Etruscans to get their help. Seize this opportunity! Attack the Trojan camp while Aeneas is away!"

She flew away, leaving behind a rainbow.

Turnus recognized the goddess and prayed, "Iris, who gave you this message to bring to me? Whoever it was, I will obey the message. I see your rainbow, and I will obey a message this clearly stated."

Turnus went to the river, purified himself with water, and prayed to the gods. Then he mustered his army and set out. At the front of the army was Messapus, and at the rear were the sons of Tyrrhus, the gamekeeper of King Latinus. Turnus was in the middle. His forces were like the mighty Ganges River, which is fed by seven streams, and like the mighty Nile River, which floods frequently and nourishes crops.

The Trojans saw dust rising in the air from Turnus' soldiers. Caicus said, "What is that blackness coming toward us? I know — it's enemy warriors! Arm yourselves! Mount the walls and prepare to defend our camp!"

The Trojans ran through the gates and mounted the defensive walls they had built. They followed the orders that Aeneas had given them when he departed: "Should enemy soldiers arrive when I am gone, don't fight a battle in the open. Stay behind the walls, and defend the camp. You will be much safer that way." Ascanius was still young, and Aeneas wanted to keep him safe.

The Trojans, ready for battle, preferred to fight a battle in the open and win glory, but they obeyed Aeneas' orders. Fully armed, they stayed behind their walls.

Turnus and twenty horsemen arrived at the Trojan camp. Slower troops followed. He said, "I will be the first one to attack the Trojans!" He threw his spear at the Trojans — this was the beginning of Turnus' war.

Turnus and his men were surprised that the Trojans stayed behind their walls instead of coming out of their camp and fighting man to man. They shouted, "The Trojans must be cowards! They are hiding behind their walls! They are afraid to fight us man to man!"

Turnus looked for a way into the Trojan camp, but he could not find one. He was like a wolf trying and failing to find a way into a sheepfold. The wolf stays hungry — the sheep are safe in their shelter.

Angry, Turnus tried to think of a way to force the Trojans to come out from behind their walls and fight. He saw the Trojans' ships tied up in the river, and he shouted to his warriors, "Bring fire!" He and his warriors seized torches and approached the ships.

Muses, name the goddess who saved the ships from fire. Tell the famous story that will never be forgotten. Cybele saved the ships. Following the fall of Troy, when Aeneas and his men were harvesting timber on Mount Ida to use to build the ships, Cybele, the Mother of Gods, went to Jupiter and pleaded, "Grant me my prayer. On Mount Ida, I have a grove of trees that are sacred to me. Worshippers brought gifts for me there. I am gladly giving to Aeneas those trees so that he can build his fleet — he needs ships so that he can fulfill his destiny. But I pray to you that the ships built from my sacred trees will never sink at sea."

Jupiter replied, "Cybele, Mother of Gods, you are asking for too much for the ships. Mortals will sail those ships, and ships should not enjoy the rights of gods, who are safe in every storm. Aeneas is a mortal, and he should not face dangers in complete safety.

"But I promise you this: When the ships have completed their mission and are moored in western Italy, I will allow you to transform all of the ships that have not already been sunk into immortal sea-nymphs — they will be like the sea-nymphs Doto, who is the daughter of Nereus, and Galatea and be at home in the waves."

Jupiter swore this oath by the river Styx — it was an inviolable oath. When he swore this oath, Mount Olympus shook.

As Turnus and his troops carried fire to the ships, Cybele and her dancing followers from Mount Ida appeared in the sky. Cybele said, "Trojans need not defend the ships. Turnus can burn my ships no more than he can burn the ocean. Ships, run free — become sea-nymphs!"

Each ship plunged into the water of the river like a diving dolphin and then surfaced as an immortal nymph who then swam to the sea. The Trojans were in their new home in Italy; they no longer needed ships.

Turnus' Rutulians were frightened of the omen. Even Messapus was terrified. The Rutulians' horses reared into the air.

Turnus misinterpreted the omen: "This omen favors us, not the Trojans. Jupiter himself has taken away the Trojans' ships! Now we don't need to destroy them! The Trojans now have no way to escape us. They have lost the sea, and soon we will control all the land.

"The Trojans may boast about their fate, but their fate was to reach Italy. I have my own fate: to repel enemy warriors who land on Italy. I have good reason to do that — the Trojans have taken away from me Lavinia — she was to be my bride! Menelaus went to war when a Trojan stole Helen. I am going to war because a Trojan has stolen Lavinia. Troy fell because of a stolen bride. I would have thought that the Trojans would have had enough of war because of women. But, no, they have not. They have built a wall here, although they saw the Greeks conquer Troy and its high walls. Dying once is enough for people. I would have thought that stealing one bride would be enough for the Trojans.

"Troops, are you ready to attack the Trojan camp? To attack Trojans, I don't need divine armor forged by Vulcan. To attack Trojans, I don't need a thousand ships. If the Etruscans wish to fight on the side of the Trojans, let them! The Trojans need not fear that we will sneak around and steal their Palladium — their sacred statue of Minerva — and kill their guards in the dark! The Trojans need not fear that we will build a second Trojan Horse! No, we will surround their camp in the daylight and fight. For ten years, Hector fought off Greek boys. We will teach the Trojans that we are better warriors than the Greek recruits!

"But night is coming. We have done good work today. Now rest, eat, and know that tomorrow we will fight the Trojans."

Messapus set up guards and fires around the Trojan camp. Fourteen Rutulians who each commanded a hundred troops watched the Trojan walls and served as guards. They took turns doing duty. While off duty, they drank wine or played at dice.

From their walls, the Trojans looked out at the fires. The Trojans made sure that the gates were strong, the camp was well guarded, and troops had plenty of weapons.

Because Ascanius was so young, Aeneas had left Mnestheus and Serestus in charge. They did their duty; the camp was well defended during the night. The Trojan guards stayed alert.

Nisus and Euryalus were loving friends — Nisus was older than Euryalus — who had competed in the footrace during the funeral games held on Sicily to honor Anchises, Aeneas' father. Now they guarded a gate together. Euryalus was young — he was just starting to grow a beard. They did everything together, including fighting side by side in battle.

Nisus said, "I have in mind doing a great deed. Perhaps the gods have given me this desire. Look out at the Rutulians, and what do you see? They are careless. They have not paid enough attention to detail. They have watch fires, but the watch fires are far apart. I hear silence — I do not hear the sounds of still-awake guards. The Rutulians are asleep after drinking too much wine.

"This is what I want to do. Our leaders want Aeneas here. They need someone to carry a message to him and let him know that the Rutulians have arrived and will attack our camp. I can do that — as long as they give to you the reward that I will ask for. I myself will be satisfied with the glory of the exploit. Over there, I see a way through the Rutulians and to Aeneas."

Euryalus replied, "Do you wish to leave me out of your exploit? You want me to let you face so much danger alone? My father, who raised me during the Trojan War, did not raise me to act in that way. And I have not acted in that way as we have followed Aeneas. I want a share of the glory of the exploit even if it means risking my life!"

Nisus said, "I know that you are brave, but I want to do this alone. It is risky, and I hope that Jupiter and the gods will allow me to return safely to you. If I should die, you should continue to live. You are younger than I am, and therefore your life is worth more than my life. If I die, I want you to give my body a proper funeral. You may be able to ransom it or get it some other way. But if you cannot bury my body, build an empty tomb for me. I want you to stay alive because of your aged mother who came with you here although so many Trojan mothers stayed on Sicily. She did not want to live there without you."

Euryalus said, "I won't accept your arguments that I should not go with you. I have decided to go, so let's get started."

Euryalus got guards to replace Nisus and him, and the two loving friends went to see Ascanius and get permission to leave the camp and carry a message to Aeneas.

Nearly everyone except the guards was asleep, but the Trojan leaders stayed awake and debated what they ought to do. Send a message to Aeneas? Yes. But who should bear the message?

Nisus and Euryalus arrived, and asked to speak to the Trojan leaders: "It's urgent!" Ascanius heard them and admitted them to the council and asked Nisus, the older man, to speak.

Nisus said, "Listen to us, although we are fairly young. We have been guards tonight, and we have observed the enemy. Their soldiers are drunk and asleep. They are lax in their guard. We have seen a place where we can get through their ranks: a road that forks along the coast. There it is dark: the watch fires are dying, and the dark smoke obscures vision. Let us leave the camp and carry a message to Aeneas. Along the way, we can kill some of the enemy. Don't worry. We can find our way in the dark. Because we are hunters, we know this area, and we know the river. We can find our way to Aeneas. Aeneas and we will return soon to the camp."

Aletes, an aged Trojan advisor, said, "The gods must be looking out for us if they are making our young warriors so courageous."

He touched the hands of Nisus and Euryalus and said, "What reward can we give you for the risky exploit that you are about to undertake? I know that the gods will reward you, and I know that you will take pride in your exploit. But Aeneas will also reward you, as will Ascanius, who will never forget what you are about to do."

Ascanius said, "Aletes is correct: I will never forget this. I need my father back here in this camp. By our household gods and by Vesta, the goddess of the hearth, I swear that I will reward you if you bring back my father.

"I will give you two silver cups that Aeneas received as booty when he conquered the city of Arisba. I will also give you two tripods and two bars of gold. I will also give you an ancient wine bowl: a gift from Dido to Aeneas.

"If we conquer western Italy, I will give you more gifts. You will receive twelve beautiful Italian women and you will receive twelve defeated soldiers and their armor to be your slaves or to be released for ransom. You will also receive the private land of King Latinus.

"Nisus, you will receive Turnus' stallion and his gold armor.

"Euryalus, you are only a year older than I am. You will be my friend and my comrade. We will share glory together as long as we two shall live."

Euryalus replied, "These are notable rewards, and I hope that we are successful in our dangerous mission. But I ask you for one more thing because I know that our mission may not be successful. I have an aged mother who has come all this long way with me. She would not stay behind on Sicily. I have not told her of this mission because I know that she will be afraid for me and she will cry. Please, swear that whatever happens you will take care of her."

Euryalus' *pietas* — his devotion to his mother — impressed the Trojans and especially Ascanius, who said, "I swear that your mother will be my mother. All she will lack will be the name Creusa. She gave birth to a brave son, and she deserves to be rewarded for that. You will be successful in your mission, and she will receive great honor, as you will."

The Trojans made sure that Nisus and Euryalus were well armed for their mission. Ascanius gave them a sword made of gold and a sheath made of ivory; Lycaon of Crete had made both. Mnestheus gave Nisus the hide of a lion. Aletes exchanged helmets with Nisus; Aletes' helmet was better than Nisus' helmet.

The Trojans escorted Nisus and Euryalus to a gate, and Ascanius gave them many messages to give to his father — but his father would never hear the messages because the winds scattered the words among the clouds.

Nisus and Euryalus left the gate and crossed the trench. Their mission would fail, they would die, but they would kill many enemy warriors. They saw many drunken soldiers lying beside weapons and wine cups and lying amid the harnesses of their horses.

Nisus said, "Euryalus, this is a time to slaughter enemy soldiers. Watch the rear so no one comes up behind us as I slaughter soldiers. I will clear a way for us through these warriors."

Nisus thrust his sword into King Rhamnes, the favorite prophet of Turnus. Although Rhamnes had the gift of prophecy, it did not save his life. Nisus also killed three guards lying by Rhamnes — they were sleeping, not guarding.

Then Nisus cut the throats of the armor-bearer and the charioteer of Remus, and he cut off the head of Remus, whose torso spurted red, hot blood.

Nisus also killed Lamyrus, Lamus, and Serranus. Serranus had won at gambling before falling asleep. He would have been luckier had he gambled all night and lost.

As Nisus killed enemy soldiers, he was like a hungry lion tearing sheep into bloody pieces of corpses.

Euryalus also killed enemy soldiers. He killed Fadus, Herbesus, Rhoetus, and Abaris. Rhoetus woke up — too late. He started to rise so he could hide, but Euryalus thrust a sword into his body. Rhoetus vomited red wine and red blood.

Euryalus moved closer to the camp of Messapus, but Nisus stopped the killing: "Dawn is near. We have cleared a path through the enemy. We have done enough killing."

They left behind much valuable booty: silver armor, mixing bowls, and expensive rugs. Euryalus, however, took Rhamnes' sword-belt. Long ago, Caedicus had given it to Remulus of Tiber. When Remulus died, he had given it to his grandson. When the grandson died, the Latins seized it as booty. Now Euryalus seized it. He also took Messapus' shiny, polished helmet.

Nisus and Euryalus moved forward. They were past the enemy warriors and seemed to be safe, but on the road ahead came a troop of enemy cavalry bringing messages to Turnus. Volcens commanded the three hundred mounted enemy warriors.

Nisus and Euryalus heard the horses and turned off from the road — too late. Euryalus' shiny, polished helmet reflected moonlight, and Volcens saw the two warriors heading to the left.

Volcens shouted, "Identify yourselves!" Nisus and Euryalus ran, but the cavalry troops fanned out and looked for them. The woods were thick, and they were dark. Nisus was able to follow a barely visible path to safety, but

Euryalus was young and afraid, and he got lost and was not able to follow Nisus.

Nisus came to the fields where King Latinus pastured his sheep and cattle. He looked around for Euryalus, but his friend was not there. Nisus said, "My friend, where did you get lost? Will I be able to find you now?"

Nisus could have gone forward and taken Ascanius' messages to Aeneas. That was his duty, but Nisus instead went back to look for his friend. He heard the sound of hoofs, he heard a chase, and he heard a cry. Then he saw Euryalus, who had been captured. The enemy soldiers were dragging him away.

Nisus did not want to leave his friend behind. Should he rush the enemy and fight and die a noble death? Should he try to kill some of the enemy warriors from afar and hope to rescue Euryalus? He lifted one of his spears and prayed to Diana, goddess of the moon, "Help me now! Remember my father's many sacrifices to you. Remember my own sacrifices to you. Help me to kill the enemy!"

He threw the spear, which hit Sulmo in the back. Sulmo fell, vomited blood, and died. The Rutulians looked all around, but they did not see Nisus in the darkness.

Nisus aimed another spear at the enemy and threw it. It hit Tagus in the head and splattered his brain. Another quick death of an enemy soldier.

Volcens was furious. Two of his men had died, and he could not see the man who had killed them. He shouted, "Whoever you are, this captive here will pay the punishment for your crimes!" He then pulled out his sword and moved toward Euryalus.

Terrified for his friend, Nisus came out into the open and shouted, "I killed your men! Let him live! Kill me instead!"

Too late. Volcens plunged his sword into Euryalus' body. Euryalus' blood flowed out of his body, and his head drooped. It became limp like a flower that a plow has cut. It drooped like a poppy droops when rain falls on it and makes it heavy.

Nisus drew his sword and charged among the Rutulians, charging straight at Volcens, who screamed. Nisus plunged his sword into Volcens' open mouth and killed him. The Rutulians attacked Nisus, inflicting wound upon wound. Nisus fell on Euryalus' body and died.

The two men had failed in their mission. Euryalus was sidetracked by a love for booty, and the shiny, polished helmet he seized caused his death. Nisus was sidetracked by his love for his best friend. Instead of taking the messages to Aeneas, Nisus tried to rescue his friend, failed, and then sacrificed his life to avenge his friend's death. Nevertheless, as long as the *Aeneid* exists, the two friends will be remembered.

The Rutulians celebrated the deaths of Nisus and Euryalus, but they mourned the deaths of Volcens and the many warriors whom Nisus and Euryalus had killed. Many Rutulians gathered around the corpses. Rhamnes' body was white because all of his blood now soaked the ground. The Rutulians returned Messapus' helmet to him.

Dawn arrived and brought light to the world. Turnus called his warriors to battle. News of the deaths of Nisus and Euryalus and of the deaths caused by them spread, and the Rutulians decapitated their bodies and spiked the two Trojans' heads on pikes and displayed them before the Trojan camp.

On the walls of the camp, the Trojans lined up for battle and saw heads that they knew well. They mourned for Nisus and Euryalus and for a mission left unfinished.

Rumors of the deaths of Nisus and Euryalus swept through the Trojan camp and reached Euryalus' mother. She stopped weaving. Grieving, crying, and tearing her hair, she went to the Trojans' walls and looked out at the enemy and saw the two pikes topped with decapitated heads. She screamed, "Euryalus, how can you die and leave me alone? I am an old woman. You left on a deadly mission and did not allow me to say goodbye to you. Now you are dead in Latium, and the dogs and birds will feast on your flesh. I, your mother, will not be able to lead a funeral procession or close your eyes or bathe your wounds or dress your body in a shroud that I have woven.

"What will happen to me now? What is left to me? Only your head?

"Rutulians, if you have any mercy in you, kill me now. Or, Jupiter, show mercy to me by killing me with a thunderbolt — send this body to the Land of the Dead so that I can be with my son. The life I have left to me is not worth living!"

The Trojans mourned along with Euryalus' mother. Ilioneus and Ascanius, who also mourned, ordered Idaeus and Actor to take her away from the wall.

An enemy trumpet sounded, and enemy soldiers held their shields over their heads, forming a tortoise shell of protection. They ran forward, seeking to cross the trench and tear down the Trojans' wall. Some enemy soldiers pushed ladders against the wall and attempted to climb them.

The Trojans defended their walls by thrusting with pikes and by dropping huge rocks on the enemy. Because of their years of fighting in the Trojan War, they were experienced in this form of warfare. The Rutulians were brave, but the Trojans' rocks broke their tortoise-shell defense. The Rutulians backed away and hurled spears and shot arrows at the Trojans. In a different part of the assault, Mezentius carried fire to the Trojan wall. Messapus broke down a section of the wall and shouted, "Bring ladders! Climb the walls!"

Muses — especially you, Calliope, Muse of epic poetry — help me to tell of the death and destruction that Turnus caused that day. Help me to tell about the many Trojans he sent to the Land of the Dead. This is an important story. Help me tell it.

The Trojans had built a defensive tower. The Italians attacked it, working hard to bring it down. The Trojans in the tower defended it with rocks and spears. Turnus threw a burning torch at the tower, and it hit the tower's side and stuck there. The wind whipped the fire, which climbed upward toward the Trojans, who backed away from it. The shift in weight to one side and the damage caused by the fire on one side caused the tower to fall outward, away from the Trojan camp and into the midst of the enemy.

Most of the Trojans in the tower died in the fall. They were crushed on the ground and impaled by their own weapons and by the splintered timber of the falling tower.

Two Trojans were left alive: Helenor and Lycus. Helenor was young. His parents were a slave woman named Licymnia and the King of Maeonia. Helenor went to Troy and fought, although slaves were forbidden to have weapons. Now Helenor was surrounded by thousands of enemy warriors, closing in on him the way that hunters close in on a wild beast that knows that it will die and that attacks the hunters. Helenor knew that he would die, and he charged the enemy, rushing toward the place where enemy weapons were thickest.

A fast runner, Lycus darted through the enemy warriors and reached the Trojan wall. He tried to climb it and grab the friendly hands that could pull him up to safety, but Turnus reached him and shouted, "Did you think that you could escape death?" He grabbed Lycus and pulled him down from the wall and killed him. Turnus was like an eagle that grabs with its talons a rabbit or a white swan. He was like a wolf that enters a sheepfold and kills a lamb as its mother bleats in grief.

Cries of war filled the air as the enemy attacked. Some enemy warriors filled the trench with dirt, and some flung burning torches onto the roofs of the Trojan camp.

The Trojan Ilioneus hurled a rock that killed Lucetius as he ran toward the Trojan gates with a flaming torch in his hand.

Liger, an Etruscan who was loyal to Mezentius, killed the Trojan Emathion.

The Rutulian Asilas, who fought with javelins, killed Corynaeus, who fought with arrows.

The Trojan Caeneus killed Ortygius, but immediately Turnus killed Caeneus.

Turnus also killed Itys, Clonius, Dioxippus, and Promolus, and he killed Sagaris and Idas.

The Trojan Capys killed Privernus, who had been grazed by a spear thrown by Themillas. Privernus foolishly dropped his shield to put his hand over his wound, exposing himself to the arrow shot by Capys that killed him.

Mezentius, the cruel Etruscan fighting on the side of Turnus, swung a sling three times around his head and hurled a shot that split the skull of the son of the Sicilian Arcens. Arcens' son was wearing fine, colorful clothing. Arcens had raised his son by the Symaethus River in a place where were a grove that was sacred to Mars and a shrine that was dedicated to some gods of Sicily.

Ascanius now achieved his first kill in combat. He had achieved skill in archery through hunting, and now he took the life of a boastful enemy warrior: Numanus, who was also called Remulus.

Numanus had recently become the brother-in-law of King Turnus, having married Turnus' younger sister, and he was proud of the connection. Numanus yelled, "You Trojans are pitiful. Twice now, at Troy and here, you have been besieged. Twice now, you have been forced to stay behind your walls. You are the people who wish to steal Italian women? Why are you even here? Menelaus is not here. Agamemnon is not here. Lying Ulysses is not here. Here are real men. When boy babies are born, we dip them in cold river water to make them tough. Italian boys hunt constantly. They ride horses, they shoot arrows, and they work hard. They can work the land, and they can conquer cities. All our lives we work with weapons. Even in old age, we are able to fight, even though we put on helmets over gray hair. We revel in taking booty from other peoples.

"But you Trojans concern yourselves with dressing up, with fashion. You wear yellow and purple. You like easy lives. You like to dance. You like to wear ribbons. You are Trojan women — not Trojan men! Go back to Troy and play music and dance for Cybele on Mount Dindyma and Mount Ida! Leave fighting to real men like us Italians!"

Ascanius was angered by the insults. He drew his arrow, aimed, and prayed, "Jupiter, make this arrow hit its target. Each year, I will bring gifts to your temple. I will sacrifice to you a bull."

Jupiter heard the prayer and sent thunder on the left: Ascanius would kill his man, but boys as young as Ascanius should not fight in war.

Ascanius' arrow went through Remulus' head. Ascanius shouted, "Now let us hear you insult us! This is the reply to you from Trojan 'women' who have been twice besieged!"

The Trojans shouted in support of Ascanius and his words.

Apollo, god of archery, was by chance flying by. He witnessed Ascanius' first kill. He said about Ascanius, "Well done. You will be a success in life, and your children will be successes. All wars that you and your descendants fight will end in peace. They will not end the way that the Trojan War ended."

But Ascanius was still young — very young — and so Apollo flew down to him. Apollo assumed the form of Butes, an elderly man who had once served Anchises but who now, at the request of Aeneas, served Ascanius. Apollo, who now looked exactly like Butes, said, "Ascanius, you have done enough in the battle. Numanus is dead, and you are alive. Let's keep you alive. Apollo supports you; you used his weapon of choice. You will fight in future battles, but for now, stop fighting."

Apollo vanished, but the Trojans heard the arrows in his quiver as he flew away and so they recognized the god. The Trojans had heard his words to Ascanius, and they made Ascanius stop fighting, eager as he was to continue.

The Trojans were also eager to fight as the battle continued. Cries of war filled the air, as did flying weapons of war. On the ground were shields and helmets and corpses. The battle was as violent as a storm that hurls hailstones at the earth.

The Trojans Pandarus and Bitias, two brothers of huge size, so trusted in their strength and fighting ability that they disobeyed orders and opened the gate that they had been entrusted to guard. They dared the enemy soldiers to attack them and try to get inside the Trojan camp.

Pandarus and Bitias stood tall in the gateway like armed towers or mighty oaks.

The Rutulians saw the open gate and charged, but Pandarus and Bitias repelled them. Pandarus and Bitias made the enemy leaders Quercens, Aquiculus, Tmarus, and Haemon, along with their warriors, retreat — or die. The battle grew hotter, and some Trojans dared to leave the camp, and — against Aeneas' orders — fight in the open.

The Trojans' lack of *pietas* turned the battle against them. They were neglecting their duty, not doing their duty.

Turnus learned that Pandarus and Bitias had opened a gate, and he charged them and all other Trojan warriors. Turnus killed Antiphates, the bastard son of Sarpedon and a mother who had been born in Thebes. Turnus threw his spear — it pierced Antiphates' chest.

Turnus also killed Merops, Erymas, Aphidnus, and the massive Bitias. To kill Bitias, he used not a spear — to kill Bitias took more than a mere spear — but a massive pike. Turnus thrust the massive pike through Bitias' shield of two bull's-hides and through his breastplate. Bitias fell and his massive shield made a sound like that of a structure that men destroy by pushing it over so that it lies in the shallows of the sea. The sound made mountains tremble, and the shock of the fall shook the earth under the sea. The corpse of Typhoeus, the hundred-headed, fire-breathing monster that Jupiter had killed with a thunderbolt and buried, trembled when Bitias fell.

Mars put courage into the hearts of the Latins, and he sent fear to the Trojans. The Latins attacked the Trojans. Pandarus, now that his brother was dead, knew that the enemy had the advantage, and so he put his shoulder to the gate and closed it. Outside the gate were many Trojans who fought and died, but many Trojans rushed inside the gate with Pandarus before it closed.

But the Trojans were not safe — Turnus also rushed inside the gate before it closed. Now he was in the Trojans' camp the way that a tiger sometimes gets into the pen of a flock of sheep.

The armor and weapons of Turnus glowed as the Trojans recognized him and knew him for the enemy he was.

Pandarus, angry at the death of Bitias, his brother, shouted at Turnus, "You are not among friends here! This is not the palace of Amata, the mother of Lavinia! You are in the camp of your enemy, and you will not escape!"

Turnus, unafraid, replied, "Fight me if you dare. I will send you to the Land of the Dead with a message for Priam, defeated king of Troy: A new Achilles has arisen in Italy."

Pandarus used all his strength to hurl a spear at Turnus, but Juno protected him and flicked it away — the spear stuck in the gate.

Turnus yelled, "I escaped your spear, but you won't escape my sword! You won't escape a fatal wound!" Turnus brought his sword down on Pandarus' head, splitting his skull and splattering his brain. Pandarus fell, his head divided in two, the halves dangling over his shoulders.

The Trojans backed away from Turnus, who — if he had not been overcome with *furor* — could have won the war if only he had opened the gate and let his soldiers into the camp. That would have been the end of the Trojans, the end of Ascanius. Turnus would have changed future history forever.

But Turnus' *furor* made him attack the Trojans all on his own. He killed Phaleris, and he cut the leg tendons of Gyges. He then used their spears to kill Trojans as they fled from him. Juno put courage in his chest as he killed Halys and Phegeus. Turnus also killed men on the Trojan wall who were unaware that he was in the Trojan camp: Alcander, Halius, Prytanis, and Noëmon.

The Trojan Lynceus attacked Turnus and shouted for his fellow warriors to attack him in a mass, but Turnus spun and used his sword to cut off with one stroke Lynceus' head. Turnus then killed Amycus, a gifted hunter and a warrior gifted at dipping the points of arrows and spears in poison. Turnus also killed Clytius and Cretheus. The Muses regarded Cretheus as a friend; he played the lyre and sang songs of heroes.

Now all the Trojans knew that Turnus was fighting in their camp. Mnestheus and Serestus, who led the Trojans while Aeneas was gone, ran to the scene and saw Turnus routing the Trojans. Mnestheus shouted at the Trojans, "Why are you running? Do you have other walls to be safe behind? Cannot all of you kill *one* enemy warrior? Will one Rutulian kill so many first-rate warriors and live on without even a scratch? Aren't you ashamed for what just one warrior has done to you? Aren't you ashamed for your gods and for Aeneas to learn of the destruction that just one enemy warrior has wrought?"

Mnestheus' words stopped the rout of the Trojans. In a mass, they fought Turnus and forced him back. He slowly backed up to the part of the Trojan camp that was beside the Tiber River. The river — not walls — provided the protection there. The Trojans fought him the way that many hunters attack a lion. Under attack by so many hunters, the lion is afraid, but it is dangerous as it backs away from the many spears. The lion will not flee, but it cannot defeat so many hunters and so it slowly backs away.

Turnus now slowly backed away from the Trojans. Twice he charged them, and the Trojans fled, but they quickly regrouped and more Trojan warriors arrived to fight him. Juno could not give Turnus enough courage and power to fight all these Trojans — Jupiter had sent Iris to her to tell her that Turnus must leave the Trojan camp — or else.

The Trojans with their many weapons kept forcing Turnus back. Their weapons hit his helmet and damaged it. Mnestheus and the other Trojans attacked Turnus with their spears. Sweat streamed down Turnus' body. He gasped for breath. His knees and body grew weak with exhaustion.

Then Turnus dived into the Tiber River, which washed away his sweat and others' blood and carried him — triumphant — to his fellow warriors.

Chapter 10: Deaths of Loved Ones in Battle

On Mount Olympus that night, Jupiter called a council of the gods. The gods arrived, and Jupiter said to them, "Why are you gods taking sides and fighting? I did not want the Trojans and the Italians to fight each other. Why are you resisting my wishes? Why is there a war now? The time for war will come — later. It is fated that Carthage will cross the Alps into Italy and fight Rome. That is the time for war. Now peace should be in Italy. Gods, stop the fighting and obey my wishes."

Jupiter spoke briefly, Venus spoke at length in her reply to him: "Father, the Trojans must fight. The Rutulians are actively making war. Turnus is actively fighting the war and planning fresh assaults following his success in the Trojan camp. The Trojans' walls did not protect them. Turnus fought inside their walls. Aeneas, the Trojans' leader and best fighter, is far away from the camp and knows nothing of the siege. The Greeks attacked old Troy, and now another enemy threatens new Troy. Another Diomedes wishes to kill Aeneas. Diomedes once wounded me when I saved my son Aeneas from him. I see that I will probably be wounded again in this new war.

"If the Trojans had come to Italy against your will and against the will of the Fates — which they have not — I would tell you to punish them. But the Trojans have followed rightful oracles from the gods and from the ghost of Anchises in the Land of the Dead, and so they deserve no punishment. They have not gone against your will or against the will of the Fates.

"And yet they have suffered punishment. On Sicily, some of their ships burned. A storm at sea sank one ship and drove the remaining ships to Carthage. Iris even took a message to Turnus telling him to attack the Trojan camp while Aeneas is absent. And Allecto even left the Land of the Dead to cause trouble for the Trojans. She was wild like a Maenad as she started this war.

"I once hoped for an empire for the Trojans' descendants. But Fortune is against the Romans. Whoever you support, let them be the victors. If Juno is so against the Trojans that she will not let them stay in Italy, then at least let Ascanius, my grandson, survive. You can do what you like to Aeneas — let him travel on an unknown sea. But let me take Ascanius somewhere safe, somewhere I am worshipped: the towns of Amathus or Paphos in Cyprus, or the island of Cythera. Ascanius can live the rest of his life safely, without weapons, without glory. And if you wish, allow Carthage to defeat Italy, which will have no Rome to resist the Carthaginians' invasion.

"The Trojans fled their conquered city, and for what? They have risked danger at sea and on land to found a new Troy in Italy. But apparently it would have been better for the Trojans not to have left Troy, but to have rebuilt a new Troy on the ashes of old Troy. If the Trojans cannot live in Italy, at least give them back their Xanthus and Simois rivers, if they must now be conquered in Italy."

Angry, Juno said, "I must speak up now, although it means revealing my wounded feelings to all. Did I force Aeneas to come to Italy to make war on King Latinus? Aeneas came to Italy, but why? Because of the Fates — and the ranting of Cassandra. Did I force Aeneas to leave the Trojan camp and seek allies? Did I force Aeneas to leave Ascanius behind in the Trojan camp? Did I force Aeneas to inflame the Etruscans and drive them to war? Is either Iris or I responsible for these things?

"Venus, you think it is wrong for the Italians to fight the Trojans at their camp. Is it wrong for Turnus to be on Italian soil? Turnus has impressive ancestors, including Pilumnus, a woodland god. His mother is Venilia, a sea-nymph. Turnus is a king and a warrior.

"Haven't the Trojans fought the Italians? Haven't the Trojans settled on land that is not their own? Haven't the Trojans arranged for Aeneas' marriage to Lavinia, a woman who was already betrothed to Turnus? Don't the Trojans plan to take other Italian daughters as their brides?

"Aren't the Trojans pleading for peace with one hand in front holding an olive branch and the other hand in back holding a spear?

"You, Venus, think that you are allowed to help the Trojans, but I am not allowed to help the Italians. You think that you are permitted to save the life of Aeneas on the battlefields of the Trojan War. You think that you are permitted to change into sea-nymphs Trojan ships threatened with fire. You do not think that I am permitted to help the Italians.

"You pointed out that Aeneas is far away and does not know that the Trojan camp is under attack. Wonderful! Let Aeneas stay far away, and let him continue to be ignorant that the Trojan camp is under attack. You have areas of the world devoted to you: the towns of Paphos and Idalium on Cyprus, and the island of Cythera. So why are you messing around with Italy?

"You think that I am trying to destroy the Trojans. Am I the one who sent Paris to Sparta to steal Helen? Am I the one who caused the Trojan War? Am I the one who supported Paris? If you really care for the Trojans, you ought to have helped them then. If you did not help them then, you ought not to help them now — and you ought not to blame me for helping the Italians!"

As Venus and Juno had spoken, the gods had listened, sometimes agreeing and sometimes disagreeing with what they heard. Their murmurs were like the first stirrings of a wind that warns sailors of the coming of a storm.

Jupiter spoke, and all the gods grew silent: "Listen to what I tell you. The Italians and the Trojans are now at war, and Juno and Venus oppose each other. I am not going to personally help either side: Italian or Trojan, Turnus or Aeneas. Why is the Trojan camp besieged? Perhaps because of fate. Perhaps because of Trojan foolishness. I will not take sides. Let Italians and Trojans, Turnus and Aeneas, take action as they will. Their own actions will lead to their glory or to their grief. I am the king of all, and I will allow the Fates to find their own way."

Jupiter had made his judgment, and he swore an inviolable oath by the river Styx that what he had said would be so. Jupiter nodded his head, and Olympus shook. The council of the gods was over.

At dawn, the Rutulians again attacked the Trojan camp. The Trojans were trapped inside their camp with not enough warriors. Manning the walls in a thin line were Asius, Thymoetes, the twin sons of Assaracus, Castor, and aged Thymbris. With them were Clarus and Thaemon, the brothers of Sarpedon who were new allies from Lycia. All of them were fighting. Acmon struggled to lift a boulder to drop on the enemy. Others were hurling javelins and rocks and burning torches. Still others were shooting arrows.

Ascanius was present. He was a favorite of his grandmother Venus: handsome, shining like a gem surrounded by gold, glowing like ivory set in a work of art. He wore a circlet of gold around his long hair.

Others also fought. Ismarus, who dipped his arrowheads in poison, shot arrows at the enemy. Mnestheus, who had the previous day driven Turnus from the Trojan camp, fought notably. Capys, whose name is remembered today in the city of Capua in southern Italy, also fought notably.

During the night, Aeneas had been sailing on the coastal sea back to the Trojan camp. He had found Tarchon, King of the Etruscans, and had identified himself. Aeneas had explained what the Trojans could do for the Etruscans and what the Etruscans could do for the Trojans — both peoples would benefit from a pact. Aeneas had talked to Tarchon about Mezentius and about Turnus. The two leaders had sworn to a pact, and now the Etruscans had — as the oracle demanded — a foreign leader. And so the Etruscans and Aeneas and the Trojans with him had set sail on the sea to the Trojan camp.

The ship Aeneas was on led the other ships. The ship's prow was decorated with an image of Mount Ida and its lions — an image dear to Trojans. Aeneas thought about the upcoming battles, and Pallas sometimes asked him about the stars used for navigation and sometimes about his past battles on land and hardships at sea.

Muses, sing now and tell who were Aeneas' allies. Who sailed with Aeneas? Who were his Etruscan allies?

Massicus sailed in the ship *Tiger*, which had bronze sides. He led a thousand warriors who came from the cities of Clusium and Cosae. Their weapons of choice were arrows.

Abas led six hundred warriors from the city of Populonia, a city on the coast. Another three hundred warriors came from Ilva, an island rich with iron ore. They sailed in a ship decorated with a gilded Apollo.

Asilas, a prophet who could read the entrails of animals, the position of stars, the flashes of lightning, and the cries of birds, led a thousand warriors from Pisa, a city settled by Greeks.

Astyr led three hundred warriors from Caere and other cities.

Cunarus of Liguria, a brave man in battle, also led warriors.

Cupavo, the son of Cycnus, led a small band of warriors. Cycnus had loved Phaëthon, who died when he attempted to drive the chariot of his father the Sun-god. Phaëthon could not control the chariot's immortal horses and nearly destroyed the Earth, and so Jupiter killed him. Cycnus grew old and white mourning for Phaêthon, remembering him in song, and Apollo transformed him into a swan and put him in the night sky as the constellation Cycnus. Cupavo, his son, now sailed on the ship *Centaur* with warriors under his command.

Ocnus also led warriors. His mother was the seer Manto, and his father was the river-god of the Tiber. He founded Mantua, naming the city after his mother. Mantua is a diverse city, with many people living in it. Mezentius, Aeneas' enemy, so angered the Mantuans that five hundred warriors from Mantua sailed on the sea to fight him.

Aulestes also led warriors. They sailed on the *Triton* with her hundred oars. The blast of her sea-horn shook the waters, and on her prow was a figure that had the head and torso of a man and the tail of a dragon.

In all, thirty ships were sailing to the Trojan camp.

The day passed, and the moon rose. Aeneas was on deck when sea-nymphs swam up to him. They had been his ships before Cybele had turned them into sea-nymphs. The sea-nymph named Cymodocea gripped the stern of the ship Aeneas was on and said to him, "Sail quickly, Aeneas! We used to be your ships, made of timber harvested from Mount Ida, which is sacred to Cybele. Now we are sea-nymphs, transformed when Turnus tried to destroy us with fire. We have been looking for you to bring you news.

"Your Trojan camp is under attack. Ascanius is trapped behind its walls as the Italians hurl spears at Trojans. The cavalry of Pallas and your Etruscan allies are approaching the Trojan camp, as Turnus knows. He plans on using his troops to keep your allies from reaching the Trojan camp.

"At dawn, put on your divine armor, call your warriors to battle, and fight. Tomorrow will see the deaths of many Rutulians."

Cymodocea dove into the water, got behind the ship, and sped it forward with her right hand — she knew ships and how to make them go fast! The ship sped faster than a spear or arrow.

Aeneas prayed, "Cybele, please be my leader in battle and help the Trojans."

Dawn immediately came, and Aeneas ordered his troops to prepare for battle.

Aeneas saw his Trojan camp, and he lifted his shining shield. The Trojans on the walls saw Aeneas and his ships filled with allies, and they shouted cries of greeting and relief and hurled spears at the enemy — the spears were as numerous as the cranes flying above the Strymon River.

Turnus and his allies didn't understand why the Trojans were shouting cries of greeting and relief until they looked toward the sea and saw Aeneas and his ships filled with warriors. Flames came from the armor of Aeneas. Flames shot from his helmet and from his sword. The flames were like the light from a bright comet that is a bad omen and brings death to many and like the light from the bright star Sirius, called the Dog Star because of its prominent location in the constellation called *Canis Major*, or Big Dog. Sirius, the brightest star, is thought to bring plague and thirst to mortals.

Turnus remained confident in his ability to fight the Trojans and their reinforcements. He wanted to fight Aeneas and his allies on the beach as they landed. Turnus told his troops, "Here is an opportunity! Let's take advantage of it! Let's defeat the Trojans on the beach! Think of your wife and home that you are defending. Think of the glory of your fathers and how you can add to the glory of your family. Let's fight the Trojans and their Etruscan allies on the beach! They are not ready to fight yet. Just now getting off the ships, they don't even have their land-legs yet!"

Turnus decided to lead the attack on the shore and leave other warriors to continue to attack the Trojan camp.

Aeneas' men walked on planks to the shore, or they jumped into shallow water and ran to shore, or they rowed to shore.

Tarchon looked for a safe place for his ships to land on shore, but his main priority was reaching the land and fighting. He told his men, "Row hard. We may wreck our ship, but we need to reach the shore." Tarchon's ship was the only ship that did not make it to the shore. His ship hit a rock in the sea and teetered and then broke into pieces. He and his men fell into the water amid broken oars and pieces of the ship. They fought the undertow and struggled to shore.

Turnus and his warriors charged the beach. Aeneas was the first warrior to kill a man. Theron attacked Aeneas, but Aeneas' sword pierced his tunic and his body.

Aeneas then killed Lichas, whose mother had died trying to give birth to him. The infant Lichas had been cut out of his mother's womb. He had avoided the knife then, but he did not avoid Aeneas' sword now.

Aeneas next killed Cisseus and Gyas, who fought with clubs, a favorite weapon of Hercules, who had been a friend of their father, Melampus.

Pharus opened his mouth to hurl a threat at Aeneas, but Aeneas hurled a javelin that flew into Pharus' open mouth.

Aeneas next targeted Cydon, a man who had loved many men and now loved young Clytius. Cydon would have died, but his seven brothers rescued him. They threw seven spears at Aeneas. Some hit his helmet and shield, which protected him. Some lightly grazed him as Venus ensured that none seriously wounded her son.

Aeneas cried to Achates, his aide, "Bring me more spears! I killed many Greeks at Troy with my spears, and I won't miss here!"

Aeneas threw a spear at Cydon's brother Maeon. It went through his shield and breastplate and his chest. The same spear struck the arm of Maeon's brother Alcanor, who had run up to assist him. Alcanor's arm dangled, useless. A third brother, Numitor, grabbed Aeneas' spear and pulled it out of Maeon's body and threw it at Aeneas hoping to kill him, but missed him and managed only to graze the thigh of Achates, Aeneas' aide.

Clausus, one of Turnus' young, proud warriors, hurled his spear and struck Dryops under the chin. Dryops tried to speak but could not, and he fell to the ground and vomited blood until his breath stopped.

Clausus also killed three Thracians and three sons of Idas.

Turnus' allies Halaesus and Messapus brought troops to the shore, and the Trojans and the Italians fought on equal terms. Winds can fight each other with no wind winning. Just like that, the Trojans and the Italians fought man against man, and neither side had an advantage.

In another part of the battle in a place filled with boulders where a storm had knocked down trees, Pallas' Arcadians had dismounted from their horses because of the rough terrain. But because they were untrained in fighting on foot, they were being defeated and so they backed away from the enemy.

Pallas took action as their leader. He shouted at them, "Why are you fleeing? Think of your reputations! Think of what people will say about you! Think of your own past victories and of the victories of King Evander! Don't flee! Fight! I will lead you into battle! I will be at the front! That is what our country demands of us. We are mortals fighting mortals — we are not fighting gods! The enemy warriors do not have more hands for holding weapons than we have. The enemy warriors do not have more lives than we have. And we have the Ocean at our backs. Where can you flee? Can you flee to Troy?"

Pallas then started to fight. Lagus lifted a huge rock to throw at Pallas, but Pallas hurled a spear that hit Lagus' sternum in between his ribs. Pallas pulled out the spear as Hisbo — angry at the death of his friend — rushed toward him. Pallas plunged his sword into one of Hisbo's lungs.

Pallas next attacked and killed Sthenius and Anchemolus — Anchemolus had slept with his own stepmother.

Pallas also attacked Thymber and Larides — identical twins whose own parents sometimes had difficulty telling them apart. Pallas made it easy to tell them apart. Using his father's sword, he cut off the head of Thymber and the hand of Larides. On the ground, Larides' hand kept moving, trying to grasp a sword.

Pallas' fighting rallied his troops. They no longer thought to flee — they were ready to fight.

Pallas threw a spear at Ilus, a Rutulian warrior. He missed, but his spear struck and killed Turnus' ally Rhoeteus, who had the bad luck to drive his two-horse chariot between Pallas and Ilus. Rhoeteus had been fleeing from the brothers Teuthras and Tyres, two of Pallas' warriors. Rhoeteus fell from his chariot and kicked the ground.

Pallas' warriors came to him and fought with him. They were like a fire that a shepherd starts and the wind blows and suddenly the fire grows and burns everything in its path.

But the enemy fought back. Halaesus, Turnus' ally who had been the companion of Agamemnon, killed Ladon, Pheres, and Demodocus. With his sword, he cut off the hand of Strymonius, who was trying to choke him. Halaesus crushed the skull of Thoas with a rock that smashed in his face and splattered blood and brain.

Halaesus' father, wanting to keep him safe, had hid him long ago deep in the woods. Halaesus' father knew how Halaesus was fated to die. But when Halaesus' father's eyes grew blind in death, the Fates took command and put Halaesus in Italy to die.

Pallas attacked Halaesus. As he did so, he prayed, "River-god of the Tiber, let this spear of my father go through the chest of Halaesus. I will strip his armor and give it to you!" The river-god heard Pallas' prayer. Halaesus used his shield to guard his ally Imaon. This left his chest exposed, and Pallas threw his spear and hit the target.

Lausus, the son of cruel Mezentius, also fought well as he sought to match the exploits of Pallas. Lausus killed the Trojan captain Abas first, and he killed other Trojans as well as Etruscans who fought for Aeneas.

The two sides fought fiercely. They were close together — too close to fight by throwing spears.

Pallas fought on one side; Lausus fought on the other side. They were young men who loved their fathers, who loved them in return. Pallas and Lausus were nearly matched in age and in handsomeness. They were matched in fate — neither would survive this battle. But neither would kill the other — Jupiter would not allow the two to fight face to face.

Turnus' sister Juturna had been a mortal, but Jupiter had raped her and then turned her into an immortal sea-nymph. She loved Turnus and advised him now to go to Lausus.

Turnus raced his chariot to where Lausus and Pallas were fighting with their men and shouted, "I will fight Pallas. He is mine! I wish that his father were present to watch me kill him!"

Lausus and the other warriors withdrew, and Pallas faced Turnus. Pallas looked Turnus over and then said to him, "We will fight, and I will win glory in one of two ways. Either I will kill you, or you will kill me. Either way, my father will be able to bear it. No more talking! No more threats! Let's fight!"

Pallas and Turnus faced each other in the center of the field. Turnus had dismounted from his chariot and now faced Pallas like a lion faces a bull just before attacking it.

Pallas lifted his spear and prayed to Hercules, who had been mortal but was now an immortal god: "Hercules, you came to my father's land, where you were welcomed, although you were a stranger. Help me now to kill Turnus and strip his bloody armor from his bloody body!"

Hercules heard Pallas' prayer, but the gods know the fates of mortal men, and so Hercules groaned in mourning. Tears streamed down his face as Jupiter said to him, "Each mortal man is fated to die after a brief life. For mortal men, life will never come again. All that they can do to achieve a kind of immortality is to achieve fame with their courage.

"Even the mortal sons of gods die — just look at the Trojan War! In that war, I lost my own son Sarpedon. Pallas will die now. Turnus will die, and soon. Every mortal man will at some time reach the end of his life."

Jupiter stopped speaking, and his eyes moved away from the battle.

Pallas hurled his spear at Turnus. It pierced Turnus' shield and grazed Turnus' skin. Pallas drew his sword, and Turnus lifted his spear and hurled it at the young warrior, saying, "Let us see whether my spear will do more damage to you than your spear has done to me!"

Turnus' spear pierced Pallas' shield and his breastplate and his chest. Pallas pulled out the spear from his chest, and his blood and life exited his body with the spear. His mouth bloody, Pallas fell to the ground and died.

Standing over Pallas' body, Turnus said, "Take a message to Pallas' loving father, King Evander. Tell him that I am giving him his son's body back. He is welcome to whatever comfort giving his son a proper burial will give him, but he has paid much for the welcome he gave to Aeneas."

Turnus put his foot on Pallas' corpse and pulled from the corpse a trophy: Pallas' sword-belt. It was decorated with a scene depicting the marriage of the fifty daughters of Danaus to the fifty sons of Aegyptus. Danaus was suspicious of Aegyptus and his fifty sons, who wanted to marry Danaus' fifty daughters, so he fled with his daughters, but Aegyptus and his fifty sons pursued them. To avoid a battle, Danaus told his fifty daughters to marry the fifty sons of Aegyptus, but although he allowed the marriages he also ordered his fifty daughters to kill the fifty sons of Aegyptus. All of his daughters except Hypermnestra, who had married Lynceus, obeyed. Hypermnestra spared Lynceus because he treated her with respect and did not force her to have sex with him their first night together. The gods did not like what the forty-nine women who had killed their husbands had done, and so those forty-nine daughters are punished in Hades with meaningless work. They are condemned to spend all their time trying to fill up with water a container that has a big leak and so can never be filled. Only one daughter avoided this eternal punishment. Only one daughter out of fifty gave *clementia* to her husband. Only one son out of fifty gave *clementia* to his wife. Giving *clementia* to another person can be difficult, but some people find a way to do it although most people may do the wrong thing. Lynceus showed *clementia* to Hypermnestra, and Hypermnestra showed *clementia* to Lynceus.

Turnus gloried in the sword-belt, which the artist Clonus had created. But Turnus did not know his fate, and soon he would wish that Pallas were still alive and still wore this sword-belt.

Pallas' friends carried his corpse away on his shield as they mourned. Pallas would return dead to his father, having been killed on his first day of battle after killing so many of the enemy.

A messenger quickly brought news of the death of Pallas to Aeneas, who needed to rally his troops and the troops of his allies. Angry, he killed the enemy warriors nearest to him, and then he sought Turnus, killing as he went. Turnus was proud that he had killed Pallas, and Aeneas was angry at Turnus. Aeneas remembered King Evander and the welcome that Evander and Pallas had given to him.

Aeneas took eight enemy warriors alive so that they could be sacrificed later at the funeral of Pallas: They were four sons of Sulmo and four sons of Ufens. Aeneas wanted their blood to soak Pallas' funeral-pyre.

Aeneas next threw a spear at Magus, but he ducked and then ran to Aeneas, clasped his knees, and pleaded for his life: "I beg you not to kill me. I beg you by the spirit of your father, and I beg you by your son, don't kill me! I also have a father and a son, and I beg you not to kill for their sakes! I have wealth: gold and silver. Allow me to ransom myself. I am just one person. Whether you win or lose this war will not depend on me — I can make little difference in this war."

Aeneas replied, "Save your gold and silver for your sons. Let them have it. When Turnus killed Pallas, he also killed all chances of ransom. My living son and the ghost of my father want me to kill you."

Aeneas grabbed Magus' helmet and forced it back, exposing the throat, into which he plunged his sword to the hilt.

Aeneas next chased Haemon's son, who was a priest of Apollo and Diana. Haemon's son stumbled and fell to the ground. Aeneas stood over him and slaughtered him, staining his white robes red. Aeneas' aide Serestus stripped off Haemon's son's armor, which was later dedicated to the god Mars.

Caeculus and Umbro tried to rally the other enemy soldiers, but Aeneas cut off the left arm of Anxur, who had been boasting, thinking that his strength would keep him alive with all his limbs until he reached old age.

Tarquitus stood in Aeneas' path and challenged him. Aeneas hurled his spear and pinned Tarquitus' shield to his breastplate. Tarquitus begged for mercy, but Aeneas' sword cut off his head, and Tarquitus' head and torso rolled on the ground. Aeneas said, "Lie there! Your mother will not bury you. You will not be laid to rest in the tomb of your ancestors. Either birds will eat your flesh as you lie on the ground, or your corpse will end up in the sea and fish will feed at your wounds."

Aeneas attacked the finest enemy warriors he could find: warriors whom Turnus put in the front lines. He killed Antaeus, Lucas, Numa, and Camers. Camers was the son of Volcens, a wealthy man who had killed Euryalus and then been killed by Nisus.

Aeneas was like the monster Aegaeon, who had a hundred arms and a hundred hands and fifty shields and fifty swords and fifty mouths that spewed fire when he battled Jupiter and Jupiter's thunderbolts.

Aeneas' sword was hot from blood and friction as he continued to fight. He saw Niphaeus' four-horse chariot and ran toward it. The four horses reared in terror, knocked Niphaeus out of the chariot, and then ran away.

Two brothers, Lucagus and Liger, rode together in their chariot. Liger held the reins, and Lucagus held a sword. On foot, Aeneas charged them. Liger shouted, "These horses do not belong to Diomedes, this chariot does not belong to Achilles, and this battlefield is not that of Troy. You will meet your death on *our* territory!"

Aeneas did not reply — with words. He hurled his spear at Lucagus, who held a shield as he slapped the horses with the flat side of his sword. Aeneas' spear went through Lucagus' shield and into the left side of his groin. Lucagus fell to the ground, writhed, and died. Aeneas shouted, "Lucagus, your horses have not deserted you — you have deserted your horses!"

Aeneas stopped the chariot by seizing the yoke, and Liger jumped from the chariot and begged for his life: "I beg you by your ancestors not to kill me. You are a great hero of Troy — please spare me!" Aeneas replied, "What you are saying now is much different from what you yelled at me before. Your new words will not save you. You will accompany your brother as he travels to the Land of the Dead!" Aeneas plunged his sword into Liger's chest.

As Aeneas continued to slaughter many enemy warriors, Ascanius and his troops left the Trojan camp and reached a safer location.

On Mount Olympus, Jupiter teased his wife, Juno, "It is Venus, just as you thought, who makes the Trojans victorious — Aeneas' strong hands have nothing to do with it."

Juno replied, "Why try to anger me? I am saddened by what will happen. If only you loved me the way you used to love me, you would allow me to take Turnus away from the battlefield — unharmed. But I know what you want. You want him to die at the hands of Aeneas. But remember that Turnus has a notable heritage. One of his ancestors was Pilumnus, a woodland god. Also remember that Turnus has made many sacrifices to you."

Jupiter replied, "If you are asking for a temporary reprieve from death for Turnus, knowing all the while that he must soon die, then save his life for now. Take him away from the battle. I will allow you to do that much. But if you are asking for more than that — an ending to the war different from the ending that is fated — realize that that will not happen."

Crying, Juno said, "I wish that your heart were different from your words. I wish that Turnus could live a long life. However, although Turnus is innocent, he is fated to endure an early death. I wish that you would — you have the power to do it — give him a long life."

Juno flew down to the battle and created a phantom of Aeneas wearing Trojan armor. The phantom of Aeneas taunted Turnus, who threw a spear at it and then charged it. The phantom ran away, and Turnus ran after it, thinking that he was running after the real Aeneas.

Holding his sword in his right hand, Turnus shouted at the phantom, "To where are you fleeing, Aeneas? Why are you abandoning Lavinia, the bride you want so much? You have sought land in Italy, and my right hand will give you a few feet of land in which your corpse shall rest."

Nearby was the ship that the Etruscan Osinius had sailed in. Aeneas' phantom ran on board and hid itself. Turnus pursued the phantom, and once Turnus was on board, Juno cut the ropes that moored the ship and it sailed out to sea.

Turnus challenged the phantom of Aeneas, but the phantom vanished. The real Aeneas was still fighting and still looking for Turnus on the battlefield. Turnus then discovered that he was far from shore with no way of getting back. Not knowing that Juno had saved him from death, and thinking only about how what appeared to be his flight would result in a loss of honor, Turnus cried, "Jupiter, why are you punishing me? Where is this ship taking me? Is this ship taking me home? Why are you making me look like a coward? I had brave soldiers fighting for me — without me to lead them, they will probably die in battle. I see them dying. I see me in disgrace. I wish that the earth would open and swallow me! I wish that the winds would wreck this ship on rocks that are so far away that no one will know my shame!"

Turnus thought about what he should do. Should he commit suicide by falling on his sword? Should he jump into the sea and swim to shore and fight once more? Three times he thought of doing one thing. Three times he thought of doing the other thing. Juno would not allow him to do either. The ship carried Turnus to his home.

With Turnus gone, Mezentius led the attack, obeying the command of Jupiter. The Etruscans whom he had formerly cruelly ruled fiercely attacked him. They hated him, and they made him their sole target in the battle. He was like a rock standing up out of the ocean. The waves and winds batter it, but it still stands.

Mezentius killed Hebrus. He threw a rock and smashed Latagus' face and mouth. Palmus tried to run away, but Mezentius cut the tendons in the backs of his knees. Palmus writhed on the ground, and Mezentius gave to Lausus, his own son, Palmus' armor.

Mezentius then killed Euanthes and Mimas. Mimas was exactly the same age as Paris, Prince of Troy. Mimas' mother, Theano, gave birth to him the same day that Hecuba gave birth to Paris. Paris' corpse lay in Troy; Mimas' corpse lay in Italy.

Mezentius was like a wild boar that packs of dogs pursue down a mountain and toward the nets of hunters. The boar stops and the hunters attack him from a distance with spears — no hunter is brave enough to get close to him. Now, no warrior is brave enough to attack Mezentius up close with a sword. Instead, they stay at a distance from him and throw spears at him.

Mezentius saw Acron, a newly arrived Greek ally of Aeneas. Acron had gone into exile and left behind a marriage. Like a hungry lion that sees a goat or stag and pounces and bloodies its jaws with meat, Mezentius pounced on Acron and killed him.

Orodes ran away from Mezentius, who would not kill him with a spear from behind. Mezentius caught Orodes and turned him around and stabbed him with a sword in the front. Orodes fell, and Mezentius stabbed him with a spear.

Mezentius shouted, "Here lies a warrior who was among Aeneas' strongest!"

Dying, Orodes prophesized, "You don't have long to boast — you don't have long to live! Soon, you will lie dead on this battleground!"

Mezentius replied, "Jupiter will see about my death and when it will occur. As for you, you will die now!"

Mezentius pulled his spear out of Orodes' body, and Orodes' eyes saw the darkness that never ends.

Even without Turnus, the Rutulians and Mezentius' Etruscan allies were fighting well — although most Etruscans hated Mezentius and wanted him dead, a few Etruscans were loyal to him and fought for him. They had gone into exile with him.

Mezentius' Etruscan friend Caedicus killed Alcathous, Sacrator, and Hydaspes.

The Rutulian Rapo killed Parthenius and Orses.

Turnus' ally Messapus killed Clonius, who had been thrown from his horse. He also killed Erichaetes, who was fighting on foot.

Valerus, an Etruscan who fought for Mezentius, killed Agis, who fought for Aeneas.

The Rutulian Salius killed Thronius, and the Trojan Nealces killed Salius. Nealces fought well with spears and arrows.

If Aeneas had killed Turnus on the battlefield, the war would have been over. By saving Turnus' life, Juno had prolonged the war, getting more warriors killed. Mars, enjoying the slaughter, made both sides equal so that the battle would be long and many warriors on both sides would die. Other gods pitied the dying mortals. Venus watched the battle, as did Juno. In the midst of the battle, the Fury Tisiphone, snakes writhing in her hair, wreaked destruction.

Mezentius marched on the battlefield like the giant hunter Orion, whose shoulders rose above the water when he stood in the middle of the sea. When he stood on land, clouds hid his head.

Aeneas saw Mezentius and moved to fight him. Unafraid, Mezentius stood his ground and judged the distance between them. When Aeneas had come within range of Mezentius' spear, Mezentius cried, "My right arm is my only god. I pray to it that it will make my spear deadly! If I kill Aeneas, Lausus will wear Aeneas' armor. Lausus will be a living trophy of my victory over Aeneas."

Mezentius hurled his spear. It hit Aeneas' strong shield, bounced off, and hit Antores in between his side and groin. Antares had been the aide of Hercules, but had decided to serve Evander and stay in Italy. Killed by a spear that Mezentius had meant for Aeneas, Antores looked up at the sky and died as he thought of his Greek homeland.

Aeneas then hurled his spear at Mezentius. The spear tore through all the metal and bull's-hide layers of his shield and planted itself in Mezentius' groin, but the spear did not make a mortal wound.

Happy to have wounded Mezentius, Aeneas drew his sword and prepared to kill him, but Lausus, the loving son of Mezentius, protected him, although it meant that he — the good and loving son of a loving father who had been a cruel king — could die.

Mezentius backed away from Aeneas. Mezentius carried his shield, through which Aeneas' spear still stuck. Aeneas raised his sword, but Lausus stepped in front of his father and blocked Aeneas' sword. Mezentius' allies threw javelins at Aeneas. Imagine a storm with hailstones pelting the ground. Farmers and travelers seek shelter and safety until the sun returns and they can work or travel again. Aeneas stood behind the shelter of his shield until the hail of javelins stopped, and he said to Lausus, "Your love for your father will get you killed. You are not a match for me."

Lausus did not back away; instead, he attacked Aeneas, who was overcome by *furor*. The Fates finished spinning the thread of Lausus' life, and Aeneas plunged his sword to the hilt through Lausus' shield and tunic and embedded it in his body. Blood reddened Lausus' tunic, and his spirit, sorrowing, fled to the Land of the Dead.

Aeneas saw the look on Lausus' face as he died, and he pitied Lausus, a son who had deeply loved his father. Aeneas said to Lausus' corpse, "Is there anything I can do for your spirit now? Your love for your father is impressive. Keep your armor; I will not strip it off your body. You will receive a proper burial. And take comfort in that you died at the hands of a great warrior, for I am Aeneas."

Aeneas lifted Lausus off the ground, where the blood was soaking his hair, and he ordered Mezentius' Etruscan allies to come and carry away the corpse.

Mezentius had left the battlefield. He had bathed his wound by the river and now he was resting. His armor lay on the ground, and his helmet hung from a tree branch. Young soldiers stood guard around him. Mezentius was in pain, and he kept asking about his son, wanting Lausus to leave the battlefield — alive — and come to him.

Soon, Lausus' friends came carrying his body on his shield to Mezentius. Even while they were far away, Mezentius saw and heard them grieving and realized what had happened. He poured dust over his head, and then he held the corpse of his son and said, "Was I so fond of life that I wanted you to die for me? Did I want your death to save my life? No. I did not want this. This wound is worse than any mortal wound. I have been evil, but you have not, and you should not have died because of my sins. I have long owed my death to the Etruscans I so harshly ruled. I wish that I had paid that debt before you died. I am still alive — but not for long!"

Despite his painful wound, Mezentius stood up. His body was weak, but his spirit was strong. He ordered that his horse, Rhaebus, be brought to him, and he said to it, "We have been together for a long time, if that concept has any meaning in this world of mortality. Today, either we will kill Aeneas and avenge the death of Lausus, or you and I will both die. I do not believe that you would ever serve another master."

Mezentius armed himself and then mounted Rhaebus. He carried several spears as he rode toward Aeneas. Mezentius shouted to Aeneas three times. Aeneas recognized his voice and prayed to Jupiter and Apollo for victory. He shouted to Mezentius, "Let us fight!"

Mezentius replied, "You have already done to me the worst thing that you could do to me: kill my son. You have destroyed me in the only way you could ever destroy me. I do not fear death or the gods. So yes, let us fight!"

Mezentius rode Rhaebus in a circle around Aeneas and threw lances at him, but Aeneas' shield protected him. Aeneas kept tearing away the lances that lodged in his shield so he could continue to hold it up for protection.

Tired of being always on the defense, Aeneas decided on a course of action. He threw his spear at the head of Mezentius' horse — a direct hit! Rhaebus reared and then fell and died, dazing Mezentius and pinning him to the ground. Warriors on both sides shouted as Aeneas drew his sword and stood over Mezentius and said, "You used to be fierce. Where is your fierceness now?"

Mezentius recovered from his daze and said, "You have defeated me, so kill me — why bother to taunt me? In war, killing the enemy is not a crime. Neither of us has made an agreement to spare the other's life. My son made no pact with you that you would spare my life. I do ask one favor, if that is permitted. I know that the Etruscans hate me, and I ask that you bury my body. I want to share a burial-mound with my son."

Mezentius lifted his head and exposed his throat, and Aeneas drove his sword deep. Blood poured over Mezentius' chest.

Chapter 11: Camilla and Other Warriors

After the battle, the enemy warriors retreated to Latium, the country of King Latinus. Turnus was also there. The Trojans stayed at their camp.

At dawn, Aeneas made a trophy for Mars. He cut the branches off the trunk of an oak tree, and he hung Mezentius' bloody armor and weapons on the trunk so that it resembled the fallen warrior. Mezentius' breastplate had been pierced a dozen times — the result of the Etruscans' hatred for him.

Aeneas then spoke to his warriors: "We have won the battle, troops. We will win the war. You see here the armor and weapons of one of our most important enemies: Mezentius. I killed him. Now we will march against Laurentum: King Latinus' city. Make sure that you are prepared to fight. When we go to war, we must be prepared to be victorious.

"But now we must do two things. We must bury our dead with the honors that they deserve. They have died for a good cause, and we must show them respect. But even before that we must prepare Pallas' body so that he can be sent to his father, our ally, King Evander."

Aeneas, in tears, grieved for Pallas. Acoetes, an old man, was with Pallas. As a younger man, Acoetes had been King Evander's armor-bearer. At that time, the omens were favorable. But when Acoetus left Pallanteum with Pallas and Aeneas, the omens were not favorable.

Around the corpse of Pallas was an honor guard of soldiers. Also present were many Trojan women with their hair unbound. They cried and shouted with grief and beat their breasts.

Aeneas looked at the corpse of Pallas. Because of the loss of blood, Pallas' face was very white. His chest bore a savage spear wound.

Aeneas said to the corpse, "A little while ago, you were alive and happy. Now you will never see the Trojans build a city. You will never return home to your father alive and triumphant. I promised your father to watch after you, but I failed to keep you alive. Your father warned me that the warriors we would fight were dangerous and brave and used to battle. Right now, not knowing that you are dead, your father is likely sacrificing and praying to the gods for your safe return. But we will bring to him only your corpse.

"King Evander, you will suffer the worst thing that a parent can suffer: the funeral of your child. The son who would have ruled Pallanteum after your death is now dead.

"But at least Pallas died bravely. He did not run from danger. He did not run away and disgrace himself so that he could continue to live. King Evander, you will know that you have a brave and honorable son. But Italy has lost a man who would have been a good king, and my son has lost someone who would have been a good friend to him."

Aeneas then sent Pallas' body back to King Evander. He chose a thousand troops to carry the corpse back and to mourn at the funeral. A funeral can offer only little comfort, but King Evander deserved whatever comfort he could find. Aeneas' people built a bed of wickerwork on which to place the corpse and carry it. Pallas' corpse lay on the wickerwork like a flower that a girl has cut. The flower is dead, but it is still beautiful. Aeneas brought two robes that Dido had made and given to him. These were used to cover Pallas' body — a body that would soon be burned on a funeral-pyre.

Aeneas ordered much of the plunder that his troops had seized after winning the battle to be sent to King Evander along with Pallas' body. Aeneas also sent horses and weapons. In the battle, Aeneas had captured twelve enemy warriors. He sent them — their hands tied behind their backs — so that they could shed their blood as a human sacrifice at the funeral. He also ordered trophies to be sent: tree trunks with limbs cut off that bore the armor and weapons and names of fallen enemy warriors.

Old Acoetes mourned, beating his chest and clawing at his face and stumbling and falling on the ground. The Trojans helped him up and journeyed with him to King Evander. In the procession were chariots that were covered with the blood of enemies. Aethon, Pallas' horse, mourned, tears trickling down his face. Pallas' spear and helmet would be returned to King Evander — Turnus had the rest of Pallas' armor, including the sword-belt.

The long cortege set off to bear Pallas' corpse to King Evander, and Aeneas mourned, "I cannot go with you. The war continues, and I must fight and lead my troops into battle. Farewell, Pallas." He returned to the Trojan camp.

Envoys came to Aeneas from King Latinus' city. They displayed olive branches to show that they did not intend to fight but had come for a different reason. They asked for a truce in which to bury the dead: "It is time for us to return these defeated, dead warriors to the earth. They need a proper burial. There is no need to punish them by not allowing their bodies to be buried — they have already been defeated and killed and so will never fight again, and at one time you regarded them as your hosts."

Aeneas agreed to the truce, saying, "Why have you fought us and then fled from us? We should be your friends. You want peace for the dead? I grant that. I am also willing to grant peace to the living. Why are we Trojans here in Italy? Because it is our fate to make our home here. If not for fate, we would never have come here. I did not start the war. King Latinus and I had a pact of peace, but the Latins who serve him broke the pact and started the war — a war that Turnus fights. Many people would live if Turnus were to die. Turnus and I should have fought a single combat to the death, thus sparing the lives of many warriors. I agree to this truce. Go and bury your dead."

The envoys were impressed by the way that Aeneas had spoken.

Drances, an aging Rutulian and a personal enemy to Turnus, was willing to build Aeneas up and to tear Turnus down. He said, "Great Aeneas, you are worthy of praise. You are just, and you are a mighty warrior. We will carry news of the truce you have consented to back to King Latinus. If we can, we will make you friends with King Latinus and let Turnus find new allies. We will even help you, if we can, to build a new Troy!"

The other envoys agreed with Drances. The truce held for twelve days, and the Trojans and their enemies worked close to each other without incident during that time as they cut wood with which to build funeral-pyres.

Rumors now reached King Evander. He had heard news at first of Pallas' triumphs, but now came news of his death. Pallas' body arrived with its long cortege of mourners; in Pallanteum, the citizens greeted the cortege with funeral torches. The mothers of the city wailed with grief.

King Evander went to the corpse of his son and threw himself on it. He cried, "Pallas, you promised me that you would be careful, that you would do nothing rash. I know that a young man can be overeager to do mighty deeds in battle and not realize the battle's dangers. I prayed to the gods for your safety, but the gods did not grant my prayer. In contrast to me, my wife, your mother, was blessed — she died before you died. She cannot feel the grief that I feel. My fate is evil: I outlived my son! I should have gone to war alongside the Trojans and been killed with a spear in battle. Better it would have been if the Trojans had brought my corpse — not yours — to Pallanteum. I do not blame the Trojans for your death — the Trojans and we are friends. I blame fate for your early death. But at least I know that you gained glory in battle!

"Now we will give you a proper funeral that will be attended by the trophies of the enemy warriors whom you killed in battle. One trophy, however, is missing — the trophy of Turnus, the trophy that will bear Turnus' bloody armor. If you, Pallas, had been as old and as strong as Turnus, his trophy would be here now.

"Trojans, tell Aeneas that the reason I keep on living now that my son is dead is that I wait for Aeneas to kill Turnus. Aeneas owes me the life of Turnus, the warrior who killed my son. Killing Turnus will bring Aeneas glory; it will not bring me joy, for it is now impossible for me to feel joy. But when I die, I want to take to my son the news that Turnus is dead."

When dawn arrived, Aeneas and his Etruscan ally Tarchon erected funeral-pyres on which to burn their dead. They put the dead on the pyres, set the pyres on fire, and performed the proper rites, riding three times on horseback around the burning pyres. They wept, and they shouted cries of grief.

Some mourners heaped the property of enemy warriors on the pyres: helmets, swords, bridles, and chariot wheels. Others heaped the shields and spears of the fallen friendly warriors on the pyres. Others made sacrifices to the gods: swine and cattle and sheep. All day the funeral-pyres burned.

Elsewhere, the enemy also built funeral-pyres for their dead. Some dead were sent back to their hometowns for burial rites. Many of the dead could not be recognized, so they were burned in a common funeral-pyre. After the bodies were burned, the mourners piled earth over the bones.

Cries of grief filled the city of King Latinus. Mothers and brides and sisters and fatherless boys mourned. They hated the war, and they said, "Turnus wants to marry Lavinia. Turnus wants to rule western Italy. Turnus is the one who should fight Aeneas. This is his fight — it ought not to be our fight!"

Drances deliberately caused hate and discontent. He swore that Aeneas had challenged Turnus to single combat. But many people still supported Turnus, including Amata, the queen. Turnus was still respected — he had achieved notable victories in battle.

Now the envoys who had traveled to Diomedes' city to ask him for his support in the war returned — with bad news for Turnus: "Diomedes will not fight with us against Aeneas. If we are to have allies, we must find them elsewhere — or we must ask Aeneas for peace."

After hearing this news, King Latinus believed that the Fates really must have ordered Aeneas to come to Italy. By opposing Aeneas, his warriors deserved their new graves. King Latinus called a council. Unhappy, he ordered the envoys who had seen Diomedes to make their report.

Venulus, the leader of the envoys, said, "We have seen Diomedes and his city, and we have talked to him. We traveled through dangerous lands, and we clasped Diomedes' hand — the hand that conquered Troy. He is in the midst of building his city, which he has named Argyripa, in northwest Italy.

"We gave him our gifts and talked to him about Aeneas, our enemy. He replied, 'You have been happily at peace, so why do you now seek war? You do not know the evils of war. Those of us who fought at Troy know the pain of fighting and the pain of losing warriors. We still suffer pain. Many of us are strewn around the world, far from the lands that we used to call home. We have been punished for our crimes, and now even Priam might pity us. Minerva has been angry at us, and she has shown us the consequences of her anger. Menelaus has been driven far from his homeland; he has been long an exile. Ulysses, far from home, has seen the Cyclopes. The son of Achilles, Pyrrhus, reigned only briefly and is now dead. Idomeneus returned to Crete, but his citizens banished him after he killed his son. The Locrians fought at Troy, but on their way home they were shipwrecked in Libya. Agamemnon returned home, but immediately his wicked wife murdered him. Agamemnon had conquered Asia, but an adulteress killed him.

"'What about me? The gods have not allowed me to stay at my old home and be with my wife. The omens I see terrify me — they show my comrades turned into lamenting birds! I deserve my punishment — at Troy, I dared to attack and wound Venus!

"'I am not willing to fight with you against Aeneas. I have not fought the Trojans since the Trojan War, and I see no need to fight them now. After all, I hardly look back on the Trojan War with joy. You have brought gifts for me, but I advise you to take the gifts and give them to Aeneas. I have fought him face to face. I know what a mighty warrior he is! If Troy had had two more warriors like Aeneas, Troy would have won the war and then would have crossed the sea and attacked Greece. The Greeks would now be in mourning. If Troy had had two more warriors like Aeneas, the Fates would have decreed a good destiny for Troy. We Greeks fought for ten years at Troy on equal terms with the Trojans because of Aeneas and Hector, who kept the Greeks from victory for so many years. Aeneas and Hector were both courageous, and both were mighty warriors, but Aeneas was first in *pietas*. My advice to you is to make peace with Aeneas and the Trojans. It is not wise to make war against them.'

"This is what Diomedes said to us. This is Diomedes' advice to us."

Troubled conversations broke out among the Italians. The sound was like rocks resisting the swift water in a river, and the banks of the river echo the sound. When the conversations died down, King Latinus said, "We would have done much better if we had made peace with the Trojans long ago. Now the Trojans are our enemies, and they are camped nearby. The Trojans are descended from the gods, and the Trojans are mighty warriors. They may have been defeated in the Trojan War, but they are far from laying down their swords. Even after defeat, they are dangerous. Diomedes will not become our ally; if we fight the Trojans, we must alone fight them. We have fought as well as we can fight, but we have been defeated. None of us is to blame; the Trojans are simply mightier warriors than we are.

"I want to make a proposal of peace to the Trojans. Our kingdom has land along the Tiber River. Much of it is good cropland; the other parts are good for grazing herds. I want to give the Trojans this land and some good timberland if they wish to stay here and build a city. But if they wish to sail to another land, we will build them twenty ships — more if the Trojans need more ships — out of timber. We have the metal and the shipwrights needed to build the ships.

"I want to send one hundred envoys to the Trojans to bear news of this offer of peace. The envoys will carry olive branches to show that they want peace. They will bring the Trojans gifts: gold, ivory, and other good things.

"Talk over my proposal. I think that my proposal is the best for our kingdom."

Drances then rose to speak. He hated Turnus, and he envied Turnus' glory. Drances spent money freely, and he spoke even more freely. In battle, he was a weakling. His strengths were debate and power politics. His mother was noble, but no one was quite sure who was his father.

Drances said, "Obviously, our situation is poor. Everyone knows that, although many do not want to admit it. Turnus needs to allow us to speak the truth. He is a proud man, but his leadership is poor. He can threaten me with death if he likes, but I will speak up. Many of our best people have died in battle — a battle from which Turnus sailed away alone in a ship!

"King Latinus, your offer of peace to the Trojans is good, but I advise you to add one more gift for Aeneas. Allow him to marry your daughter. You are her father, and Aeneas will make you a good son-in-law. A marriage will result in peace.

"Let Turnus agree to let Aeneas marry Lavinia. Why should Turnus get so many of us killed because he wants to marry Lavinia? He is the cause of the war — we are the ones who suffer! We need peace!

"Turnus, I am the first one to speak out against you, and you believe that I am your enemy. Should it matter that I am your enemy? Do the right thing! Take pity on the families of the warriors who have died, and seek peace! You have been defeated, so act like it! We are tired of death. We are tired of seeing our kingdom devastated.

"Turnus, if you want to be a hero, you can be a hero by meeting Aeneas in single combat. That is the way for you to win your bride! That is better than letting us die so that you can marry Lavinia. You regard our lives as being worth less than your own. Our corpses are the ones littering the battlefield. Aeneas is challenging you to single combat — accept the challenge!"

Drances would be happy if Aeneas were to kill Turnus in single combat.

Filled with *furor*, Turnus replied, "You are a mighty warrior, Drances — but with words, not weapons! At councils, you are always the first citizen to speak. You keep talking — that is what you are good at. You are brave as long as you are behind high defensive walls and a trench.

"But you are saying that I am a coward. I will believe you as soon as I see heaps of Trojans that you have slain. When you have killed as many Trojans as I have killed, I will believe what you say about courage and cowardice.

"Drances, march with me against the Trojans. They are near; they will not be difficult to find. What? You aren't willing to fight the Trojans? You find it much safer to fight with words than with weapons.

"Drances, you say that I am defeated, but many Trojans are dead — the Tiber River swelled because of their blood. Ask King Evander if I am defeated. Ask his warriors if I am defeated. Ask Pandarus and Bitias and the many warriors I killed when I was the only Rutulian inside the Trojan camp if I am defeated.

"Drances, you say that we cannot win the war. Go and tell that to Aeneas and make him happy; you can find a way to personally benefit from being a traitor. Here you are, trying to create panic in your hearers by criticizing the warriors of your own country.

"Drances, I suppose that you believe that everyone is afraid of the Trojan warriors. The warriors of Achilles are afraid of them, Diomedes is afraid of them, and you seem to think that we are supposed to believe that even Achilles was afraid of them.

"Drances, you are putting on an act right now. You are pretending to be afraid of me and you are cowering. You have attacked my courage. Now you are attacking my character by pretending that I am a bully. You need not be afraid. I am not going to attack you. I am not going to kill you. Your heart will keep on beating inside the body of a coward.

"King Evander, if you truly think that we are defeated, then we should beg for peace, but are we defeated? At one time, we were courageous. The best men are those who reject surrender. A good man is one who will not surrender, but who will fight and die.

"King Evander, if we still have warriors and weapons, if we still have Italian allies, if the Trojans have also suffered in battle and have lost many warriors, then why should we give up and surrender now? Why should we lack courage?

"The Wheel of Fortune turns, and those once brought low are then raised high. Many men have been defeated before, but Fortune has then made them victorious. True, Diomedes declines to fight with us. But Messapus will fight with us, Tolumnius will fight with us, and many other men will. So will Camilla, who is the head of many horsemen.

"If Aeneas calls on me to fight him in single combat, and if you want me to accept, I will. I am no stranger to victory in combat. I am willing to fight Aeneas even if he is strong enough to defeat Achilles and even if he is wearing armor the equal of Achilles' divine armor. Let he and I fight! That is something that Drances is not willing to do."

Aeneas had been busy. He and his warriors had left the Trojan camp, and they were prepared for battle. He had sent out some troops ahead of the others.

A messenger now came into the Italian council and blurted, "The enemy army is advancing against us! The Trojans and their allies are coming!" Panic and confusion spread in King Latinus' city. Many young warriors shouted, "To battle!" But their elderly fathers mourned. The many cries in the city were like the cries of a flock of birds in a grove of trees or the cries of swans in the Padusa River.

In the council, Turnus said, "While you are praising peace, your enemies are preparing to kill you!"

Turnus left the council and gave orders: "Volusus, lead your warriors outside the city. Messapus, you and Coras, and Catillus, Coras' twin brother, lead the cavalry. One group of warriors will stand here and guard the city. All other warriors, come with me!"

King Latinus left the council. Now he could not put his plans for peace into effect. He blamed himself for not making peace earlier — he blamed himself for not making Aeneas an ally instead of an enemy.

The warriors prepared for war. Boys and mothers were on the walls, ready to defend them. The queen and other ladies rode on horseback and took gifts to the temple of Minerva to pray for her protection. Beside Queen Amata rode Lavinia, the bride over whom the war was being fought and warriors were dying. Lavinia's eyes looked down at the ground. At the temple, the ladies burned incense and prayed, "Minerva, shatter the spear of Aeneas, and shatter Aeneas!"

Turnus armed himself and went out to lead the army. He was like a stallion that has broken free of its tether and now runs to a pasture to mingle with mares or to plunge into a river.

Camilla, the warrior woman, met Turnus. Camilla and her horsemen dismounted, and Camilla said to Turnus, "Let me meet the enemy troops. Aeneas has sent his cavalry ahead of his other troops. Let me and my cavalry fight them. You can stay here and guard the walls of the city."

Turnus said, "Camilla, warrior princess, thank you. You are courageous, but I will share the fight with you outside the walls of the city. As you say, Aeneas has sent his cavalry ahead of his other troops. I have learned that Aeneas himself is marching here with his infantry through hilly terrain, and I am going to set an ambush at a path Aeneas will take through a gorge. You and your cavalry can fight the Etruscan cavalry Aeneas has sent ahead of his other troops. You can lead the attack; backing you up will be Messapus and his cavalry and Tiburtus' warriors."

Turnus knew the terrain around the city, and he knew well the path that Aeneas and his infantry would take. It was a narrow path, and alongside it were walls of rock from the tops of which warriors could throw weapons or drop boulders or ride down and attack Aeneas and his troops. Turnus and his warriors went there and waited to ambush Aeneas.

On Mount Olympus, Diana, who knew the fates of mortals, called for Opis, an immortal nymph who served her. Diana was a virgin goddess, and her followers — whether immortal or mortal — were also virgins. Opis and Camilla were both virgin followers of Diana.

Diana said to Opis, "Camilla is putting on armor to fight in war, but her fighting will be in vain. She will not get the result she wants. I love and respect her, and she loves and respects me.

"This is Camilla's story. Her father, Metabus, became a tyrant and his people hated him and drove him away. They pursued him as he ran away with Camilla, his daughter, who was then an infant. Her mother's name is slightly different: Casmilla.

"Metabus fled through woods, and enemy weapons forced him to go to the Amasenus River, then in flood. To escape his enemies, Metabus had to swim the river, but he loved his daughter and would not risk her life. He tied her to a spear and cushioned her with corkwood. He then threw his spear and Camilla across the river, first praying to me, 'Diana, I give this baby girl to you. She will worship you. I ask you for your mercy. Protect my infant daughter as she travels through the air to the opposite shore!'

He hurled the spear that carried his daughter across the river, and as his enemies arrived, he jumped into the river and swam across it. With joy, he discovered that I had protected Camilla — she was safe.

Metabus stayed away from cities, preferring to live in the woods and raise his daughter there. He fed Camilla with milk from a wild mare, squirting milk from its udders directly into her mouth. When Camilla began to toddle and take her first steps, he gave her a tiny spear and a tiny bow and arrows. She did not wear a gold band around her head. For clothing, she used the skin of a tiger. She hurled her tiny spears. With a slingshot, she killed birds.

"When Camilla reached puberty, many mothers wanted her to marry their sons, but she remained devoted to me and stayed a virgin. She loves chastity and hunting, but now she is going to war against the Trojans. I wish that she had stayed at her home. She would continue to live and continue to serve me.

"I have orders for you, Opis. Go down to the battle, where the omens are bad for Camilla and for Turnus. Take my bow and quiver of arrows. Watch the battle, and after Camilla is killed, take one of my arrows and avenge her death by killing the person who killed her. I myself will take Camilla's body to her home so that it can receive a proper funeral."

Opis obeyed the orders of Diana. Taking Diana's bow and quiver of arrows, she flew down to the battlefield. No one saw her; she had wrapped herself in a whirlwind.

Some Trojan forces and the Etruscan cavalry advanced toward King Latinus' city: Laurentum. Warriors carried many spears across the plain in front of the city. Messapus, Coras, and Camilla and their troops also appeared with their weapons and marched against the forces opposing them.

When the two forces of warriors had come so close that a spear could be thrown from one army to the other, the two armies rushed forward and fought. The Etruscan Tyrrhenus and the Italian Aconteus rode against each other, charging with spears. Their horses crashed together and broke ribs. Aconteus fell off his horse. Badly injured, he gasped and died.

The Italians fled on their horses, and the Trojans and the Etruscans chased them. The Italians carried their shields on their backs for protection as the Etruscan seer Asilas and his horsemen chased them. When the Italians had nearly reached the walls of their city, they turned around and attacked. Now the Trojans and the Etruscans turned around, and their enemy chased them.

Waves wash up on a shore, going high, and then they reverse direction and retreat. So it was with the Trojans and the Etruscans and their enemy. They kept reversing direction: The first group chased the second group, and then the second group chased the first group.

But then the two groups closed together and fought warrior to warrior. The air filled with the groans of dying warriors, weapons and blood and dead warriors and horses covered the ground, and dying horses writhed.

The Trojan Orsilochus was wary of fighting the Rutulian Remulus on horseback, so he threw his lance at Remulus' horse, spearing it below an ear. In agony, the horse reared and threw Remulus, who rolled on the ground.

Catillus, an ally of Turnus, killed Iollas and the huge warrior Herminius, who fought with his shoulders bare because he did not fear injuries. But Catillus speared him, and the head of the spear exited through Herminius' back, and Herminius felt the agony of the wound.

The battlefield was filled with pools of blood, the crashes of weapons against shields, death, and wounded warriors and horses.

Camilla fought with one breast bared — her weapons were spears and arrows and a double-headed battle-ax. Even when she retreated on horseback, she shot arrows at her pursuers. Fighting with Camilla were other warrior maidens: Tulla, Larina, and Tarpeia, who fought with an ax. They were like the Amazons of Thrace who fought around Queen Hippolyte or who cried out to welcome Queen Penthesilea.

Camilla killed and killed again. She ran toward Eunaeus and speared him, and he vomited blood and writhed on the ground and died. The Trojan Liris fell to the ground when his horse was injured, and his friend Pagasus ran to help him. Camilla killed both of them. Camilla then killed Amastrus. Throwing spears, she killed Tereus, Harpalycus. Demophoön, and Chromis. She did not miss with her spears.

Ornytus, a hunter who was an Etruscan ally of Aeneas, wore unusual armor to the battle. He wore a bull's-hide over his shoulders. For a helmet, he wore the head of a wolf. For a weapon, he carried a hunter's javelin. He was taller than the other warriors by a head, but when he and the warriors with him were retreating, Camilla chased him and pierced his body with a spear, saying, "This is a battle, not a hunt. My spear has made that clear to you. You will be able to tell the other ghosts in the Land of the Dead that you were killed by no ordinary warrior — Camilla killed you!"

Camilla then killed the Trojans Butes and Orsilochus. While Butes' back was turned toward her, she speared him in the neck, under his helmet. Then she outsmarted Orsilochus. She fled from him and raced her swift horse in a circle so quickly that the pursued became the pursuer. He begged her for mercy, but she raised her battle-ax and smashed his head many times, cutting through his helmet and his skull and splattering his brain onto his face.

Camilla then faced Aunus' son, a noted liar who was terrified to see her. He tried to trick his way out of death. Both Aunus' son and Camilla were on horseback, and Aunus' son said to her, "Your horse deserves much of the credit for your victories in battle. Meet me face to face on the ground, and we will see who is victorious!"

Camilla was willing to fight Aunus' son on the ground. She dismounted and gave her horse to an aide and stood with a sword waiting for Aunus' son to dismount, but he immediately attempted to gallop away from Camilla and his death.

She said, "Fool and liar! Your trick will not work! You will not return to your homeland alive!"

She ran and grabbed the horse's bridle and killed the son of Aunus. She was like a falcon diving down from the sky and seizing a dove and ripping it to bloody pieces. Drops of blood and bloody feathers fall from the sky.

Jupiter was watching the battle. He now sent courage in battle to the Etruscan leader Tarchon, one of Aeneas' allies. Tarchon led his cavalry and spurred them on with words: "Are you cowards? Look at the damage that a woman is doing to us! Are our swords useless? Are our spears useless? When it is time to have sex or dance or eat and drink, you show no fear. Isn't the battlefield another place where you should have no fear?"

Ready to die if his death were fated, Tarchon rode his warhorse into the midst of the battle. He rode straight at Venulus, grabbed him and pulled him off his horse, and holding him tightly, he rode away with his enemy. Tarchon first broke off the tip of Venulus' spear and then searched for a mortal spot so that he could kill him. Venulus fought to keep Tarchon's hand from his throat. Tarchon was like an eagle that has seized a snake — the snake fights back, but the eagle clasps its talons all the more tightly around the snake. Tarchon, triumphant, rode away with Venulus.

Tarchon's Etruscans were inspired by his success. Arruns, an Etruscan ally of Aeneas, began to stalk Camilla, wanting to kill her without losing his own life. He did not know that on this day he would die. He followed Camilla, and whenever she turned around and came toward him, he retreated. Continually, he tried to get close enough to her — without her seeing him — to kill her.

Camilla saw the Trojan Chloreus, a priest of Cybele, the Great Mother of Gods. Cybele was the wife of Saturn and the mother of many of the Olympian gods, including Jupiter and Poseidon. Works of art often showed Cybele seated with lions by her side. Worship of her included dancing to the music of drum and fife. The priests of the Phrygian goddess Cybele were known as Corybantes, whose worship of Cybele included an ecstasy in which they castrated themselves.

Chloreus was dressed in gaudy armor with lots of red and purple and yellow. He carried a bow made of gold, and he wore a gold helmet. His cape was saffron, and he wore a golden brooch. Camilla may have wanted to dedicate Chloreus' armor and clothing to Diana, or she may have wanted his armor and clothing for herself, but she was attracted by the gaudy armor and clothing and she wanted it. She stalked Chloreus, neglecting to pay enough attention to the other enemy warriors.

Arruns saw his chance to kill Camilla. He prayed, "Apollo, we worship you and we even walk on fire for you as part of our worship of you. Let me be victorious over Camilla, who has killed so many of our warriors. I am not out for plunder or even for glory. I can gain those with other feats in battle. Just let me kill this girl, even though I gain no plunder from the kill. And let me return to my father's land alive and unharmed."

Apollo heard the prayer, but he would grant only part of it. Yes, Arruns would kill Camilla. But no, Arruns would not return to his father's land alive and unharmed. That part of the prayer Apollo allowed the winds to scatter.

Arruns threw his spear. Camilla's warriors heard the spear and turned and watched as it struck Camilla beneath her naked breast and sank deep in her body. Camilla's attendants ran to catch her as she fell off her horse. Arruns did not stay to glory over his kill, but instead quickly galloped away, hoping to outrace death.

Arruns was like a wolf that has killed a shepherd or an ox. The wolf knows that men with spears will be out for revenge, so it runs away, its tail between its legs, hoping to disappear before the armed men can take revenge. Arruns hoped to escape, and so he ran away.

Camilla tried to pull out the spear, but she could not. She had lost much blood, and she was weak and growing weaker. Her eyes were becoming useless, she was growing colder, and her face was growing paler. With only a few breaths remaining to her, she told her fellow woman warrior Acca, "This is my last battle. Go to Turnus and tell him that he must return and defend the city from the Trojans and their allies. Goodbye."

Camilla died. She dropped her weapons, and her breath left her body. Her spirit went to the Land of the Dead.

Her warriors and their allies grieved for her, and their cries reached the golden stars. The Trojans and their allies attacked more fiercely now that Camilla had died, and they shouted cries of war.

Opis, the attendant of Diana, had kept watch. She saw Camilla die, and she mourned, "Your death is cruel. You should still be alive. But Diana has remembered you. You have gained honor in battle, and your death will gain you honor. An arrow of Diana shall avenge you.

Opis flew to the burial-mound of Dercennus, a king of old. She saw Arruns, who was proud of his kill, galloping away from the battle and toward the burial-mound. Opis shouted, "Why are you galloping so quickly? You are racing toward your well-deserved death!"

Opis fitted one of Diana's arrows to the bow and drew back the bow until its ends almost touched each other. She loosed the arrow. Arruns heard the arrow coming toward him, and he heard it enter his flesh. He fell from his horse and gasped his final breath, alone. Opis returned to Diana and Olympus.

The Trojans and their allies routed the enemy. Left without a leader, Camilla's cavalry fled first, followed closely by the Rutulians. Atinas, a brave Rutulian leader, also fled. The Trojans' enemies raced for their city's walls, and the Trojans and allies pursued and killed them. The mothers of the Trojans' enemies wailed.

The Trojans and their allies killed many Rutulians and their allies in front of the gates. Some warriors closed the gates, leaving friends outside — friends begging for the gates to be opened so that they could reach safety. Warriors fought, and some fell in the trenches. Mothers on the walls of the city emulated Camilla and fought, dropping heavy wooden beams from the walls onto their enemies. Their hands trembled as they lifted the heavy beams, but the mothers were willing to die for their city. They fought with weapons of wood, not metal.

Turnus was still lying in ambush, waiting for Aeneas and his troops. Acca brought him the news that Camilla had died and the Trojans were routing Turnus' allies. As Jupiter desired, Turnus was filled with *furor* and abandoned the ambush. Almost as soon as Turnus abandoned the ambush, Aeneas and his troops arrived. If Turnus had stayed only a little while longer, he could have inflicted heavy damage on his enemy.

Now two armies sped toward the walls of Laurentum: Turnus' army and Aeneas' army. The two armies were close, and Turnus and Aeneas looked at each other. They would have fought immediately, but darkness arrived. Aeneas' army camped in front of the city; Turnus' army fortified the walls of the city.

Chapter 12: A Destiny Fulfilled

Turnus knew that his troops had been defeated again in a major battle. Twice they had faced Aeneas' troops, and twice Aeneas' troops had defeated them. Turnus knew that he should meet Aeneas in single combat. Turnus was like a lion that fights hunters more fiercely after the hunters have deeply wounded it. Then the lion is willing to fight. The lion bites and breaks off the spear in its body, and it roars, unafraid of wounds.

Inside the walls of Laurentum, Turnus said to King Latinus, "I will not keep the Trojans waiting. Aeneas and I will fight in single combat. The Trojans have no reason to avoid the single combat. Start the sacred rites and form a pact with the Trojans for the single combat. I will fight and defeat Aeneas, who fled from Troy. I alone — with my warriors watching — will show that we are not cowards. The alternative is that Aeneas will rule a defeated people and Lavinia will be his bride."

King Latinus calmly replied, "Turnus, no one doubts your courage, but I need to consider what is best for my people as a whole. You have a kingdom of your own. Your father, Daunus, has many towns for you to rule, and you have conquered other towns with your sword. I, King Latinus, have wealth and am willing to share it. Listen. In my kingdom are many unwed girls who need husbands. They can marry any of several suitors. But the gods have plans for Lavinia. The gods forbid me to marry Lavinia to an Italian suitor. The gods and the prophets have clearly stated that that would be wrong. But out of my love for you, and because of our kinship and the wishes of my wife, I allowed Lavinia to be engaged to you, although the gods want Aeneas to be her husband. We are wrong when we wage war against the Trojans.

"You have seen the results of our unjust war. Twice we have fought major battles, and twice we have been defeated. Our enemies, who should be our friends, camp outside our city. The Tiber River is still red with our blood. Our bones still lie on the battlefield.

"I must obey the gods. If you, Turnus, were to die in battle, I would accept Aeneas as my son-in-law. Why should I not accept Aeneas as my son-in-law now, while you are still alive? If I let you fight and die, what will your Rutulians think of my people and me? Give up your desire for marriage with my daughter. Do what is best for your aged father, who does not want you to die."

King Latinus' words made Turnus only more eager to fight Aeneas. He replied, "Do not worry about my death. I am willing to trade death for glory and fame. And remember that I have weapons and that I am a warrior — the wounds that I inflict make much blood flow. When I fight Aeneas, I think that his mother, Venus, will be far away and unable to hide her son in fog to keep him safe."

Queen Amata, worried about the single combat, said to Turnus, "Let my tears influence your decision. Do not fight Aeneas in single combat. In your warrior's hands rest the fate of our kingdom. In your warrior's hands rest my own fate. If you fall in single combat, I will also die. I am not willing to stay alive if it means seeing Aeneas marry Lavinia."

Lavinia was present and listening to the debate. Hearing her mother's words, she wept and blushed. Her cheeks were like ivory dyed red. Her cheeks were like white lilies that take on a ruddy hue when surrounded by red roses.

Turnus looked at Lavinia as she blushed. Inflamed with love, he said to Queen Amata, "I will fight Aeneas in single combat, so don't say anything that can be interpreted as an evil omen. My fate, whatever it is, is already set."

Turnus then said to Idmon, a fellow Rutulian, "Take a message to Aeneas — a message that I doubt he will like. At dawn, he must not attack the city; instead, he and I will meet in single combat. The blood of our warriors shall not end this war; instead, either his blood or my blood will end this war."

Turnus left and went to his horses to make sure that they would be ready. His horses were magnificent and swift. They were gifts from Orithyia, who had married Boreas, the North wind. She had given them to Pilumnus, an ancestor of Turnus. Turnus' charioteers were grooming them and getting them ready for the next day.

Turnus then armed himself with breastplate, shield, helmet, and a sword that had been made for his father, Daunus, by the fire-god himself, Vulcan, who had plunged it into the Styx River. He also armed himself with a spear that he had taken as plunder from Actor, an enemy. Turnus shook the spear and said, "You have never failed me in battle. The great warrior Actor wielded you in battle, and now I wield you. Help me to kill Aeneas and strip his breastplate and destroy it. Aeneas is nothing but a eunuch! Let me make his perfumed hair bloody in the dust!"

Furor consumed Turnus. Fire consumed him. Turnus was like a bull before it goes into battle. It bellows, it buries its horns in tree trunks, and it challenges the wind as it prepares to do battle.

Aeneas had received Turnus' message and was happy that a single combat would end the war. He spoke to his friends and his son about fate, and he sent envoys to King Latinus to set the terms of the peace that would follow the single combat.

Just before dawn, the Trojans and their enemies prepared the dueling ground in front of the city and set up altars to their common gods. Both armies were present; thousands of warriors would witness the single combat. Among the leaders present were the Trojan Mnestheus, the Etruscan seer and Trojan ally Asilas, and the Rutulian Messapus. The time for the single combat arrived. The warriors put aside their spears and shields. Watching from the walls of the city were unarmed mothers and old men.

Juno watched from a mountain. At that time, it had no name, but now it is called the Alban mountain. She saw the two armies, and she saw the dueling ground. Always ready to interfere and cause trouble for Aeneas, she called Juturna to her. Juturna was the sister of Turnus. She had once been a mortal girl, but Jupiter had raped her and as recompense for her stolen virginity, he had made her an immortal nymph. Juno normally hated the women whom Jupiter had slept with — it made no difference to her whether they had slept with him willingly or unwillingly — but Juturna was perhaps the only former sex partner of her husband whom she liked.

Juno said to Juturna, a water nymph whose name combined the names Juno and Turnus, "I like you by far the most of all the Italian women who have slept with my husband. You have a place among the gods. Sorrow is coming to you, but I am not to blame. I have protected your brother, Turnus, but his day of death is approaching. Today, he is supposed to fight in single combat against a warrior who is stronger than he is. I cannot and will not watch the single combat, but you are Turnus' sister. Perhaps you can help him. You may be able to stave off his day of death."

Juturna wept and beat her breasts.

Juno said to her, "You have no time to weep. You must hurry if you are to help your brother. If you can, save your brother's life as he fights this duel. Or you may be able to avoid the duel by breaking the truce and starting the war again. These are my ideas, but only you can put them into effect!"

Juno left Juturna mourning for her brother, Turnus.

King Latinus rode a four-horse chariot to the dueling ground. Turnus carried two javelins and arrived in a two-horse chariot. Aeneas walked to the dueling ground, carrying his shield and wearing his divinely made armor. Ascanius walked by Aeneas' side.

A priest wearing white robes brought a boar and a sheep for the sacrifice.

Aeneas stated the terms of the duel: "Gods, witness what I say! If Turnus achieves victory in the duel, then the Trojans will go to Pallanteum, the city of Evander, and Ascanius will leave your land. The Trojans will never again attack your city and your land.

"But if I achieve victory in the duel — as I think I will, gods willing — I will not make Italians be the servants of Trojans. I will not seek to be king over Italians. Instead, Trojans and Italians will both be at peace and obey the same laws. I will worship my gods here and follow my religious rites. King Latinus will keep his army and his power. I will be his son-in-law. We Trojans will build our city, which we will name Lavinium, after Lavinia."

King Latinus then raised one hand and put his other hand on the altar and said, "I swear by the gods that we will never break this pact. That will never happen just as this wooden scepter I am holding will never again sprout green leaves."

They sealed the pact of peace and sacrificed the animals.

The Rutulians, however, believed that the duel would be unequal — they believed that Aeneas had much the advantage over Turnus. They looked at both Aeneas and Turnus — Aeneas seemed much the stronger of the two warriors.

Turnus sincerely prayed at the altar, and the Rutulians pitied him.

Juturna assumed the form of the Rutulian Camers, the son of Volcens. She took advantage of the pity that the Rutulians were feeling for her brother. She spread uncertainty and rumors: "We Rutulians should be ashamed to allow Turnus to fight Aeneas in single combat. We are as strong as the troops of Trojans and their allies. We outnumber them. If only half of us were to fight the Trojans and their allies, some of us would find it difficult to find a warrior to fight. If Turnus dies in single combat, he will gain glory and fame, but we will lose our kingdom and become slaves."

Her words worked. Even the warriors of King Latinus began to want war, although previously they had wanted peace. They pitied Turnus, and they wanted to fight.

Juturna then created a sign in the sky. An eagle — the bird of Jupiter — attacked a swan, killed it, and began to carry it away. The other birds rose in the air and attacked the eagle, which dropped the dead swan and flew away.

The Italians watched the bird-sign with awe, and the Rutulian seer Tolumnius said, "I have hoped for a sign like this from the gods. We must go to war — now! Get your swords! We have been like terrorized birds, but together we can repel the invader just like these birds repelled the eagle. Fight!"

Tolumnius threw his spear and broke the pact of peace. He threw his spear into a group of nine brothers whom one mother had bore. The spear hit one brother in the ribs, and his brothers rose up and grabbed their swords and spears and fought. King Latinus fled, his peace broken. Some warriors mounted their chariots; other warriors mounted their horses. Both sides grabbed weapons and fought.

Messapus, an ally of Turnus, charged his horse at Aulestes, who backed up and tripped, falling against an altar. As Aulestes begged for mercy, Messapus speared him and shouted, "This one's dead. He is a better sacrifice to the gods than mere animals!" Messapus' warriors ran to strip the armor off Aulestes.

The Trojan Corynaeus grabbed a burning torch and threw it into the bearded face of the Rutulian Ebysus. His beard caught fire, and Corynaeus forced him to the ground and stabbed him in the side.

The Trojan Podalirius tried to kill Alsus, once a shepherd but now a warrior. Podalirius stood over him with a sword, but Alsus swung his ax and split his head in two — Podalirius' blood sprayed and his eyes saw the darkness that never ends.

Aeneas remembered the pact of peace. He did not wear a helmet, and his hands did not carry weapons. He shouted to his warriors, "We have a pact of peace! Only I should be fighting now! I should be fighting Turnus!"

As Aeneas tried to make peace so that he could fight Turnus in single combat, an arrow wounded him. Who shot the arrow was and is not known. No one admitted to wounding Aeneas.

When Turnus saw that Aeneas was wounded and forced to leave the battlefield, he began to fight. He jumped in his chariot and started running over the enemy warriors and fighting them. He chased the warriors fleeing from him, grabbed their spears, and killed them. As he killed, he resembled the war-god Mars, who is attended by his aides Fear, Anger, and Ambush as he rides in his war chariot and his shield clangs. Turnus drove his horses and chariots over enemy warriors, and their blood sprayed into the air.

Turnus killed Sthenelus, Thamyrus, and Pholus. At long range, he hurled spears and killed warriors, including Glaucus and Lades, the two sons of Imbrasus. They had been born and raised in Lydia, and their father had given them matching weapons.

The Trojan Eumedes was fighting nearby. Eumedes had the same name as his grandfather, but his father, Dolon, was more famous. Dolon had volunteered to spy on the Greeks during the Trojan War. Dolon had asked that the immortal horses of Achilles be given to him as his reward for undertaking the dangerous mission, but Diomedes had killed him.

Turnus spotted Eumedes and hurled a spear and hit him. Turnus then drove his chariot close, dismounted, put his foot on Eumedes, took his sword away from him, and then drove the sword through Eumedes' neck, saying, "Trojan, these are the fields that you fought to win. Lie there and enjoy them. This is the reward that all Trojans who challenge me will enjoy."

Turnus then speared Asbytes, Chloreus, Sybaris, Dares, Thersilochus, and Thymoetes, who had been bucked off his panicking horse. Turnus was like the North wind whipping up waves and sending them to shore, and he charged enemy warriors and sent them fleeing from him.

Phegeus attempted to stop Turnus by grabbing the bridles of the horses pulling his chariot, but Turnus speared him in the side and inflicted a minor wound. Phegeus tried to defend himself with his shield and even to attack Turnus with a sword, but he fell and the wheels of Turnus' chariot ran over him. Turnus hacked Phegeus' neck with a sword and left his corpse headless in the sand.

Meanwhile, Mnestheus and Achates had taken the wounded Aeneas to the Trojan camp. Aeneas bled and supported himself by using his spear as a cane. Eager to get back into the battle, he insisted that the arrowhead be removed as quickly as possible: "Use a sword to open the wound and dig out the arrowhead. I need to fight!"

Iapyx, the son of Iasius, was the healer of the Trojans. Apollo, the god of prophecy, music, archery, and medicine, respected him, and offered him his choice of gifts. He could have been a prophet, a musician who played the lyre, or an archer, but Iapyx' father was deathly ill, and so Iapyx chose to be a healer. He learned the properties of herbs, and he healed people. He forsook the glory and fame that would have come to him as an excellent archer in battle. Iapyx, now aged, attempted but failed to remove the arrowhead despite his experience and knowledge as a healer. Ascanius grieved for his father. With Aeneas in the Trojan camp, the battle favored Turnus and his warriors. The battle neared the Trojan camp.

Venus, a mother grieving for the pain her son was suffering, went to Mount Ida on Crete and harvested dittany, a plant with medicinal properties. Even wild goats are aware of its healing properties, and they eat its leaves and purple flowers when an archer has shot an arrow into them but failed to kill them.

Venus harvested the dittany and soaked it in water from the Tiber River and added drops of liquid from ambrosia, the food of the immortal gods — and she added a panacea. She then slipped this potion among the other potions of Iapyx without his knowledge. Iapyx rubbed Venus' potion onto Aeneas' wound. Aeneas' pain ended, his blood stopped flowing, the arrowhead easily exited the wound, and Aeneas' strength returned to him.

Iapyx gave credit where credit is due. He said, "Give Aeneas back his weapons — he is ready to fight. This strong recovery is not due to my medicine — a god is helping Aeneas."

Aeneas put on his armor, and then he hugged Ascanius and kissed him through the visor of his helmet. He said to Ascanius, "From me you can learn about courage and hard work in times of adversity. From other people you can learn about good luck. Today I will fight for you so that you can achieve your destiny. Listen. When you are a man and are looking for role models, remember me and your uncle Hector!"

Aeneas strode back to the battle with Antheus and Mnestheus and other warriors by his side. The Trojans and their allies kicked up a cloud of dust as they marched, and Turnus and his warriors saw the advancing army and were afraid.

Juturna heard the sound of the marching Trojans and Trojan allies. She fled.

Aeneas kept marching. He was like a storm that blocks the sun. Farmers see the storm and know that it will uproot trees and destroy their crops. Aeneas and his warriors charged into the enemy warriors.

The Trojan Thymbraeus killed the Rutulian Osiris, a giant of a man.

The Trojan Mnestheus killed Arcetius.

The Trojan Achates killed Epulo.

The Trojan Gyas killed Ufens.

The Rutulian prophet Tolumnius also died. He had interpreted Juturna's bird-sign and broken the truce.

Turnus' warriors fled from the Trojans and their allies. Aeneas would not kill those fleeing from him, and he would not kill those who challenged them, and he would not chase and kill those who hurled spears at him from long range. Instead, Aeneas looked for Turnus — Turnus was the warrior whom Aeneas wanted to kill.

Juturna was terrified that Turnus, her brother, might die. She took on the form of Metiscus, Turnus' charioteer. She knocked the real Metiscus from Turnus' chariot and took his place. She had his voice, his form, and his armor. A bird can swiftly fly in the hall of a wealthy man and scavenge bits of food for its nestlings. Just as swiftly Juturna drove Turnus' chariot around the battlefield, showing Turnus to the Trojans, but keeping him well away from Aeneas, the stronger warrior. Aeneas followed Turnus, keen to meet him in battle, and he kept shouting at Turnus to stop and fight him. But Juturna ignored Aeneas' cries and kept Turnus away from the deadly warrior, frustrating Aeneas.

Messapus, Turnus' ally, hurled one of his two spears at Aeneas. Aeneas saw the spear coming and knelt on one knee. The spear missed him, but cut off the plumes on the top of his helmet. Aeneas was angry at Messapus, and he was angry as he once more saw Turnus' chariot drive away from him. Aeneas called on Jupiter to remember that the enemy had broken the pact of peace, and then he entered the battle. Filled with *furor*, he killed and killed again, no longer trying to chase down Turnus.

If slaughter can win glory, then Aeneas won much glory. Jupiter must enjoy deaths in battle — the people who were now trying to kill each other on this battlefield would later live in lasting peace as people of one country.

Aeneas stabbed the Rutulian Sucro in the side; Aeneas' sword split his ribs and stopped his heart.

Turnus attacked Amycus and Diores, two brothers. He knocked them off their horses, and he dismounted from his chariot and stabbed one with a spear and one with a sword. Then he cut off their heads and tied the heads to his chariot, where they dripped blood.

Aeneas killed Talos, Tanis, and Cethegus in one charge, and then he killed Onites, whose mother was named Peridia.

Turnus killed two brothers who came from Lycia, and then he killed Menoetes, who when he was young had hated war. Menoetes was a fisherman, his house was humble, and he did not experience the luxuries of the rich. His father farmed land that he did not own.

Aeneas and Turnus were like fires on two sides of a wood filled with dry timber. Both fires burn everything in their path. Both Aeneas and Turnus were filled with *furor*, and both killed and killed again.

The Rutulian Murranus was proud of his ancestry, and he was able to recite the names of his many ancestors who had been kings. Aeneas threw a rock at him and hit him. Murranus fell on the ground, and his own chariot and horses ran over him, trampling him to death.

The Trojan Hyllus charged Turnus, who hurled a spear at him and split his helmet and splattered his brain. Turnus then killed Cretheus, a Greek soldier who fought for Aeneas.

Aeneas killed the Rutulian warrior-priest Cupencus — his worship of the gods did not save his life.

The Trojan Aeolus, whom the Greeks at Troy could not kill, now died. Achilles had killed many Trojans, but he could not kill Aeolus, whose home had been in the city Lyrnesus under Mount Ida near Troy, but who found his tomb in Italy.

All were fighting. Strong warriors fought on both sides. Neither side let up.

Venus inspired Aeneas to attack Laurentum, the city of the enemy. This would panic its citizens and warriors. Still trying to get to Turnus to fight him, Aeneas saw the city at peace and untouched by bloodshed. Aeneas gathered Mnestheus, Sergestus, Serestus, and other warriors and told them, "Now we must attack the city. This is the stronghold of the enemy, and I will conquer it unless it surrenders to me. I can't wait until Turnus decides to fight me — that is taking too long. Better to attack the city immediately. Bring fire, and we will set the city aflame!"

The Trojans and their allies attacked the city, placing ladders against its walls and bringing fire. Some killed sentries at the gates. Arrows and spears filled the sky.

Aeneas shouted, "The gods know that our enemies have twice broken their pacts of peace! Twice they have started battles!"

Inside the city, citizens were divided. Some thought they should open the gates and surrender to the Trojans and give King Latinus to the Trojans. Others rushed to arm themselves and fight the Trojans.

The city, part of which was now burning, was like a beehive that a shepherd has found. The shepherd lights a fire to fill the beehive with smoke. The bees are angry and swarm as the beehive fills with smoke.

Another disaster hit the citizens of Laurentum. Queen Amata had witnessed the attack on the city. The enemy warriors were climbing ladders on the walls, and the city was burning. She could not see Turnus — he must be dead! Filled with *furor,* she ripped off part of her gown and made a noose and hung herself. The women inside the city mourned. Lavinia tore her hair and raked her fingernails across her cheeks. The air filled with the sounds of laments of women. The news spread, and King Latinus ripped his clothing and poured dust over his head.

Juturna kept Turnus away from the city. They were on the other side of the battlefield, where few warriors could be found. He heard sounds coming from the city and asked, "Why are sounds of grief coming from Laurentum?" He pulled back on the reins and made the chariot stop.

Juturna, desperate to keep her brother alive, said, "Let's keep fighting out here and let others defend the walls of the city. You will be able to kill just as many warriors as Aeneas!"

Turnus replied, "I recognize you. I know that you are my sister Juturna. I have known for a while — ever since you broke the pact of peace and started this battle. You can't hide your divinity from me. Why have you come here? Has one of the gods made you come down to see me die? What can I do now but die? My warriors are dying. I saw Murranus die — he called out 'Turnus!' to me as he died. He was a great warrior. Ufens died, and the Trojans took his armor and his body. Next, the city of Laurentum will be conquered and its houses destroyed. Must I see that and not fight? Can't I show Drances that I am not a coward? It is better for me to die fighting than to run away! I will go to the Land of the Dead, but I will win glory!"

The Rutulian Saces, his face bearing a slash made by an arrow, rode up to Turnus and said, "We need you — now! Aeneas is attacking the city, which is on fire. Your warriors need a leader. King Latinus himself is despairing — he does not know what to do. Queen Amata is dead — she committed suicide. Before the gates of the city, Messapus and Atinas fight bravely while you are out here in an empty field!"

Turnus felt shame. He looked at the city and saw a tower go up in flames — he himself had helped to build that tower.

Turnus said to his sister, "My fate is calling me. Do not try to keep me from it. The Fates and the gods are in control, not us. I will fight Aeneas face to face. No longer will you see me in disgrace. I must fight, and I must die."

He jumped from the chariot and ran to the city. His sister stayed behind and mourned. Dashing through his enemies and his enemies' spears, Turnus was like a boulder crashing down a mountain after a storm or erosion has freed it. The boulder crushes trees, cattle, and men.

Reaching the wall of the city, Turnus shouted, "Troops, stop fighting! Let my sword decide the outcome of the war! Aeneas and I will fight alone!"

The warriors stopped fighting and backed away from the opposing warriors. In between was an open area where Aeneas and Turnus could fight.

Aeneas heard Turnus and was happy. He hit his shield, and his shield sounded like thunder. Aeneas seemed to be as huge as Mount Athos, Mount Eryx, or Father Apennine, the god of the Apennine mountains of central Italy.

All warriors took off their armor and prepared to watch the single combat between Aeneas and Turnus. King Latinus knew that this would be an impressive fight — it would decide which side won the war.

Aeneas and Turnus charged at each other like two bulls fighting to decide which would rule the herd. Their swords clanged against each other's shields. The sounds of fighting reached the sky. Jupiter listened, and he placed the fate of Aeneas and the fate of Turnus onto his scales, and he lifted them up. One warrior's scale would fall, and that warrior would die. One warrior's scale would rise, and that warrior would live. Which warrior would die, and which warrior would live?

Turnus raised his sword high and brought it swiftly down on Aeneas' divine armor — the sword broke. In his eagerness to fight Aeneas, Turnus had taken the wrong sword. He had taken the sword of Metiscus, his charioteer; he had not taken the sword of his father. Metiscus' sword worked well when Turnus fought ordinary warriors wearing ordinary armor, but it could not withstand the divinely made armor of Aeneas.

Without a weapon, bearing only a hilt, Turnus had no choice but to run from Aeneas. Turnus could not escape. Trojan warriors on one side, a swamp on another side, and the walls of the city on the remaining side enclosed him.

Aeneas, filled with *furor*, chased Turnus, but his arrow wound slowed him. Aeneas was like a hunting dog chasing a stag. The hunting dog comes close and closer and almost is able to close the gap and kill the stag, but not quite. The sky fills with the cries of the dog.

Turnus, running from Aeneas, shouted to his warriors by name to get him his own sword. Aeneas shouted that he would destroy the city if anyone armed Turnus. Aeneas kept chasing Turnus five times in a big circle. The prize for the victor of the race was the life of Turnus.

Within the circle was a wild olive tree's stump in which Aeneas' spear had stuck. The olive tree was dedicated to Faunus, the horned god of the forest. Sailors saved from drowning hung gifts and clothing dedicated to Faunus on the branches of the tree. The Trojans, however, had chopped down the tree — dedicated though it was to a god — to clear the field for fighting.

Aeneas grabbed his spear and tried to pull it loose. If he could not catch Turnus and kill him with a sword, he wanted instead to kill him with a spear.

Terrified, Turnus prayed, "Faunus, have pity on me! Hold on to that spear! Do not let Aeneas pull it out! I have always treated you with respect — unlike Aeneas' warriors, who chopped down your tree!"

Faunus answered Turnus' prayer: Aeneas struggled to pull out the spear, but he could not. Juturna, having again taken on the form of Metiscus, gave Turnus his own sword. Venus witnessed this help, and being a more powerful god than Faunus, pulled out Aeneas' spear and gave it to him. Aeneas and Turnus faced each other.

Jupiter and Juno had been watching the single combat together. Jupiter said to Juno, "You know the fates of these two heroes. You know that Aeneas' fame will eventually rise to heaven. You know that Aeneas will eventually become a god in heaven. Why resist what you know is fated to happen? All you can do is to delay what you know will happen. You helped guide an arrow so that it would wound Aeneas — a future god. Was that the right thing to do? You have helped Juturna to help Turnus. You have given strength to a warrior whom you know will be defeated. Why not stop resisting what you know is inevitable? Listen to me. Stop resisting the inevitable. Do not grieve for what is inevitable. Do not complain to me about what is inevitable. Accept it. You have sent trouble to the Trojans both on land and sea. You have started a war. You have brought grief to many. You have brought the grief of a war to what should be the happiness of a wedding. You have done enough. I order you to do no more."

Juno replied, "I know what you want, and that is why I am not down on earth helping Turnus myself, although I would like to. If I could do what I want, I would start the war again and make sure that Aeneas is in great danger. I admit that I greatly encouraged Juturna to help her brother. I did not, however, encourage anyone to shoot the arrow that wounded Aeneas. This I swear — an inviolable oath — by the river Styx.

"I will do what you wish. I will interfere no more in this war. But I have a request to make of you — a request that does not go against fate. Soon, Aeneas and Lavinia will be married. I request that the Italians continue to be known as Italians and not be known as Trojans. I request that the Italians continue to keep their own language and their own style of clothing. Let Italy continue to be Italian and not Trojan. The city of Troy fell — let it stay fallen!"

Jupiter smiled and said, "It shall be done. Italians will keep their own language and their own customs. The Trojans will marry Italians and will become Italian. Some Trojan religious rites will survive, but they will become Italian religious rites. The descendants of the Trojans and Italians will worship you more than any other people worship you."

Juno consented to the will of Jupiter. Now she was a model of *pietas*, but in the future the Carthaginians she loved would fight three wars against Rome. Juno left.

Jupiter now wanted Juturna to leave her brother. The Furies number three: Allecto, Tisiphone, and Megaera. Snakes are entwined in their hair, and they have wings that make them as fast as the wind. The Furies serve Jupiter, and at his command they bring death and plague and war to men.

Jupiter commanded one of the Furies, "Go down to the world of men and cross the path of Juturna. That will let her know that she must leave Turnus."

The Fury flew down to earth like a speeding arrow. She assumed the shape of the small bird that often sings an ominous song while perched on a tombstone. The Fury flew against the face of Turnus, and beat its wings against him and screeched. Turnus felt dread, his skin seemed to crawl, and he could not speak.

Juturna recognized the Fury and knew what it meant. Juturna tore her hair and scratched her face and beat her breasts as she grieved. She cried to Turnus, "Brother, I can do nothing now to help you. I cannot lengthen your life. This Fury is the omen that you will die. Now I am forced to leave you — against my will. Jupiter thought to reward me with immortality after he raped me. Was immortality really a reward? Is death always bad? If I were mortal, I could die with you and be with you in the Land of the Dead. Instead, I am doomed never to die, always to live without you. Rather than live without you, I would like the earth to open and take me, a minor goddess, to the Land of the Dead!"

Juturna moaned with grief and left.

Aeneas lifted his spear and shouted at Turnus, "Why delay your death any longer? Stop running. Start fighting. Call up whatever courage you have and face your fate. With your death, you will either fly to heaven or sink to hell."

Turnus said to Aeneas, "I do not fear you, but I do fear Jupiter, who hates me."

Turnus saw a huge rock that property owners had set out to mark boundaries. Today, a dozen men could not lift it, but Turnus picked it up and threw it at Aeneas. But Turnus weakened as he threw the rock, and the rock did no damage — it did not reach Aeneas.

Turnus felt as if he were in a dream in which he was not in control of himself. The dreamer tries to race, but cannot. The dreamer tries to speak, but cannot. Turnus tried to take some kind of action, but the Fury prevented all action and confused his mind. Turnus could not run. Turnus could not attack Aeneas. His sister and his charioteer had left him. His Rutulians could not help him. He was without friends. Facing him was Aeneas.

Aeneas hurled his spear at a vulnerable spot. His spear made a sound like a rock hurled by a catapult or like lightning. The spear pierced the edge of Turnus' shield and his armor and buried itself in Turnus' thigh. Turnus dropped to his knees. His warriors groaned, and their groans echoed.

Turnus, a suppliant, said to Aeneas, "I know that I deserve this. I do not ask you for mercy for myself. This is your moment of victory. If you can respect the grief of an aged father, then send me — alive or dead, as you wish — to Daunus, my father. Your father, Anchises, was much like my father. I hold out my arms to you. You are the victor, and I am the vanquished. All the warriors here — yours and mine — have witnessed my defeat. You shall marry Lavinia. Whatever decision you make about whether I shall live or die, I ask that you do not make that decision in hatred."

Aeneas thought about whether he should let Turnus live or die: *Good reasons for killing Turnus exist. Good reasons for allowing Turnus to live exist.*

Turnus and I have been fighting a single combat. Single combats end in death. The victorious warrior kills the defeated warrior.

If I allow Turnus to live, Turnus could rebel later. Warriors who pity Turnus now could fight for him later.

I should avenge the death of Pallas. King Evander, the father of Pallas, wants me to kill Turnus.

Some kinds of anger are justified. When anger is justified, it is not negative. I should be angry at the deaths that Turnus has caused.

Perhaps a good leader ought to kill Turnus.

However, the choice between choosing to kill Turnus or to allow Turnus to live is a choice between furor *and* clementia*. Furor* can be a bad thing. When I gave in to* furor *in the sense of sexual passion and had an affair with Dido, it was a bad thing — I forgot my destiny and the destiny of my son.*

When I visited Anchises, my father, in the Land of the Dead, he gave advice to future Romans — advice that my father must want me to follow. My father said, "Romans must remember to rule well the peoples of the world, including their own people. Romans must remember to rule while encouraging peace. Romans must remember to spare the defeated, just as Romans must remember to defeat the proud." Turnus was proud, but now he is defeated. Because he is defeated, he should be spared, according to my father's words. I should give Turnus clementia*; I should show him mercy.*

Perhaps a good leader ought to allow Turnus to live.

Sword in hand, Aeneas stood above Turnus as he considered whether to kill him or to let him live. Aeneas had won the war; he and Lavinia would marry. He would achieve his destiny and found the Roman people. The decision that Aeneas must make now would determine whether the Roman people would be founded on an act of *furor* or an act of *clementia*.

As Aeneas stood above Turnus, he saw that Turnus was wearing the sword-belt of Pallas. The sword-belt depicted the marriage of the fifty daughters of Danaus to the fifty sons of Aegyptus. Forty-nine of the marriages were characterized by *furor*. Forty-nine husbands gave in to the *furor* of sexual passion and slept with their wives without first giving the wives a chance to get to know and love them. The husbands did not respect the wives' wishes to keep their virginity a while longer in their forced marriages. The forty-nine wives killed these forty-nine husbands. One husband resisted *furor* and did not force his wife to have sex with him. They did not have sex until after she had had a chance to get to know and to love him. He showed *clementia* to his wife, over whom he had power, and they enjoyed a good marriage, had children, and started a line of kings.

When Aeneas saw that Turnus was wearing the sword-belt of Pallas, he remembered that Turnus had killed Pallas. Aeneas said to Turnus, "Pallas was my friend, you killed him, and you stripped him of his sword-belt, which you are now wearing. Pallas strikes you with my sword! Pallas takes your life!"

Aeneas plunged his sword into Turnus. Turnus' heart was filled with the metal of Aeneas' sword; Aeneas' heart was filled with *furor*.

Conclusion

Now that you have read this retelling of Virgil's *Aeneid*, read the real thing. Here are some recommended translations:

Virgil. *The Aeneid*. Trans. Robert Fagles. New York: Penguin, 2006.

Virgil. *The Aeneid*. Trans. Robert Fitzgerald. New York: Vintage, 1990.

Virgil. *The Aeneid*. Trans. Rolfe Humphries. New York: Charles Scribner's Sons, 1951.

I also recommend this course on Virgil's *Aeneid* from the Teaching Company:

Vandiver, Elizabeth. *The Aeneid*. Course No. 303. The Teaching Company.

<http://www.teach12.com/ttcx/CourseDescLong2.aspx?cid=303>.

Appendix A: Important Terms

Furor means rage or passion. It is excessive rage or passion. Juno's hatred for Aeneas and the Trojans is an example of *furor*.

Pietas means proper, dutiful behavior. It means respect for things for which respect is due, including gods, family, and destiny. Aeneas is noted for his *pietas*, as when he carries his father on his back out of Troy.

Another important Latin term is *clementia*, from which we get our word "clemency." A person is clement when he or she gives a mild rather than a harsh punishment. Julius Caesar was noted for his *clementia*. *Clementia* can mean calmness, clemency, compassion, forbearance, gentleness, humanity, indulgence, mercy, mildness, etc. *Clementia* is especially mercy shown by a person who has much power to a person who has less or no power.

Appendix B: Background Information

- *What are the Greek and Roman names of the major gods and goddesses?*

Here is a list of some gods and goddesses with their Greek and (Roman) names:

Aphrodite (Venus)

Ares (Mars)

Artemis (Diana)

Athena (Minerva)

Dionysus (Bacchus)

Hades (Pluto)

Hephaestus (Vulcan)

Hera (Juno)

Hermes (Mercury)

Poseidon (Neptune)

Zeus (Jupiter)

Note: The god Apollo has the same name in Greek and in Roman mythology.

Note: The Greek mortal Odysseus has the Roman name Ulysses.

- *What is the* Iliad *about?*

The *Iliad* tells the story of the quarrel between Achilles and Agamemnon. Following the quarrel, Achilles (the mightiest Greek warrior) withdraws from the fighting, which allows the Trojans to be triumphant in battle for a while. The *Iliad* tells about Achilles' anger and how he finally lets go of his anger.

- *What is the* Odyssey *about?*

The *Odyssey* is about a different Greek hero in the Trojan War: Odysseus, whose Roman name is Ulysses. Following the ten years that the Trojan War lasted, Odysseus returns to his home island of Ithaca, where he is king. It takes him ten years to return home because of his adventures and mishaps. Much of that time he spends in captivity. When he finally returns home, he discovers that suitors are courting his wife, Penelope, who has remained faithful to him and who wants nothing to do with the suitors, who are rude and arrogant and who feast on Odysseus' cattle and drink his wine as they party all day. In addition, Telemachus, Odysseus' son, has found it hard to grow up without a strong father-figure in his life. The *Odyssey* tells the story of how Odysseus returns home to Ithaca and reestablishes himself in his own palace.

- *What is the* Aeneid *about?*

The *Aeneid* is a Roman epic poem by Virgil that tells the story of Aeneas, a Trojan prince who survives the fall of Troy and leads other survivors to Italy. His adventures in part parallel the adventures of Odysseus during his return to Ithaca. In fact, they visit many of the same places, including the island of the Cyclopes. One of Aeneas' most notable characteristics is his *pietas*, his respect for things for which respect is due, including the gods, his family, and his destiny. His destiny is to found the Roman people, which is different from founding Rome, which was founded long after his death. Aeneas journeys to Carthage, where he has an affair with Dido, the Carthaginian queen. Because of his destiny, he leaves her and goes to Italy. Dido commits suicide, and Aeneas fights a war to establish himself in Italy. After killing Turnus, the leader of the armies facing him, Aeneas marries the Italian princess Lavinia, and they become important ancestors of the Roman people.

- *What is the basic story of the Trojan War?*

Paris, Prince of Troy, visits Menelaus, King of Sparta, and then Paris runs off with Menelaus' wife, Helen, who of course becomes known as Helen of Troy. This is a major insult to Menelaus and his family, so he and his elder brother, Agamemnon, lead an army against Troy to get Helen (and reparations) back. The war drags on for 10 years, and the greatest Greek warrior is Achilles, while the greatest Trojan warrior is Hector, Paris' eldest brother. Eventually, Hector is killed by Achilles, who is then killed by Paris (with the help of Apollo), who is then killed by Philoctetes. Finally, Odysseus comes up with the idea of the Trojan Horse, which ends the Trojan War.

- *Who is Achilles, and what is unusual about his mother, Thetis?*

Achilles, of course, is the foremost warrior of the Greeks during the Trojan War. His mother, Thetis, is unusual in that she is a goddess. The ancient Greeks' religion is different from modern religions in that they were polytheistic (believing in many gods) rather than monotheistic (believing in one god). In addition, the gods and human beings could mate. Achilles is unusual in that he had an immortal goddess, Thetis, as his mother and a mortal man, Peleus, as his father. Achilles, of course, is unusual in many ways. Another way in which he is unusual is that he and Thetis have long talks together. Often, the gods either ignore their mortal offspring or choose not to reveal themselves to them. For example, Aeneas' goddess mother is Venus. Although Venus does save Aeneas' life or help him on occasion, the two do not have long talks together the way that Achilles and Thetis do.

• *Which prophecy about Achilles was given to his mother, Thetis?*

The prophecy about Thetis' male offspring was that he would be a greater man than his father. This is something that would make most human fathers happy. (One exception would be Pap, in Mark Twain's *Adventures of Huckleberry Finn*. Pap does not want Huck, his son, to learn to read or write or to get an education or to live better than Pap does.)

• *Who is Jupiter, and what does he decide to do as a result of this prophecy?*

Jupiter is a horny god who sleeps with many goddesses and many human beings. Normally, he would lust after Thetis, but once he hears the prophecy, he does not want to sleep with Thetis. For one thing, the gods are potent, and when they mate they have children. Jupiter overthrew his own father, and Jupiter does not want Thetis to give birth to a greater man than he is because his son will overthrow him. Therefore, Jupiter wants to get Thetis married off to someone else. In this case, a marriage to a human being for Thetis would suit Jupiter just fine. A human son may be greater than his father but is still not going to be as great as a god, and so Jupiter will be safe if Thetis gives birth to a human son.

• *Who is Peleus?*

Peleus is the human man who marries Thetis and who fathers Achilles. At the time of the *Iliad*, Peleus is an old man and Thetis has not lived with him for a long time.

• *Why is Eris, Goddess of Discord, not invited to the wedding feast of Peleus and Thetis?*

Obviously, you do not want discord at a wedding, and therefore, Eris, Goddess of Discord, is not invited to the wedding feast of Peleus and Thetis. Even though Eris is not invited to the wedding feast, she shows up anyway.

• *Eris, Goddess of Discord, throws an apple on a table at the wedding feast. What is inscribed on the apple?*

Inscribed on the apple is the phrase "For the fairest," written in Greek, of course. Because Greek is a language that indicates masculine and feminine in certain words, and since "fairest" has a feminine ending, the apple is really inscribed "for the fairest female."

• *Juno, Minerva, and Venus each claim the apple. Who are they?*

Three goddesses claim the apple, meaning that each of the three goddesses thinks that she is the fairest, or most beautiful.

Juno

Juno is the wife of Jupiter, and she is a jealous wife. Jupiter has many affairs with immortal goddesses and mortal women, and Juno is jealous because of these affairs. Jupiter would like to keep on her good side.

Minerva

Minerva is the goddess of wisdom. She becomes the patron goddess of Athens: The Greeks called her Athena. Minerva especially likes Odysseus, as we see especially in the *Odyssey*. Minerva is a favorite of Jupiter, her father. Jupiter would like to keep on her good side.

Venus

Venus is the goddess of sexual passion. She can make Jupiter fall in love against his will. Jupiter would like to keep on her good side.

• *Why doesn't Jupiter want to judge the goddesses' beauty contest?*

Jupiter is not a fool. He knows that if he judges the goddesses' beauty contest, he will make two enemies. The two goddesses whom Jupiter does not choose as the fairest will hate him and likely make trouble for him.

Please note that the Greek gods and goddesses are not omnibenevolent. Frequently, they are quarrelsome and petty.

By the way, Athens, Ohio, lawyer Thomas Hodson once judged a beauty contest featuring 25 cute child contestants. He was running in an election to choose the municipal court judge, and he thought that judging the contest would be a good way to win votes. Very quickly, he decided never to judge a children's beauty contest again. He figured out that he had won two votes — the votes of the parents of the child who won the contest. Unfortunately, he also figured out that he had lost 48 votes — the votes of the parents of the children who lost.

• *Who is Paris, and what is the Judgment of Paris?*

Paris is a prince of Troy, and Jupiter allows him to judge the three goddesses' beauty contest. Paris is not as intelligent as Jupiter, or he would try to find a way out of judging the beauty contest.

• *Each of the goddesses offers Paris a bribe if he will choose her. What are the bribes?*

Juno

Juno offers Paris political power: several cities he can rule.

Minerva

Minerva offers Paris prowess in battle. Paris can become a mighty and feared warrior.

Venus

Venus offers Paris the most beautiful woman in the world to be his wife.

• *Which goddess does Paris choose?*

Paris chooses Venus, who offered him the most beautiful woman in the world to be his wife.

This is not what a Homeric warrior would normally choose. A person such as Achilles would choose to be an even greater warrior, if that is possible.

A person such as Agamemnon is likely to choose more cities to rule.

When Paris chooses the most beautiful woman in the world to be his wife, we are not meant to think that he made a good decision. Paris is not a likable character.

• *Does the Judgment of Paris appear in the* Iliad *and the* Aeneid?

We are not certain that Homer knew of the myth of the Judgment of Paris; however, we know that Virgil knew of the myth because he mentions it near the beginning of Book 1 of the *Aeneid*.

• *Does myth develop over time?*

Myth does develop over time. Possibly, the myth of the Judgment of Paris was created after Homer had created the *Iliad* and the *Odyssey*.

• *As a result of Aphrodite's bribe, Paris abducts Helen. Why?*

Aphrodite promised Paris the most beautiful woman to be his wife. As it happens, that woman is Helen. Therefore, Paris abducts Helen, with Aphrodite's good wishes.

• *Did Helen go with Paris willingly?*

The answer to this question is ambiguous, and ancient authorities varied in how they answered this question.

• *To whom is Helen already married?*

Helen is already married to Menelaus, the King of Sparta. Paris visits Menelaus, and when he leaves, he carries off both a lot of Menelaus' treasure and Menelaus' wife, Helen. Obviously, this is not the way that one ought to treat one's host.

• *Who are Agamemnon and Menelaus?*

Agamemnon and Menelaus are the sons of Atreus. They are brothers, and Agamemnon, the King of Mycenae, is the older brother and the brother who rules a greater land, as seen by the number of ships the two kings bring to the Trojan War. Menelaus brings 60 ships (Fagles, *Iliad* 2.678-679). Agamemnon brings 100 ships (Fagles, *Iliad* 2.667-672).

• *Who is responsible for leading the expedition to recover Helen?*

Agamemnon is the older brother, so he is the leader of the Greek troops in the Trojan War.

• *Why do the winds blow against the Greek ships?*

When the Greek ships are gathered together and are ready to set sail against Troy, a wind blows in the wrong direction for them to sail. The goddess Diana is angry at the Greeks because she knows that the result of the Trojan War will be lots of death, not just of warriors, but also of women and children. This is true of all wars, and it is a lesson that human beings forget after each war and relearn in the next war.

• *Why does Diana demand a human sacrifice?*

Diana knows that Agamemnon's warriors will cause much death of children, so she makes him sacrifice one of his daughters so that he will suffer what he will make other parents suffer.

• *Who does Agamemnon sacrifice?*

Agamemnon sacrifices his daughter Iphigenia. This is a religious sacrifice of a human life to appease the goddess Diana.

• *Did Homer know about this sacrifice?*

Very possibly, he did. In Book 1 of the *Iliad*, Agamemnon tells the prophet Calchas that he always brings bad news to Agamemnon. Calchas is the prophet who told Agamemnon that he had to sacrifice his daughter in order to get winds that would sail the ships to Troy.

• *What do Menelaus and Agamemnon do?*

After the sacrifice of Iphigenia, Agamemnon and Menelaus set sail with all the Greek ships for Troy. They land, and then they engage in warfare.

• *Who are Achilles and Hector?*

Achilles is the foremost Greek warrior, while Hector is the foremost Trojan warrior. Both warriors are deserving of great respect.

• *Does Homer assume that Achilles is invulnerable?*

Absolutely not. Achilles needs armor to go out on the battlefield and fight.

• *What happens to Hector and Achilles?*

Hector kills Achilles' best friend, Patroclus, in battle. Angry, Achilles kills Hector.

Later, Paris and Apollo kill Achilles.

• *What is the story of the Trojan Horse?*

Odysseus, a great strategist, thinks up the idea of the Trojan Horse. Epeus builds it.

The Greeks build a giant wooden horse, which is hollow and filled with Greek warriors, and then they pretend to abandon the war and to sail away from Troy. Actually, Agamemnon and his troops sail behind an island so that the Trojans cannot see the Greek ships. The Greeks also leave behind a lying Greek named Sinon, who tells the Trojans about a supposed prophecy that if the Trojans take the Horse inside their city, then Troy will never fall. The Trojans do that, and at night the Greeks come out of the Trojan Horse, make their way to the city gates, and open them. Outside the city gates are the Greek troops led by Agamemnon, who have returned to the Trojan plain. The Greek warriors rush inside the city and sack it.

Virgil's *Aeneid* has the fullest ancient account of the Trojan Horse. Of course, he tells the story from the Trojan point of view. If Homer had written the story of the Trojan Horse, he would have told it from the Greek point of view. For the Greeks, the Trojan War ended in a great victory. For the Trojans, the Trojan War ended in a great disaster.

• *Which outrages do the Greeks commit during the sack of Troy?*

Achilles' son, Pyrrhus, aka Neoptolemus, kills King Priam at an altar. This is an outrage because anyone who is at the altar of a god or gods is under the protection of that god or gods. When Pyrrhus kills Priam, an old man (old people are respected in Homeric culture), Pyrrhus disrespects the god or gods of the altar.

Hector's son is murdered. Hector's son is a very small child who is murdered by being hurled from the top of a high wall of Troy. Even during wartime, children ought not to be murdered, so this is another outrage.

Cassandra is raped by Little Ajax even though she is under Minerva's protection. Cassandra is raped in a temple devoted to Minerva. This is showing major disrespect to Minerva. Again, the Greeks are doing things that ought not to be done, even during wartime.

The Greeks sacrifice Priam's young daughter Polyxena. The Trojan War begins and ends with a human sacrifice of the life of a young girl. This is yet another outrage.

• *How do the gods and goddesses react to these outrages?*

The gods and goddesses make things difficult for the Greeks on their way home to Greece.

• *What happens to the Greeks after the fall of Troy?*

Nestor is a wise, pious, old man who did not commit any outrages. He makes it home quickly.

Odysseus' patron goddess, Minerva, is apparently angry at all of the Greeks because she does not help him on his journey home until 10 years have passed.

Little Ajax, who raped Cassandra, drowns on his way home.

Agamemnon returns home to a world of trouble. His wife, Clytemnestra, has taken a lover during his 10-year absence, and she murders Agamemnon.

Menelaus is reunited with Helen, but their ship is driven off course, and it takes them years to return home to Sparta.

• *What happens to Aeneas?*

Aeneas fights bravely, and he witnesses such things as the death of Priam, king of Troy; however, when he realizes that Troy is lost, he returns to his family to try to save them. He carries his father on his back, and he leads his young son by the hand, but although he saves them, his wife, who was following behind him, is lost in the battle.

Aeneas becomes the leader of the Trojan survivors, and he leads them to Italy, where they become the founders of the Roman people.

• *Who were the Roman people?*
The Romans had one of the greatest empires of the world.

Appendix C: About the Author

It was a dark and stormy night. Suddenly a cry rang out, and on a hot summer night in 1954, Josephine, wife of Carl Bruce, gave birth to a boy — me. Unfortunately, this young married couple allowed Reuben Saturday, Josephine's brother, to name their first-born. Reuben, aka "The Joker," decided that Bruce was a nice name, so he decided to name me Bruce Bruce. I have gone by my middle name — David — ever since.

Being named Bruce David Bruce hasn't been all bad. Bank tellers remember me very quickly, so I don't often have to show an ID. It can be fun in charades, also. When I was a counselor as a teenager at Camp Echoing Hills in Warsaw, Ohio, a fellow counselor gave the signs for "sounds like" and "two words," then she pointed to a bruise on her leg twice. Bruise Bruise? Oh yeah, Bruce Bruce is the answer!

Uncle Reuben, by the way, gave me a haircut when I was in kindergarten. He cut my hair short and shaved a small bald spot on the back of my head. My mother wouldn't let me go to school until the bald spot grew out again.

Of all my brothers and sisters (six in all), I am the only transplant to Athens, Ohio. I was born in Newark, Ohio, and have lived all around Southeastern Ohio. However, I moved to Athens to go to Ohio University and have never left.

At Ohio U, I never could make up my mind whether to major in English or Philosophy, so I got a bachelor's degree with a double major in both areas, then I added a master's degree in English and a master's degree in Philosophy.

Currently, and for a long time to come (I eat fruits and veggies), I am spending my retirement writing books such as *Nadia Comaneci: Perfect 10*, *The Funniest People in Dance*, *Homer's* Iliad: *A Retelling in Prose*, and *William Shakespeare's* Othello: *A Retelling in Prose*.

By the way, my sister Brenda Kennedy writes romances such as *A New Beginning* and *Shattered Dreams*.

Appendix D: Some Books by David Bruce

Retellings of a Classic Work of Literature

Ben Jonson's The Alchemist: *A Retelling*

Ben Jonson's The Arraignment, or Poetaster: *A Retelling*

Ben Jonson's Bartholomew Fair: *A Retelling*

Ben Jonson's The Case is Altered: *A Retelling*

Ben Jonson's Catiline's Conspiracy: *A Retelling*

Ben Jonson's The Devil is an Ass: *A Retelling*

Ben Jonson's Epicene: *A Retelling*

Ben Jonson's Every Man in His Humor: *A Retelling*

Ben Jonson's Every Man Out of His Humor: *A Retelling*

Ben Jonson's The Fountain of Self-Love, or Cynthia's Revels: *A Retelling*

Ben Jonson's The Magnetic Lady, or Humors Reconciled: *A Retelling*

Ben Jonson's The New Inn, or The Light Heart: *A Retelling*

Ben Jonson's Sejanus' Fall: *A Retelling*

Ben Jonson's The Staple of News: *A Retelling*

Ben Jonson's A Tale of a Tub: *A Retelling*

Ben Jonson's Volpone, or the Fox: *A Retelling*

Christopher Marlowe's Complete Plays: Retellings

Christopher Marlowe's Dido, Queen of Carthage: *A Retelling*

Christopher Marlowe's Doctor Faustus: *Retellings of the 1604 A-Text and of the 1616 B-Text*

Christopher Marlowe's Edward II: *A Retelling*

DAVID BRUCE

Christopher Marlowe's The Massacre at Paris: *A Retelling*

Christopher Marlowe's The Rich Jew of Malta: *A Retelling*

Christopher Marlowe's Tamburlaine, Parts 1 and 2: *Retellings*

Dante's Divine Comedy: *A Retelling in Prose*

Dante's Inferno: *A Retelling in Prose*

Dante's Purgatory: *A Retelling in Prose*

Dante's Paradise: *A Retelling in Prose*

The Famous Victories of Henry V: *A Retelling*

From the Iliad *to the* Odyssey: *A Retelling in Prose of Quintus of Smyrna's* Posthomerica

George Chapman, Ben Jonson, and John Marston's Eastward Ho! *A Retelling*

George Peele's The Arraignment of Paris: *A Retelling*

George Peele's The Battle of Alcazar: *A Retelling*

George's Peele's David and Bathsheba, and the Tragedy of Absalom: *A Retelling*

George Peele's Edward I: *A Retelling*

George Peele's The Old Wives' Tale: *A Retelling*

George-a-Greene: *A Retelling*

The History of King Leir: *A Retelling*

Homer's Iliad: *A Retelling in Prose*

Homer's Odyssey: *A Retelling in Prose*

J.W. Gent.'s The Valiant Scot: *A Retelling*

Jason and the Argonauts: A Retelling in Prose of Apollonius of Rhodes' Argonautica

John Ford: Eight Plays Translated into Modern English

John Ford's The Broken Heart: *A Retelling*

VIRGIL'S AENEID: A RETELLING IN PROSE

John Ford's The Fancies, Chaste and Noble: *A Retelling*

John Ford's The Lady's Trial: *A Retelling*

John Ford's The Lover's Melancholy: *A Retelling*

John Ford's Love's Sacrifice: *A Retelling*

John Ford's Perkin Warbeck: *A Retelling*

John Ford's The Queen: *A Retelling*

John Ford's 'Tis Pity She's a Whore: *A Retelling*

John Lyly's Campaspe: *A Retelling*

John Lyly's Endymion, The Man in the Moon: *A Retelling*

John Lyly's Galatea: *A Retelling*

John Lyly's Love's Metamorphosis: *A Retelling*

John Lyly's Midas: *A Retelling*

John Lyly's Mother Bombie: *A Retelling*

John Lyly's Sappho and Phao: *A Retelling*

John Lyly's The Woman in the Moon: *A Retelling*

John Webster's The White Devil: *A Retelling*

King Edward III: *A Retelling*

Mankind: *A Medieval Morality Play* (A Retelling)

Margaret Cavendish's The Unnatural Tragedy: *A Retelling*

The Merry Devil of Edmonton: *A Retelling*

Robert Greene's Friar Bacon and Friar Bungay: *A Retelling*

The Taming of a Shrew: *A Retelling*

Tarlton's Jests: A Retelling

Thomas Middleton and William Rowley's The Changeling: *A Retelling*

DAVID BRUCE

The Trojan War and Its Aftermath: Four Ancient Epic Poems

Virgil's Aeneid: *A Retelling in Prose*

William Shakespeare's 5 Late Romances: Retellings in Prose

William Shakespeare's 10 Histories: Retellings in Prose

William Shakespeare's 11 Tragedies: Retellings in Prose

William Shakespeare's 12 Comedies: Retellings in Prose

William Shakespeare's 38 Plays: Retellings in Prose

William Shakespeare's 1 Henry IV, aka Henry IV, Part 1: *A Retelling in Prose*

William Shakespeare's 2 Henry IV, aka Henry IV, Part 2: *A Retelling in Prose*

William Shakespeare's 1 Henry VI, aka Henry VI, Part 1: *A Retelling in Prose*

William Shakespeare's 2 Henry VI, aka Henry VI, Part 2: *A Retelling in Prose*

William Shakespeare's 3 Henry VI, aka Henry VI, Part 3: *A Retelling in Prose*

William Shakespeare's All's Well that Ends Well: *A Retelling in Prose*

William Shakespeare's Antony and Cleopatra: *A Retelling in Prose*

William Shakespeare's As You Like It: *A Retelling in Prose*

William Shakespeare's The Comedy of Errors: *A Retelling in Prose*

William Shakespeare's Coriolanus: *A Retelling in Prose*

William Shakespeare's Cymbeline: *A Retelling in Prose*

William Shakespeare's Hamlet: *A Retelling in Prose*

William Shakespeare's Henry V: *A Retelling in Prose*

William Shakespeare's Henry VIII: *A Retelling in Prose*

William Shakespeare's Julius Caesar: *A Retelling in Prose*

William Shakespeare's King John: *A Retelling in Prose*

William Shakespeare's King Lear: *A Retelling in Prose*

VIRGIL'S AENEID: A RETELLING IN PROSE

William Shakespeare's Love's Labor's Lost: *A Retelling in Prose*

William Shakespeare's Macbeth: *A Retelling in Prose*

William Shakespeare's Measure for Measure: *A Retelling in Prose*

William Shakespeare's The Merchant of Venice: *A Retelling in Prose*

William Shakespeare's The Merry Wives of Windsor: *A Retelling in Prose*

William Shakespeare's A Midsummer Night's Dream: *A Retelling in Prose*

William Shakespeare's Much Ado About Nothing: *A Retelling in Prose*

William Shakespeare's Othello: *A Retelling in Prose*

William Shakespeare's Pericles, Prince of Tyre: *A Retelling in Prose*

William Shakespeare's Richard II: *A Retelling in Prose*

William Shakespeare's Richard III: *A Retelling in Prose*

William Shakespeare's Romeo and Juliet: *A Retelling in Prose*

William Shakespeare's The Taming of the Shrew: *A Retelling in Prose*

William Shakespeare's The Tempest: *A Retelling in Prose*

William Shakespeare's Timon of Athens: *A Retelling in Prose*

William Shakespeare's Titus Andronicus: *A Retelling in Prose*

William Shakespeare's Troilus and Cressida: *A Retelling in Prose*

William Shakespeare's Twelfth Night: *A Retelling in Prose*

William Shakespeare's The Two Gentlemen of Verona: *A Retelling in Prose*

William Shakespeare's The Two Noble Kinsmen: *A Retelling in Prose*

William Shakespeare's The Winter's Tale: *A Retelling in Prose*